THE MARSH

Would you like to read some free novellas set in the world of this book? To get your free ebooks or audiobooks, go to rachelmclean.com/cumbria-novella or you can buy these novellas in paperback from book retailers.

Happy reading!
Rachel and Joel

Rachel McLean writes thrillers that make your pulse race and your brain tick. A proud indie author who manages her own publishing company, she has sold millions of copies digitally and hundreds of thousands in print, regularly topping the bestseller lists. She is the author of the Dorset Crime novels and five spin-off crime series, with beloved characters appearing in multiple series. In 2021, she won the Kindle Storyteller Award with *The Corfe Castle Murders*. She divides her time between Birmingham and Dorset and lives with her wife, three children and two cats Cagney and Lacey.

Joel Hames is a Lancashire-based writer of crime fiction, and the editor of million-selling books across multiple genres. Joel's own works include the Dead North series featuring lawyer Sam Williams, and the psychological thriller *The Lies I Tell*. Most recently, he has been working with titan of crime fiction Rachel McLean on the hugely successful Cumbria Crime series.

ALSO BY RACHEL MCLEAN
AND JOEL HAMES

Cumbria Crime series

The Harbour
The Mine
The Cairn
The Barn
The Lake
The Wood
The Port
The Marsh

Copyright © 2026 by Rachel McLean and Joel Hames

All rights reserved.

No part of this book may be reproduced in any form or by any electronic or mechanical means, including information storage and retrieval systems, without written permission from the author, except for the use of brief quotations in a book review.

This is a work of fiction. Names, characters, businesses, places, events and incidents are either the products of the author's imagination or used in a fictitious manner. Any resemblance to actual persons, living or dead, or actual events is purely coincidental.

Ackroyd Publishing

ackroydpublishing.com

Printed and bound in the UK by CPI Group (Uk) Ltd, Croydon CR0 4YY

THE STORY SO FAR

It's been a busy couple of years for DI Zoe Finch and her team, but as *The Marsh* opens, their longest, hardest investigation is finally bearing fruit.

Following the recovery of secret recordings implicating him in people trafficking, and the murders of Victor Parlick, Bobby Silver, Kieran Mulligan and Daria Petrescu, the trial of the biggest figure in local organised crime, Myron Carter, is underway.

A wide and familiar cast of witnesses is set to give evidence. Not just Zoe and her team, but DS Denise Gaskill, still recovering from the explosion that nearly killed her with the help of a secret painkiller habit, as well as forensic accountant Zhang Chen. Then there are the others: murder-suspect-turned-mine-of-information Ryan Tobin; Carter's one-time tame police officer Ralph Streeting, who made the recordings in the first place; his hired assassin, Kaciaryna Ilinich; Elena and the other victims of Carter's people-trafficking operation; and, after years of work tracking her down,

Olivia Bagsby, the artist who witnessed part of that operation in action, and caught it on camera.

There are still more familiar faces on hand to watch, including Miles and Stacey, Bobby's old friends, DCI Branthwaite, the head of PSD, and Sinead Conway, Carter's former ally... and Denise's one-time lover.

But the man who saved Olivia's life and brought her back to Cumbria, Zoe's former nemesis David Randle, won't be involved. Randle was killed in a fire designed to obliterate Streeting's recordings.

Among the team, Tom and Harriett have moved in together, Nina is dating a local fireman and complaining about her mum, and Aaron is wondering who leaked information about his mental state.

Zoe's secret contact with Randle has caused tension between her and her partner, PSD DI Carl Whaley. And with recent changes within her team – Nina's promotion to DS, Aaron becoming a DI – Zoe is questioning her long-term future in Cumbria, particularly as she finds herself at loggerheads with the irascible DCI Kiki Carnegie too often for comfort. The damning IOPC report into leadership at the Hub has affected Detective Superintendent Fiona Kendrick's confidence, adding to Zoe's difficulties. Zoe likes her team, and she has friends in Cumbria, people like Jake Frimpton, but will that be enough against the lure of a tempting job offer from an old friend?

Of course, there's a murder to solve, too, a new investigation that will take the team north, to the tip of Cumbria, and then back to where everything began, in Whitehaven Marina.

And the biggest question of all remains: whose chair will the antimacassar end up on?

CHAPTER ONE

THE TIDES WERE perfect this time.

Simon Miller smiled as he parked his car by the final gate before Grune Point. He'd driven through three of them already, carefully unlocking each padlock and securing them after passing through. The track ahead was too rocky for his Honda Jazz, and it was only a ten-minute walk along Skinburness Creek to reach the Point.

At half past five in the morning, the tide was out, exposing plenty of sand and marsh for the birds. Dawn was still an hour away. In February, with the bitter wind and threatening rain, he knew he'd have the place to himself for hours.

Just Simon and the birds.

He couldn't see them yet, but if he set up quietly, he could listen for their calls cutting through the wind and water. The barnacle geese would be here in their thousands for winter, along with bar-tailed godwits. If he was lucky, he might hear the honk of a whooper swan. No clumsy humans to frighten them away.

Except for himself, of course.

He walked in silence, embracing the cold, until he reached his chosen spot by Grune Point. When the sun rose, he'd have views across the Solway to the west, Scotland ahead, and the creeks to the east. He had everything he needed – his book, binoculars, coffee and a cheese sandwich.

For now, he closed his eyes and listened.

Light crept in earlier than he'd expected. He trained his binoculars to the left before sunrise, his face tightening with concentration.

Nothing clear yet. He realised that scanning westward into the darkness wasn't the best strategy, so he turned north, towards the shadowy hills of the Scottish lowlands: Dumfries, Annan, Caerlaverock, Sweetheart Abbey. The names alone stirred something inside him. But darkness still cloaked the landscape there.

It wasn't until he looked east, towards the creeks beside him, that he spotted it.

A movement above the sluggish water caught his eye – a flock of pink-footed geese heading north. As they passed over the marsh, he noticed something below them – a white flash against the brown and grey.

He blinked. Whatever it was, it was too large for a bird. And it wasn't moving.

Probably rubbish washed up from the Irish Sea onto the Solway Coast.

Simon took a few steps closer, moving from the stone and shingle onto the soft creek mud.

It wasn't rubbish.

It was a person.

"What's someone doing here at this hour?" he muttered. "Some drunk sleeping it off?"

CHAPTER ONE

He inched forward through the mud, testing each step with his stick.

"Bloody idiots coming out here, disturbing the wildlife." He shook his head. "They ruin everything."

The person lay face down in a creek tributary that would have been underwater a few hours ago. Simon's heart rate quickened as he realised what that might mean.

He hesitated, tempted to walk away and pretend he hadn't seen anything, but his feet carried him forward.

The ground was firmer here. He crouched down and rolled the body over. It moved easily. What he saw confirmed his fears.

When he released it, the body rolled back onto its front.

He'd seen enough.

He considered his options.

The body might wash down to Skinburness, or east into Moricambe Bay and the Firth. It could be in Scotland by nightfall. No one would know he'd found it first. No police interviews, no explaining how he'd got through the gates.

But it might stay put. Some tourist or jogger would spot it soon – it was almost fully light now. They might remember seeing his car on the track, a detail that would become significant once they found a body.

That would make any police conversations far more complicated.

He pulled out his phone with a frustrated sigh, taking one last look at the horizon, hoping to spot a scaup or goldeneye. Then he hunched over his phone, jabbing at the screen before raising it to his ear.

"Hello," he said. "My name's Simon Miller. I'm up at Grune Point, on the Solway Coast, and I've just found a dead body."

CHAPTER TWO

"So, how did it go?" DI Zoe Finch asked.

She sat back in her chair, trying to block out the rain beating against her third-floor office window. She listened as Stella Berry, the Crime Scene Manager for the West Cumbria Region, detailed the latest on the Myron Carter trial.

The case had been Zoe's for two years – patient work, proving that Carter headed West Cumbria's biggest organised crime network. The trial had stretched over two weeks, with witnesses giving evidence against their former boss in the hope of lighter sentences, others needing protection, and some backing out at the last moment.

"All fine," Stella said.

Zoe shook her head. "All fine? Is that it?"

"What d'you want me to say? Carter's people tried to imply I wasn't expert enough, I outlined my qualifications and previous trial work, and they went quiet."

"Excellent." Zoe felt relief wash over her.

A significant portion of their evidence had come through

CHAPTER TWO

Stella's team's analysis. Discrediting the manager would have been Carter's best shot at undermining it.

"Is Kat in now?" she asked.

"She is. Seemed particularly keen to get in there."

"Carter must have really annoyed her."

Zoe's phone beeped with an incoming call from a Dorset landline. She ignored it.

"How d'you figure that?" asked Stella.

"With what we've already got on her, she's not getting her sentence reduced."

Kaciaryna Ilinich had been Carter's enforcer and chief trigger-woman, running his people-trafficking operation. Her body count stood at four, including police officer Kieran Mulligan, plus an attempt on former officer Ralph Streeting, who was due to give evidence.

"True," Stella said. "But that's not why I called."

Zoe sat forward, frowning. The Carter trial was their work's culmination. If that wasn't Stella's reason for calling, she dreaded what might be.

"It's confirmed," Stella continued.

Zoe closed her eyes, releasing a long breath. "Site Two?"

"Yes. Full DNA match."

Zoe opened her eyes to the distant fells, watching clouds race south against the grey sky. Site Two – Red Lonning – where Carter's offices had stood before he'd blown them up as police approached. One casualty: former Detective Superintendent David Randle, who'd rushed ahead to retrieve evidence. Her old boss, a man she'd hated for years until he'd earned her grudging respect at the end.

Randle had been corrupt in West Midlands Police, had testified against his boss, and had entered the Protected Persons Programme. He'd broken every condition to come north and help Zoe bring down Carter. He'd got Streeting talking and saved Olivia Bagsby's life.

Her phone buzzed again, a mobile number now, but the same caller. Zoe ignored it.

Lesley and Dorset could wait. She needed to finish the Carter case before considering her future.

CHAPTER THREE

"Not that I don't love working with you..." DS Nina Kapoor leaned against the desk.

Aaron swallowed. He scowled at her. "Funny way you have of showing it."

She shrugged. "It's just that... Well, you're holding us back, aren't you?"

Really? At least she'd said it out loud this time. She'd been building up to it ever since he'd passed the exams and officially become a Detective Inspector. Dropping hints, talking about opportunities he might find elsewhere, referring to him by his rank rather than his name whenever she got the chance. Just that morning he'd entered the team room to find a printout on his chair – half a dozen sheets filled with vacancies from constabularies across the country and beyond.

"Holding us back?"

"You know what I mean."

Behind her, Tom looked on sympathetically. Nina had always been ambitious, but now she'd made DS, she wasn't adjusting to still reporting to the same people within the same team. DI Finch at the top. DI Aaron Keyes beneath her. DS Nina Kapoor under that, and DC Tom Willis, her best mate, at the bottom.

The truth was, nothing had changed. Nina was frustrated. And when Nina was frustrated, she took it out on the people around her. Tom knew that better than anyone.

Aaron picked up the papers and ran his eye over the top sheet. There were some interesting locations, places he'd often thought about visiting. But not places he wanted to live. Cumbria was home.

"Scilly Isles." He eyed the second sheet. "Really?"

"Sun never stops shining." Nina folded her arms.

"It's true," Tom added.

Aaron's phone rang, saving him from objecting.

"DS Keyes—" Nina shook her head, and he corrected himself. "DI Keyes."

"Aaron, it's Morris Keane. We've got something you might want to take a look at."

"What is it?"

"Body found at Grune Point this morning. Nothing immediately suspicious, but a couple of PCs went to have a look."

"Don't tell me, they didn't like what they saw."

"Have you been to Grune Point in February?"

Aaron laughed. It was desolate enough on a warm day, the tip of the Solway Coast, battered by wind rushing over open water on three sides and flat land as far as the fells on the other. There wasn't much more than mud and ancient smuggling routes up there, but it attracted tourists keen to soak up a different sort of natural beauty from the Lake District.

CHAPTER THREE

"Can't say I have," he said.

"Man found face down in the marshes. Local bird-watcher called it in. You get people up there who get lost sometimes, stumble and sink, especially if they've had a few."

"But you think there's more to it?"

"There's injuries on the poor sod's head," Morris said. "Not consistent with landing on mud. Probably find he's been pecked at by a bunch of geese, but I wouldn't be doing my job if I didn't tell you about it."

Aaron thanked him, jotted down the location, and walked out of the team room and down the corridor. He knocked on DI Finch's door and walked in to find her with her phone to her ear, staring distractedly out of the window.

He pointed to his own phone and mouthed the word 'murder'.

"Got to go, Stella," she said. "Looks like something's come up."

CHAPTER FOUR

Nina had grown to love her electric Nissan even more than the squalid Ford Fiesta it had replaced, but she was glad she wasn't in it now.

She'd parked up in Skinburness and ridden with the boss and Tom in a police Land Rover driven by PC Martinez. They passed a handful of gates and drove over a track that ran north alongside the rough creek, which would have reduced the Nissan to four wheels and a battery.

At the final gate, Nina spotted a white Honda Jazz parked beside it, in a wider area where the track branched inland. She wasn't so sure now. If that thing had managed it...

The Jazz didn't look like it was in great condition, though. And Nina had become someone who actually cared about her car.

They emerged from the Land Rover and followed Martinez up a path that stayed just above the shoreline. A light drizzle fell, but it was the wind that did the damage up here. She could hear it all around her, feel it biting through

CHAPTER FOUR

her clothes as she picked her way among the stones and patches of mud.

The landscape opened out without warning, the scrub giving way to low banks of sand and water, and beyond them, the distant hills of Dumfriesshire. Ahead she could see a small group of people. As they reached them, she could make out two in uniform, but not officers she recognised, and two she could pick out even in their masks and white forensic suits.

"Hello," she said, then moved closer and shouted it, the wind so loud that yelling was the only way to make herself heard.

Caroline Deane turned, a smile forming beneath her mask. Beside her, Keisha Middleton glanced over, nodded, and went back to staring at the ground. Stella Berry had sent out two of them, which either meant it was a slow day, or this was going to be a difficult crime scene.

Nina turned and surveyed the area. Open to the public, battered by wind and rain, half-submerged by the sea twice a day. 'Difficult crime scene' was putting it mildly.

A fifth person stood there, a tired-looking sandy-haired man in his forties or fifties, already engaged in conversation with Tom. But he could wait, whoever he was.

Nina was more interested in the dead man in front of her.

Caroline and Keisha had put down boards already, which would help to preserve any footprints or other evidence that had survived the weather, but proved particularly handy when it came to approaching the dead body without sinking into the Solway. Nina moved cautiously towards it, stopping a few feet away.

"Was he found like this?" she shouted, but nobody could

hear. The man Tom was talking to, he'd be the one who'd called it in. He'd know.

The dead man lay on his back, eyes wide, staring sightlessly at the grey sky overhead. Nina hadn't seen him for a few months and had hoped never to see him again. Not because he was a bad person, but because he was someone who she'd always expected to end up like this.

Not dead on his back in the Skinburness Creek, but dead, one way or another, and way before his time.

She made her way back to DI Finch. "I know him, boss. Femi Moorhouse."

The boss frowned. "Trouble?"

"Low-key trouble. Shoplifting. Drugs."

"Violence?"

Nina shook her head. "Not that I know of. He was a heroin addict, though. Can take you places you wouldn't otherwise want to go."

The boss looked thoughtful. "So, what was he doing up here?"

"He lives round here, last I heard. Used to live in Whitehaven, moved out a short while ago with his girlfriend. Chelsea Bright."

"Don't tell me, also a heroin addict."

"They tend to come in pairs, boss. I think—"

"What the bloody hell are you doing here?" boomed a voice, close enough to be heard clearly above the wind.

Nina whirled round to see a woman with short hair and wire-framed glasses, wearing a black trouser suit that was somehow entirely unrumpled. She could hear the boss muttering beside her as DCI Carnegie stepped towards them.

"Well?" the DCI demanded.

CHAPTER FOUR

"We're investigating a potential murder, Ma'am," replied DI Finch.

"No you're not," DCI Carnegie replied. "Not on my patch. Not without consulting me."

The boss was smiling, but her eyes were blank. "I'm sure we can—"

"I'm sure you can shut up. DI Knight here will be taking charge, and you can bugger off back to your little Hub."

The woman had a nerve, what with the Hub being three times the size of Durranhill. But she had a point, too. Carlisle was closer, marginally. And she...

Nina turned to the man standing beside the DCI, the words she'd heard finally getting through.

DI Knight.

He stood by his boss, wearing the same smug grin he'd worn last time Nina had seen him. When he'd been a DS. Same as her.

As if it wasn't bad enough that Femi Moorhouse had got himself murdered in the arse-end of nowhere. As if it wasn't bad enough that Kiki Carnegie had decided to get territorial.

Bloody hell. Today really had it in for her.

It looked like Sammy Knight had been promoted.

CHAPTER FIVE

WORKING with the same people for years had its drawbacks. Zoe caught herself making assumptions, falling into patterns that sometimes led to mistakes.

But familiarity brought benefits, too. They'd learned to communicate without words. A single look between her and Nina conveyed everything – she'd handle this while Nina and Tom got on with investigating Femi Moorhouse's murder, regardless of Kiki Carnegie's protests.

"Shall we call Detective Superintendent Kendrick?" Zoe suggested, pulling out her phone as she walked away. She hit the super's contact details.

DI Sammy Knight stood frozen on the shoreline, caught between following his boss and doing his actual job.

"Zoe." Fiona's voice came through clear. "I hear you have a murder on your hands."

"That's what I wanted to discuss." Zoe knew she had to choose her words with care. "I'm putting you on speaker – DCI Carnegie's here and there's some question about jurisdiction."

CHAPTER FIVE

"There's no bloody question," Carnegie snapped as Zoe activated the speaker.

They'd moved inland enough now that the gorse and sea grass blocked the worst of the wind. The landscape stretched out bleak but beautiful around them, and Zoe felt the chill in her bones.

"Can you both hear me?" Fiona asked.

"Yes," Zoe said. Carnegie nodded silently.

"I assume Kiki's claiming this for Durranhill since Carlisle's marginally closer?"

"That's right, Fiona." Carnegie straightened. "We're here, and DI Knight is perfectly capable of handling this type of investigation."

"Is he?"

Carnegie's brow furrowed. "Yes, of course," she said, impatience creeping into her voice.

"Because last I saw your DI Knight, he was DS Knight and making a mess of the Mulligan case."

Carnegie's frown deepened, the lines as stark as the distant hills.

"Which means," Fiona continued, "that I want—"

"I'm sorry," Carnegie cut in, "but this isn't acceptable."

"It isn't?"

"No. We're on scene, and I outrank DI Finch here by—"

"Listen to me, Kiki." Ice filled Fiona's voice. "I understand you have big plans for the future. But right now, I allocate cases to Major Crime teams, and I want my best team on this. Which means Zoe. Do you understand?"

Silence fell. Carnegie's scowl melted into resignation, her body deflating as if the fight had drained out of her.

"Do you understand?" Fiona repeated.

"Absolutely." Carnegie walked away.

Zoe watched her go and thanked Fiona. As she ended the call, she had a thought: *what were those 'big plans for the future' Fiona had referred to?*

CHAPTER SIX

"I REALLY SHOULD BE GOING." The man with the binoculars peered past them towards the track.

Tom liked to think of himself as open-minded. He rarely rushed to judgement, and if someone behaved in a particular way, he usually tried to find out why.

But the man with the binoculars was definitely beyond understanding.

His name was Simon Miller, and he'd found the body whilst out birdwatching earlier that morning.

"You came here before sunrise?" DI Knight asked. He'd attached himself to Tom the moment he'd made a move towards the witness, sticking with him like a bad smell.

"I did." Miller shifted his weight. "Which means I've been here far too long already, so if you could see your way clear to—"

"How can you use those in the dark?" Knight pointed at the binoculars hanging around Miller's neck.

Tom nodded. It was a good question.

"What a stupid question." Miller's lip curled. "You come in the dark to stake out your position."

He raised an eyebrow, looking at Knight like he was an idiot. Tom resisted a smirk.

"Lots of other birdwatchers out here that you've got to get in front of, are there?" Knight asked.

Miller didn't appear to appreciate the joke any more than Tom did.

"Don't be ridiculous. I come early, listen for the calls, and work out the best place to position myself for sunrise. Now, as I've said already, I'm sorry the man's dead, but it was only a matter of time, really, and I have to be on my way."

"Yes," Tom said. "You said that earlier. Only a matter of time. What do you mean by that?"

Miller rolled his eyes, a gesture he was several decades too old for. "I mean, I know the man. Knew him. *Of* him at least."

"You knew Femi?"

"I didn't know his name. Just that he'd moved into the North Cumbria Caravan Park with that tart of his. I suppose you know that. Druggies, the pair of them."

They were standing a little way inland now, out of sight of the body and the shoreline. The wind had dropped enough for them to speak in normal voices, but the rain was intensifying. Tom didn't envy Caroline and Keisha, down there in the mud, examining the ground.

"Druggies?" Knight repeated.

Miller nodded. "Yes. And before you ask, no, I don't know what sort of druggies they were. I have friends at the park. This one and the girl, they're really the wrong sort of person for a place like that."

"How so?"

CHAPTER SIX

"They attract trouble, don't they? And that's the last thing the decent law-abiding people who live there want. No doubt it's drugs that killed him, his dealer or some other druggie. As I said earlier, it was only a matter of time."

"No doubt," Knight agreed.

Tom stared at the man. He couldn't really think that, could he?

"I really think I should go," Miller repeated.

"We won't keep you long," Tom said. "Is that your car, by the way? The Honda we saw by the gate?"

Miller blinked. "What if it is?"

"Nothing, really. I just want to make sure it isn't anyone else's. So it is yours?"

"Yes. And I'd like to get back to it, if you don't mind."

He'd started walking away.

"How did you get it all the way up here?" Tom called after him.

Miller stopped and turned, trudging back with deliberate slowness. "I drove it."

"Past all the locked gates?"

"Look, I have the keys." Miller's voice lowered. "I have... Some of the people who work the farms, I give them tips, every now and then. They let me make copies of the keys."

"Tips?" Knight asked.

Miller sighed. "Money."

Tom eyed him. "Do you visit this site regularly?"

"At least twice a week. Some of the best birding in Cumbria, here. Just a shame about the people."

"What d'you mean by that?"

"I mean the likes of him. Femi, you said his name was?"

Tom nodded. "Had you seen him here before, then?"

"I don't know if it's him. Just, people. Any people. The

joggers and the tourists. The teenagers are the worst. Scaring away the birds. It would be nice, don't you think, if there was just one place that people didn't ruin?"

In other circumstances, it might have been a perfectly reasonable sentiment. But with one of those teenagers lying dead not fifty feet away...

"Come on!" a voice shouted from close by.

Tom looked round to see DCI Carnegie marching over, wearing the look of a woman who'd been punched, robbed and fired in the same hour.

"Boss?" Knight said.

"We're leaving," she said. "This bunch of morons are taking over."

"Oh." Knight followed her away.

Tom stood in silence, Simon Miller beside him, watching them recede along the track. DCI Carnegie walked with purpose and anger, DI Knight struggling to keep up.

"Can I go now?" Miller asked.

Tom sighed. On the plus side, he'd got rid of Knight. But that still left him with Miller.

CHAPTER SEVEN

Nina watched as Tom led the witness away from the scene, DI Knight hovering nearby.

She scowled at Knight's back. After working so hard to make DS, it grated that some useless idiot from up the road had leapfrogged to detective inspector. Though she shouldn't be surprised – the unlikeliest people got there. DI Markin at the Hub made Knight look competent by comparison.

She turned to Caroline Deane. "What have you got for me?"

"Not a lot, I'm afraid. You can see how the ground has moved?" Caroline pointed to the mud around and under the boards.

To Nina it was just mud, with occasional pools of water waiting to be absorbed. The creek meandered towards the Solway Firth through gentle undulations.

"Yes," she lied.

"The tide means everything could have moved as much as thirty metres inland and back. Any evidence could be over there." Caroline gestured to where mud gave way to rock and grass. "Or out there." She pointed towards the Solway. "And that's before considering what rain does to imprints on this surface."

Nina sighed. *Bloody typical.* "So no footprints, and even if they dumped the weapon here, we might not find it."

"I'm afraid so." A rueful smile formed under Caroline's mask.

Nina turned to leave.

"But there is something," Caroline added.

Nina turned back. "Yes?"

"Drag marks."

"Drag marks?" Nina knelt on the board to examine the ground, mud staining her trousers. "I don't see any. Wouldn't they wash away like footprints?"

Caroline shook her head. "Footprints are smaller, easier to obliterate. Dragging a body leaves deep, continuous grooves. Even with tide and rain, enough should remain to identify them clearly."

Nina stood carefully, scanning the shore. "No grooves."

"Exactly."

"So he wasn't dragged here. He probably died here."

"That would be my guess," said Caroline.

Kiki Carnegie's raised voice carried from inland, though Nina couldn't make out the words. DI Finch appeared at the boardwalk's end as Dr Robertson and his intern, both wearing white suits, approached the body.

"What happened?" Nina asked the DI.

The boss flashed her a grin. "Fiona Kendrick happened. She wants her best team on it – us."

Nina snorted. "Kiki Carnegie won't have liked that."

"Nope. But she seemed less upset than I expected. Like she was playing a long game."

CHAPTER SEVEN

"Well, as long as we don't have to deal with Sammy Knight," said Nina as Tom returned with the witness.

The DI turned to him. "Anything?" Simon Miller stood apart, occasionally tracking birds in flight.

Tom gave the witness a look that Nina couldn't quite interpret. He lowered his voice. "Our witness was out walking and found the body around dawn. Didn't see anything suspicious. He was familiar with the victim, but says he didn't know him well. He has... his own theories. I don't think they're worth much."

Dr Robertson approached.

"Initial thoughts?" asked the boss.

"Likely drowning," Robertson replied, "but your colleagues were right to call you. Clear head injury from a blunt object, which could have happened in the water, but maybe not. I'll need PM analysis to say more."

"Timeframe?"

"I can't tell you anything now," Robertson replied. "Your best bet is Caroline's tide analysis, but she's not confident. Unless there were other witnesses..."

"Apart from the man who found him," said the boss, "that's unlikely. Not really a night spot."

"As it happens," Simon Miller said, stepping closer, "that might not entirely be the case."

CHAPTER EIGHT

Zoe turned to the man, surprised. "I'm sorry?"

"It's just..." Miller wrung his hands, his face twisted into a pained expression. Zoe recognised it; he was wishing he'd kept quiet.

"What is it?" She softened her voice, aiming for encouraging rather than impatient.

"I just... it wouldn't surprise me if there *had* been people around last night."

"More birdwatchers?"

Miller's mouth puckered as if the suggestion was ridiculous. "Of course not. I mean *his* sort." He waved towards the body without looking at it.

"Black people?" Zoe's eyebrows rose.

"No. I mean, some of them, yes. Just... The younger people. Younger than him, most of them. Druggies." He all but spat the word out.

"They come here, do they?" she asked.

Miller nodded.

"But you didn't actually see anyone."

CHAPTER EIGHT

"Well, no. I wasn't here until this morning, though. I can give you their names, if you like."

"Names?"

"The druggies. If they didn't see anything, they probably know who did it. One of their friends, I'd imagine. And the sooner you get all this cleared up..."

Zoe suspected he was more interested in being left to his birds than in justice. While he could be right, an investigation like this had to start somewhere else – not with random names from a birdwatcher who'd already made his mind up about the victim.

"Tom, Nina," she said, "can you go to the North Cumbria Caravan Park? See if... What's her name again?"

"Chelsea Bright," said Nina.

"See if Chelsea's around. You'll have to tell her what's happened to her boyfriend. And maybe she can shed some light on who might have wanted him dead." Zoe kept her thoughts about Chelsea's potential involvement to herself.

"I really don't think you need to bother the residents at the caravan park," Miller interjected. "They're decent, law-abiding people. If you want to look anywhere..."

"Yes," Zoe interrupted. "If you want to give me these names you have, for some of the teenagers who hang around here, I'll pass them onto one of my colleagues and he'll follow that up."

After taking five names from Miller, she watched Tom and Nina heading down the track while she called Aaron at the station. She stepped away to explain the situation.

"You want me to interview a bunch of teenagers whose only connection to the dead man is that your witness doesn't like them any more than he liked him?" Aaron summarised.

"That's about the size of it."

"Fine, boss. You never know. They might actually know something."

And be prepared to talk to us, she thought.

"That's the spirit, Aaron."

"And pigs might fly," he muttered before hanging up.

Miller twisted his hands together. "Can I go now?"

"You can go. I need to talk to my colleagues, anyway."

She watched him follow the path Tom and Nina had taken. As she turned towards Dr Robertson and his assistant, who were moving the body onto a board, her phone rang.

She checked the display. Not Lesley – she could have waited. But this caller would only corner her later if she ignored him now.

Suppressing a sigh, she answered with forced brightness. "Hello, Carl."

CHAPTER NINE

SHE COULD FOOL plenty of people, but Carl knew Zoe well enough to tell when she was feeling impatient.

"I'll keep it brief," he said, trying not to imagine her relief.

Their relationship had been strained for months, ever since he'd learned about her secret conversations with David Randle over the past two years. Randle's death hadn't improved matters – the way she seemed to mourn him more than his victims made no sense to Carl.

The lying and distrust had driven a wedge between them. The Dorset job offer had only made things worse.

"No need," she said. "You still at the court?"

"Just came out. They don't like you using your phone in there."

"How did it go?"

He heard something in the background – the rush of wind. "Are you in the car?"

"No, up at Grune Point, on the Solway Coast. Weird place. You'd probably like it."

Carl had been to Skinburness, walked to Grune Point, come back and told Zoe all about it. She'd forgotten.

She always forgot. Or had she simply not been listening in the first place?

Best not to think about it.

"I couldn't see much of her." He stood on Earl Street by the statue of Major Aglionby. A construction crew was demolishing something on Warwick Road behind him, forcing him to raise his voice. He stepped closer to the court building, where the noise lessened.

"She gave her evidence from behind a bulletproof screen. And the security... They searched me three times before I was allowed in, and they know who I am."

Kaciaryna Ilinich had spent thirty minutes in the witness box, her voice flat, her words clear. When Zoe's team first found her, she'd pretended to be one of Carter's victims – a trafficked woman from Eastern Europe who barely spoke English.

She was, it turned out, as fluent as most natives. And as for being a victim...

"What did she have to say?" Zoe asked.

"Enough to bury Carter, if the jury believes her. She admitted to four direct murders, plus involvement in three more, all on Carter's explicit orders."

"Was she convincing?"

"She handled the cross-examination without much difficulty. Carter's barrister tried claiming she was just saving her own skin. But Kaciaryna pointed out she wasn't getting out of prison before she died anyway, and turning against Carter would make her life inside more dangerous, not less. The defence had nowhere to go after that. They've had to adjourn for now. She'll be back tomorrow."

CHAPTER NINE

"Good," Zoe said, sounding distracted.

Carl realised something must have happened at Grune Point. A murder, no doubt.

The murders just kept coming.

Movement caught his attention – the low iron gates opening onto the small courtyard beside the court building. Three grey vans waited there, engines running, tinted windows shut. Inside them, Carl knew, was enough weaponry to topple a small country.

They had everything here – High Court, Probate, Family – but he was here for the Crown Court. The reason for all the security was currently walking out of the building, behind those vans, two armed police on either side, and another two in front and back.

Kaciaryna Ilinich had already testified. If Carter had wanted her dead, the best time would have been this morning. But she'd return tomorrow to bury her former employer deeper.

Which meant the second-best time to take her out would be now.

The thought had barely formed when shouting erupted from Warwick Road – the angry voice of an irate driver.

"Watch where you're bloody—"

The rest was drowned out by an engine's roar. Carl jumped back as a black van sped onto Earl Street's cobbles.

Another black van followed.

Shit.

Carl pressed himself against the statue. The Major, carved from Caen stone, glowed golden in the weak sunlight. Time slowed as he crouched and peered out.

The first vehicle's side doors opened before it stopped.

Something long and dark protruded from the gap – Carl didn't need his years of police experience to identify it.

"Firearms!" he shouted, but the shooting had begun. When he looked up, Kaciaryna's armed guards had vanished. He scanned for bodies but saw only movement around the court building's small arched windows and in the grey police vans.

Kaciaryna Ilinich stood alone between the building and police vans as the second black van spun and reversed into the courtyard. She smiled – the smile of someone who knew the game was lost.

Carl waited for the shot, for her to fall, desperate to act but knowing he was helpless. A small, urgent voice reminded him he was still on the phone with Zoe.

She could hear it all – the shots, the revving engines and the deafening silence that followed.

No shot came. Two arms emerged from the van's side and lifted Kaciaryna inside. She didn't struggle – she wasn't stupid. She hadn't fought during her arrest, either.

Carl wondered why they hadn't killed her immediately, hoping it wasn't because they planned to torture her first. She had no information Carter's people didn't already know. But they'd want to send a message, and torturing Kaciaryna Ilinich would be exactly the kind of message Myron Carter *would* send.

The first van had turned, and Carl saw one of the gunmen – dark clothes and a black balaclava over a heavy frame.

The man raised his gun towards Carl. Time froze as Carl waited for the shot.

He closed his eyes and heard shots. But he felt nothing.

Opening his eyes, he saw the gunman shooting at the

CHAPTER NINE

police vans' tyres – one shot per tyre, fired with perfect accuracy. The vans sank lower with each shot. Then came a rush of noise, a whirl of black, and they were gone – the gunmen, the black vans, and Kaciaryna Ilinich herself.

Carl stood alone before the court building, phone in hand, Zoe's voice thin, high and desperate.

His hand shook as he raised the phone.

"I'm OK," he said. "It was... They got her, Zoe. They got Kaciaryna Ilinich."

CHAPTER TEN

Martinez drove in silence as she took Nina and Tom back to Nina's car in Skinburness, then turned around to head back to Grune Point for DI Finch.

"Sorry," Nina said.

"Not really what I signed up for," Martinez said. "But not your fault, either."

She shot Tom a pointed look, suggesting she blamed him instead. Nina wondered if Tom had ever properly addressed things with Martinez after their near-relationship during his break from Harriett. Knowing Tom, he'd avoided that conversation entirely.

Once they were alone and heading south in Nina's car, Tom pointed left. "What the hell is that place?"

Nina glanced at a field crammed with caravans. "Caravan graveyard."

"What?"

"See that machine over there?" She gestured to where a hybrid tank-digger crawled through debris of wood, metal

CHAPTER TEN

and glass. "It's where caravans go to die. There was a similar place near Skegness when I was young."

"Better them than me," Tom said, turning to look west where rain clouds obscured the view of mud and rock.

They passed two larger caravan sites before reaching North Cumbria Caravan Park, south of Silloth. A small group gathered on a patch of green watched as they drove in and parked.

A muscular, bald man in his sixties approached, with an aggressive swagger and artificial smile. "Help you?"

"It's OK," Nina said as she got out. Tom was already scanning the nearby caravans.

"Cops, are you? Want the druggies, do you? Scum, they are."

"I'm sorry?" Tom came around to stand beside Nina.

"Scum. Been causing trouble, right?"

"What's your name, sir?" Nina asked.

"Baz. What they done, then?" He stepped towards her.

Nina held her ground and turned to Tom. "Found it?"

"I think it's over there." He pointed to a row of expensive park homes alternating with shabby caravans.

"Seriously," Baz said. "If there's cops on site, we've got a right to know what's going on."

Nina gave him her most insincere smile. "If we believe you can help with our investigation, we'll be in touch."

Two more men joined Baz. On the green remained a frowning man with a cane and an elderly woman who kept glancing nervously at Baz.

Chelsea Bright's caravan was notably decrepit compared to its pristine neighbour, where a woman in her forties watched from the doorway before retreating inside.

After several increasingly forceful knocks and loud calls,

Chelsea answered. Though nineteen, she could have passed for either fourteen or thirty. Long, dirty hair partially obscured her pretty face, and her lips were covered in sores. She gripped the doorframe, squinting.

"Yeah?" she said after a long pause.

"We need to talk to you, Chelsea," Nina said.

Another "Yeah?" followed by more silence.

"You know who we are, yes?"

Chelsea peered at Nina's face. "You're cops, ain't you?"

Nina nodded. "Can we come in, please?"

Chelsea glanced behind her before looking between Nina and Tom. "Rather not."

"We really do have to talk to you, Chelsea," Tom said.

"Go on, then."

Her speech was clear but slow, with strange pauses like a lagging video call.

"I really think we need to go inside," Nina said.

Chelsea swayed slightly, eyes closing before reopening. She stared at them as if trying to place them, then nodded and stepped back.

Inside, the caravan was divided into living and sleeping areas, with a bathroom door at the back. The air was thick with the smell of unwashed clothes and something worse. Chelsea collapsed onto the unmade bed.

"Go on, then."

Nina knelt before her, hating this part but knowing it should come from her since she knew them both.

"I'm afraid something's happened to Femi."

"Yeah? Got himself nicked, has he?"

"It's worse than that, Chelsea." Nina took the girl's hands as Chelsea's attention drifted between Tom and the cramped kitchenette. "Look at me, Chelsea."

CHAPTER TEN

Chelsea slowly focused on Nina.

"It's bad news, I'm afraid. Femi's dead."

A brief, uncertain smile crossed Chelsea's face, as if waiting for the punchline. Then came confusion, fear in her eyes. She turned away, buried her face in her hands, and trembled.

CHAPTER ELEVEN

Aaron drove north into the rain, spending twenty fruitless minutes knocking on doors as the weather worsened.

Silloth was technically in Cumbria, but it felt like another world. Wide cobbled streets and a vast green with its tiny splash park and amusement arcade gave it the air of a different century. Today, though, everything was grey. He was working from a list of names – all young men and women the witness didn't like, rather than people Miller had actually seen doing anything suspicious.

The first door, just down from the flour mill, went unanswered. The second was tucked behind the Albion Inn with its dark stencilled First World War soldiers, opposite the sports ground.

A short, thickset woman opened the door. "Yeah?"

"Is Gareth in?" Aaron asked.

"Why the bloody hell d'you want to know?" She narrowed her eyes and stepped towards him. "Not one of those perverts, are you?"

"No," Aaron replied. A sharp jab to his stomach made

CHAPTER ELEVEN

him look down. The woman's finger was pushing him backwards.

"Got to be twenty years older than him, you dirty bastard. Now bugger off."

"I just want to—"

"He's not here." She slammed the door in his face.

His phone rang as he got back to the car. The journey was so short he'd have walked if not for the weather. He checked the display before answering.

"How are things?" Denise Gaskill asked.

"Fine. Why are you calling?"

She laughed. "Can't a friend just check up on another friend?"

"If that friend's a normal person, then yes. But there's always another angle with you."

"Typical suspicious copper."

He sighed. "Well?"

"Just wondering if you had any more ideas," she said.

"About what?" He pulled away from the kerb and turned down Solway Street past the takeaway.

"About Ralph Streeting having confidential details about your mental state when he wanted to be released from custody. About him refusing to say how he got those details. About the fact that neither of us knows how he got them, short of bugging Dr Filey's office. Someone's leaked, Aaron."

"And I've told you, I don't remember telling anyone else."

"But you don't remember *not* telling anyone else, either."

Aaron grunted as he turned left towards the coast. They'd been over this countless times. "That's not how memory works. I've told you. My head wasn't in a good place then. Everything's jumbled together. Have you seen her yet?"

Silence.

"Denise?"

"Yes?"

"Have you seen Dr Filey yet? I know you think it's a waste of time, but you need to—"

"Yes, Aaron."

"Yes?"

"Yes, I've made an appointment. Yes, I'll be seeing her next week. And yes, I do think it's a waste of time, but the powers that be have seen fit to demand that I sit in a room with a shrink for several hours as a condition of my return to active duty."

Aaron smiled. "Never change," he told her. "Now, talking of a waste of time, I've got to knock on a door and be told to bugger off."

He was wrong about that. This time, there wasn't even anyone there to tell him to bugger off.

CHAPTER TWELVE

"STAY CALM," Zoe said.

"I am calm," Carl replied, for the tenth time in as many minutes. His voice still carried a tremor.

Zoe had flagged Martinez down and jumped in the Land Rover before it had fully stopped, then directed her to speed back to Skinburness. Her Mini waited in a courtyard, surrounded on three sides by an ancient white building.

"They didn't shoot at you, right?" she asked.

"No." Carl's voice wavered. "Although for a moment I thought..."

Zoe let the silence settle as she drove south along the coast road through Maryport and Workington back to the Hub. Not the quickest route, but the one that needed the least concentration.

The memory of engines roaring and gunshots echoing played through her mind. What had lasted seconds felt like hours in replay.

"It was insane," Carl said. "It was so professional. They—"

"Stay calm." The response had become automatic whenever his voice pitched higher. "Tell me about Kat."

"I don't know. They dragged her in. I thought they'd shoot her right there."

"You think they'll take her somewhere else to do it?"

"I don't know, Zoe. Maybe make an example of her. Or..."

Zoe gripped the steering wheel tighter at the thought. Beyond torture and murder lay another possibility – this wasn't a kidnapping but an escape. If so, someone besides Carter had orchestrated it.

The thought made her uneasy. Cut off one head of organised crime, another grows in its place.

If that was true, Kaciaryna Ilinich could return to her previous occupation: putting bullets in strangers' heads.

Her phone buzzed. She glanced at the display and ignored it.

"Tell me about her evidence," she said to Carl.

"She was pretty straightforward. I could only see her face when she leaned forwards, but she smiled the whole way through, even describing what she'd done. The woman's psychotic, Zoe."

"That tends to be the way, with multiple murderers. What did she say, though?"

"She put Carter in the frame for everything she did, directly or indirectly. His lawyers looked worried. Carter, too."

A worried Carter was good news, but also dangerous. Had Kaciaryna Ilinich discovered just how dangerous?

Zoe pulled over on Maryport's outskirts. "Do you want me to head over there?"

"Eh?" Carl sounded surprised.

CHAPTER TWELVE

"Do you want me in Carlisle? With you?"

"Er, no. I'm fine. Really."

Relief washed over her – no need to derail her day playing nursemaid. She merged back into traffic, heading south. For a moment, she imagined driving on, hundreds of miles to Dorset and whatever awaited her there.

But it wasn't time. She hadn't decided whether a life there suited her. Carl hadn't decided if he'd join her if she took Lesley's offer.

Lesley could keep calling multiple times daily, demanding an answer. It wouldn't bring one any faster.

CHAPTER THIRTEEN

Tom watched while Nina spoke quietly to the young woman on the bed. Over several minutes, Chelsea's desolate sobs gradually subsided. Tears still tracked down her cheeks, but the shaking had stopped.

He remained still, taking in the cramped caravan. From here, he could see nearly everything he needed to.

Puddles dotted the uncarpeted sections of the floor. The stained and partially burned carpet, which had likely once covered the entire space, was now scattered with fresh mud and sand.

Someone had been out on the shore and marshes recently.

He waited until Chelsea was speaking – mostly variations of "I don't understand" and "I don't know" – before pulling on gloves and moving to the far side of the bed.

Wet, sandy clothes lay on the floor – skinny jeans and a tiny top that couldn't have fit the body from the beach. Chelsea's clothes. She'd been out on the marshes.

CHAPTER THIRTEEN

He bent down again but paused as Chelsea's voice rose.

"Why are you asking me these questions?"

"We just want to know what happened to Femi." Nina's voice was gentle. "We want to make sure whoever did this to him doesn't get away with it."

"But I don't know!" Chelsea's sobs started up again.

Tom spotted something half-hidden under the bed. He nudged it out with his foot – a metal box.

When Chelsea calmed, he examined it closer. The old rectangular box had a faded design of symbols and letters around its sides. One side was dented as if someone had tried breaking it open.

They'd found an easier way – through the clasp on top, secured by a flimsy padlock. After checking he wasn't being watched, Tom lifted the lid.

Inside was a wooden tray, like those in cigar boxes. Empty except for brownish residue – perhaps sand, perhaps not. He closed it quietly and gestured to Nina.

The caravan was too small for private conversation. He headed for the door at the far end, into what turned out to be the bathroom. The stench of vomit hit him as Nina followed, closing the door. He kept his eyes on her, avoiding looking for the source of the smell.

Nina grimaced. "Keep it brief," she said.

"There's puddles and sandy clothes, probably Chelsea's. She's been on the marsh and back."

"Right. That's not a crime."

"I know," he said. "There's also a box that's been broken open. Might be drugs. I think we need Stella's people in."

She nodded in agreement and opened the door. The smell seemed to follow them out.

Nina turned to Chelsea. "Do you mind coming outside with us?"

"Why?"

"We'd like to chat with you, and have our colleagues look over the caravan. See if Femi left any clues about why he was at Grune Point."

Chelsea looked ready to argue, but instead she deflated, nodding as she stood and shuffled outside.

Tom phoned Keisha Middleton, who answered quickly. He could hear voices in the background, the man who'd called himself Baz, waiting outside.

"Bloody scum," Baz muttered.

Nina guided Chelsea past him towards the car while Tom briefed Keisha.

"You want me to come over then?" the CSI asked.

"If you can," Tom said, hoping Keisha wouldn't bristle at being asked to do her job. He glanced up to see a woman's face watching from the opposite park home's window.

He blinked and she vanished.

"Good," Keisha said, "cos it's cold enough to freeze the bits off a brass monkey out here."

"What?"

"Me. I'm freezing. Give me the address."

By the time he finished the call, things had escalated with Baz. And Chelsea had noticed him.

"Scum," Baz repeated.

"You," Chelsea spat.

Baz stepped back, startled. "What about me?"

"You killed him, didn't you?"

A smile flickered across Baz's face before fading as he caught Nina's expression.

"Hang on..." he said.

CHAPTER THIRTEEN

"No." Chelsea shrugged off Nina's hand and stepped towards Baz. "You hated him. You'd have done it."

"Now listen up, you..."

Baz caught himself, glancing first at Nina and then at Tom. He turned on his heel and walked away.

CHAPTER FOURTEEN

THE RAIN HAD EASED when Aaron finally got an answer about Elle Frobisher's whereabouts. A sulky-looking girl who should have been at school muttered "Splash park" before shutting the door in his face.

Silloth's green stretched from the sea to the main street, nearly as vast as the town itself. Mrs Wilson's Coffee House overlooked it, its salmon pink frontage and portrait of the famous contralto standing out among the shops and cafés. At the far end, the splash park sat in the shadow of a grassy mound topped with a Victorian pagoda, blocking the view of the sea.

Around a dozen teenagers huddled around a picnic table, passing a joint between them. Aaron cleared his throat as he approached. There was a guilty shuffle from the centre of the group.

"He's on his own," someone said, and the movement ceased.

Smoke drifted upward, followed by a cough.

"Hello," Aaron said.

CHAPTER FOURTEEN

An overweight boy of about sixteen stood up and stepped away from the group. "What d'you want, copper?"

"I'd like to talk to you about your whereabouts last night. What's your name?"

"Eyal."

"Eyal what?"

"Eyal break your bloody legs if you don't piss off, copper."

The group erupted in hoots and sniggers.

"I don't care about your joint," Aaron said.

A girl with spiky hair took a drag. "Good. Coz you're not getting it."

"I just want to know if any of you were around Grune Point last night."

More laughter followed, mixed with confused looks.

A thin boy sporting a mullet like a seventies footballer spoke up. "Why would anyone be up there?"

"I understand you sometimes frequent the area," Aaron said.

"Frequent the area," a red-haired girl mimicked in a deep voice.

"I understand—"

"Not in this weather," the girl with the joint said. She took another drag before blowing smoke in his direction.

"So none of you were there last night?"

"Might have been." The red-haired girl stood, her hair cascading down to her waist.

"Well, were you?" Aaron gestured towards the group. "I really don't care about any of this."

A short boy with dark hair and shrewd eyes spoke up. "Yeah."

"Where?" Aaron asked. "When?"

"Grune Point. Six till half seven."

"Eight," the red-haired girl corrected.

The girl with the joint smirked. "Two hours, Gareth? Might give you a go myself."

Gareth shrugged as the group sniggered.

"Anyone else?" Aaron asked.

"Just the two of us," the red-haired girl said.

"And you didn't see anything unusual there? Anyone else on the marshes?"

"Wasn't really looking at the marshes," Gareth said, triggering more sniggers.

"No," the girl added. "I'd have noticed. Don't want any of those perverts watching, do I?"

"Sure you don't," the overweight boy said.

Aaron processed the information as they continued their banter. If they were telling the truth, this gave him a window for time of death. It had been light when they arrived, and they'd have noticed a body.

Which meant Femi Moorhouse had been killed after eight the previous evening.

"What's this about, then?" asked a boy who hadn't spoken yet.

"It's fine," Aaron replied. "Nothing you need to worry about."

He'd turned to leave when the boy with the mullet called out. "Dead then, is he?"

CHAPTER FIFTEEN

"Come in," said Fiona.

No one was outside the super's office to warn Zoe about Fiona's mood. Luke had transferred to the Assistant Chief Constable's office and hadn't been replaced yet, though a temp was supposedly on the way.

"I've just been on the phone with Carl," Zoe said as she closed the door behind her.

Fiona stood at her usual spot by the window, gazing at the fells. "If you're here to tell me about Kaciaryna Ilinich, don't bother. I've already had a full report."

"Oh." Zoe sat down, studying her boss carefully. These days, Fiona's moods were unpredictable.

Fiona's shoulders shifted. "Easy come, easy go. And from what I hear, she'd done a lot of damage in the witness box."

"She did," agreed Zoe.

Fiona turned to her. "As for how something like this could happen, we should be expecting this by now, shouldn't we?"

"Should we?"

"One disaster after another, Zoe. One disaster after another."

Zoe held back a sigh. Fiona was usually a good boss, willing to stick her neck out when needed. But since the IOPC's damning report about the Hub – which had been particularly harsh about her leadership – she seemed defeated. The fight had drained from her.

"How's your corpse?" Fiona asked.

Zoe had barely started outlining their findings when Fiona's phone rang.

"I need to take this." She gestured for Zoe to stay seated. "Wait here."

Fiona answered, listened briefly, then said, "I've got Zoe Finch with me. I'm putting you on speaker."

Superintendent Singer's voice filled the room. As head of Operations, he'd overseen several raids with Zoe's team over the past year.

"Ah, good," he said. "That saves me a second call. Well, not good, I suppose."

"Not good?" Zoe asked.

"Your witness. Olivia Bagsby. She's disappeared."

"I'm sorry?" said Fiona.

Zoe sat frozen. She'd spent two years tracking down Olivia Bagsby, whose photographs had been crucial in arresting Ralph Streeting and pressuring Carter. Olivia was meant to give evidence tomorrow.

"She's gone, Fiona. I'm sorry. Thanks to the debacle at the court today we're a bit stretched, had to leave her unaccompanied for a while this afternoon."

'A bit stretched' was an understatement. Zoe knew every available resource would be on the hunt for Kat and the people who had taken her. She pulled out her phone and

CHAPTER FIFTEEN

dialled Olivia's private number while Fiona wrapped up with Singer.

No answer.

"Let's think this through," said Fiona. "No need to panic."

Zoe chewed a nail, fighting down her rising anxiety. First Carl, now this.

"Her evidence," Fiona said. "She's in tomorrow, right?"

"Yes." Zoe forced herself to focus. "But the truth is, there's not much she can say that we don't have other people for now. We have Carter's actual victims. And most importantly, we have Streeting. That was what we needed Olivia for. She was the one who helped us bring in Streeting."

The super nodded, still standing behind her desk. "So Olivia gave us leverage on Streeting. Will Streeting change his tune if he knows she's gone?"

"I don't know," Zoe admitted. "And without Streeting's evidence, the recordings we have are useless."

"We can't let Streeting find out she's gone." Fiona picked up her phone.

"Agreed. But..."

They both knew what Zoe was saying. There was every chance Streeting already knew about Olivia's disappearance.

Because there was every chance he was the one who'd planned it in the first place.

CHAPTER SIXTEEN

Aaron turned back. The group fell silent, motionless except for a thin wisp of smoke rising from their midst.

"Is who dead?" he asked.

The boy with the ridiculous hair shifted his weight. "The Black lad."

Movement rippled through the group as they passed the joint to Gareth, the shrewd-looking boy who'd been up at Grune Point last night. He took a long drag, held it, then released a steady plume of smoke that hung in the air before dissipating. His gaze remained fixed on Aaron.

"He still owe you?" one of them asked.

The boy with the mullet shook his head. "Nah. COD only for the wasters."

Murmurs of approval spread through the group.

A girl who hadn't spoken yet smirked. "Smart. You don't want to go giving credit to a dead man."

"What dead man?" Aaron turned to her. "What do you know?"

CHAPTER SIXTEEN

She responded with an inscrutable grin, menacing despite her youth.

"Nothing, man," Gareth cut in. "Just leave it."

The others chimed in, their voices overlapping.

"Leave it."

"Piss off."

"We're not saying nothing."

The mullet-headed one piped up again. "Just goes to show."

Aaron turned to him, catching Gareth's warning look directed at the boy.

"Just goes to show what?"

Mullet-head shrugged. "Nothing."

"Just goes to show what?" Aaron pressed.

"Just goes to show you shouldn't mess with Ethan Reid."

"Ethan Reid?" Aaron echoed.

Gareth's eyes turned cold. "Shut it," he snapped at the other boy.

"Chill, puppy," the boy replied.

"I mean it, Fishhead." Steel crept into Gareth's voice.

"Whatever," Fishhead muttered.

Aaron watched as they turned away one by one, their conversation closing him out. But he'd learned something valuable – a timeframe for Femi Moorhouse's death and a name: Ethan Reid. The name was familiar, though he couldn't place it. He could search the system, but that was unlikely to reveal a connection to Femi Moorhouse.

As Aaron walked away towards the grey Victorian church, he realised there was another way. Fishhead might not be the lad's real name, but with that distinctive mullet, he wouldn't be hard to find again.

CHAPTER SEVENTEEN

Nina glanced back as they walked away. Baz stood with folded arms, watching them.

"Who is he?" she asked.

"Barry Joyce." Chelsea's voice cracked. "Hates us. Hated Femi. If anyone..." She dissolved into tears before they reached Nina's car.

Nina opened the front passenger door for Chelsea and walked around to the driver's side. Tom slid silently into the back seat.

They sat in silence, broken only by Chelsea's shuddering sobs. The young woman was struggling with more than grief – Nina had seen enough users to recognise the signs. Chelsea Bright was coming down.

A white van burst through the entrance to the caravan park, ignoring the ten miles per hour speed limit. Nina watched as Keisha skidded to a halt. Tom exchanged a glance with Nina, then got out of the car and walked towards the van, directing her to Chelsea's caravan.

By his return, Chelsea had settled. She sat back, pushing

CHAPTER SEVENTEEN

hair from her face to reveal a nasty cut above her left eyebrow.

"How did you get that?" Nina asked.

The young woman shrugged. "Don't remember."

Tom slipped back into the rear seat. Nina caught his eye in the mirror and gave him a *leave this to me* look.

"Chelsea, where were you last night?" she asked.

Chelsea stared ahead, dazed. "What?"

"Last night. You and Femi. Where were you?"

"Don't remember."

"Could you have got that cut last night?"

Chelsea's eyes fluttered closed. The silence stretched so long Nina thought she'd fallen asleep.

"Don't know," she mumbled at last.

A sharp bang on Nina's window made her jump.

"Bloody hell!" she gasped.

"What?" Chelsea hadn't even noticed Keisha outside.

"Wait here," Nina said as she and Tom left the car.

Barry Joyce had returned to the green by the entrance with his two friends. They watched silently while Keisha gave her report.

"Not done any analysis yet," she said.

"Course not," Tom said. "You've only been there five minutes."

Keisha ignored him. "There was heroin in the box. Tiny amount, but..."

"But what?" Nina asked.

"More around the bed. On the floor to the bathroom. Probably on your shoes if you went in wearing regular footwear instead of forensic suits and overshoes. Did you?"

"Did we what?"

"Go in like idiots without proper gear?"

"Maybe." Nina redirected. "But you think there was more heroin?"

"Yeah. Traces. In rows. We're looking at a decent amount – more than an average user's stash. It's gone now, though. Spilled, then scooped up. The rows are from collecting it."

"Thanks."

Keisha shrugged and headed back towards the caravan.

Nina looked at Tom. "Her stash, or Femi's?"

"We won't know until Keisha's spent more time examining it."

She pressed her lips together. "It might not belong to either of them. Come on." She made for the car.

Chelsea's eyes were closed when they got into the car.

"Chelsea?" Nina said.

No response.

"Chelsea!"

Her eyes flew open. "What?"

Nina shook her head. "There are things we need to discuss. About Femi. And your drugs."

A shrug. "Go on, then."

"I think we should talk under caution. At the Hub. Do you know what that means?"

"Not my first rodeo," Chelsea said with a slight smile.

As they drove past Barry Joyce and his friends, his words carried clearly through the closed windows.

"Don't come back!"

Chelsea turned to Nina, her eyes sharpening. "Them."

"What about them?"

"All of them. Bastards that live here. Had it in for us since we moved in. If anyone killed Femi, it were them."

CHAPTER EIGHTEEN

BACK IN HER OFFICE, Zoe started making calls.

Her first was to James Kirby, who ran the secure unit holding Streeting. She explained what had happened to Kaciaryna and Olivia.

"And?" His response was flat.

She felt a muscle twitch in her cheek. "And the whole point of delaying Streeting's trial was so he could give evidence at Carter's. If he finds out another witness has disappeared and changes his mind..."

"The walls have ears, Detective Inspector, and the bars tell their own stories."

"What's that supposed to mean?" She knew impatience showed in her voice.

"These things have a way of finding their way into a unit. I doubt there's much we can do to stop your man learning about the other witness absconding."

"She didn't abscond, she was taken." Zoe drilled a thumbnail into her palm. "Can't you segregate him? Fully?"

"That's a punishment. Unless Mr Streeting has done something to warrant it, I'd rather not."

Realising arguing was pointless, Zoe ended the call and made the next one: David Cohen, Kirby's senior officer. He grasped the situation's sensitivity immediately.

"I'll deal with it."

"Are you sure? James Kirby didn't seem keen to help."

"If James Kirby wants a job in the morning, he'll help," Cohen's grim tone reassured her.

Her third call was to Inspector Morris Keane, who hadn't heard about Olivia's disappearance.

"Bloody hell. It never rains but it pours, eh?"

Zoe glanced out of her window. The idiom rang especially true in Cumbria.

"Think you can get the search started?" she asked.

"I'll do what I can. But with this other woman..."

She understood. Kaciaryna was the priority – not because she mattered more than Olivia, but because her kidnappers had used semi-automatic weapons outside the Crown Court.

Her phone rang as she ended the call. Jake Frimpton. She nearly ignored it, but decided against it – Jake rarely wasted her time.

"What's this I hear about disappearing witnesses?"

Her stomach clenched at the plural. "Witnesses?"

"Witness, then. I hear your better half was caught up in it this morning. He OK?"

Relief flooded through her. Jake was a journalist with excellent sources, but those sources weren't exclusive. If he only knew about Kaciaryna, they might still keep Olivia's disappearance quiet.

CHAPTER EIGHTEEN

"He's OK," she said. "A bit shaken, although he's not admitting to it."

"He was right there, yes?"

Zoe pursed her lips. "Not right there as such, but he saw it all from across the street."

"And I imagine you've no idea what's happened to the witness."

Zoie sighed. "None."

Jake nodded and cleared his throat. "Have you decided yet?"

Zoe looked at him. "Decided what?"

"If you're going to Dorset."

"Look, Jake, it's not an easy—"

"Oh, I know, you've got factors pulling both ways. But what about Carl?"

"Jake, with all respect, I don't think—"

"He doesn't want you to go, Zoe!" Jake's tone suggested this should be obvious.

Carl had never pretended to be thrilled, but he'd said he wouldn't stop her. Maybe that was the problem – was he not willing to fight for their relationship?

"He doesn't really care, Jake."

"No, he does. He just thinks you don't."

"Look, I don't have time for this." She hung up, guilt settling in her stomach.

Jake's words stuck: *He doesn't want you to go*.

After so much distrust and lies, mostly from her, could she blame Carl for assuming the worst? Was he right?

She was considering moving three hundred miles to Dorset for her old boss, and leaving Carl behind barely factored into her decision.

They'd moved to Cumbria together from Birmingham when they both needed an escape. Now everything felt one-sided.

Was she doing it again? Was she seeking an escape?

CHAPTER NINETEEN

AARON RETURNED to find Nina and Tom just entering the team room. He called the boss, who said she'd be right down.

DI Finch looked exhausted. "There's a lot going on," she said. "So we won't waste any time. You know about Kaciaryna."

"Yes," Nina said.

Tom scowled – he'd been the one to arrest her.

The boss nodded. "Well, now Olivia's gone missing, too."

Aaron felt his mouth open. "What?"

"Olivia. They had to leave the safe house unguarded."

"Because of Kaciaryna," Tom said.

"Indeed." The boss was looking down at the carpet. "And... well, the best we can say is there's no sign of forced entry."

Aaron dropped into a chair. All that work to find her, persuade her to return to Cumbria, convince her to talk after Randle's death.

All of it wasted.

"Morris Keane has people looking for her," DI Finch

said. "Streeting is being isolated, so he can't find out. We need to get on with our jobs and let everyone else get on with theirs. There's no point worrying about Olivia."

That was easier said than done, Aaron thought. One glance at the DI told him she felt the same.

She turned to Nina and Tom. "What have you got from the caravan, then?"

Nina outlined their minimal findings. Chelsea Bright, the dead man's girlfriend, was downstairs in an interview room, sleeping off her high and trying to ward off the inevitable crash.

"There's a lot going on there that needs looking into," Tom said. "There's a metal box in the caravan with heroin in it."

"They *are* heroin addicts," Nina pointed out.

"Yes, but Keisha was talking about quantities you wouldn't expect. And that box... It was almost an antique."

Nina nodded. "She's got a cut above her eye she won't discuss. And the whole caravan park wants them gone. My guess is either a domestic or a row with the neighbours that got out of hand."

"It's drugs," Tom insisted.

Nina lifted the antimacassar from Tom's chair and let it fall back. The hideous hand-made item from Nina's mother had become the penalty for losing team bets.

"Bet?" she said.

"There's something else that might be relevant," Aaron said. "Ethan Reid."

"What about Ethan Reid?" Nina asked.

"You familiar with him?"

She nodded. "Where did you come across him?"

Aaron explained about the teenagers on Silloth Green.

CHAPTER NINETEEN

He'd checked Ethan Reid on the system while waiting for the others, and listened as Nina filled in the gaps.

"He's dangerous," she said. "Only about twenty-one, I reckon, but he's been active since he was fourteen."

"Active how?" DI Finch asked.

It was a good question. The PNC information was sketchy. Either Reid wasn't as bad as Nina suggested, or he was too clever to get caught.

"He's a gangster," Nina said. "Wannabe gangster, really, but he's working at it. Started as a kid in Wigton, moved to Silloth – probably how those kids knew him. Through older siblings, likely, since he left there a couple of years ago for Whitehaven."

"He's in Whitehaven?" Aaron asked. That explained why the name was familiar, though the PNC was clearly outdated.

"Yeah. His operation's small, but from what I hear, it's growing monthly. Same as his reputation for violence."

"How do you know him?" the DI asked.

"Back in my uniform days. Found him causing trouble in Wigton. Took three of us to bring him in."

"Well," Aaron said, "at least one of those teenagers seemed to think he might be involved. And they weren't surprised Femi was dead."

"But they wouldn't tell you more?" Tom asked.

"Not yet."

Nina turned to Tom. "Can we cancel the bet?"

"Why?"

"Because if Ethan Reid is involved, this isn't just angry neighbours or a domestic. It's drugs. And it's a lot bigger than Femi Moorhouse and Chelsea Bright."

CHAPTER TWENTY

"You're sure you don't want a lawyer?" asked Tom.

Chelsea Bright stared back at him, her eyes blank.

Tom could have flown a toy plane through the window of Interview Room Four and out through the door, and she probably wouldn't have flinched.

"Chelsea?" he said.

"Oh, yeah," she replied.

"Yeah, you do want a lawyer?"

"Oh, no. No need for that."

Tom exchanged glances with Nina, who shrugged.

"And you understand that this interview's being recorded and you're under caution?" she reminded Chelsea.

"Got it," said Chelsea.

They'd done all they could do.

"Do you happen to know where Femi's phone is?" Tom asked.

They'd checked with both the CSIs and the pathologist. There was no sign of a phone.

"He didn't have one. Neither of us have one. Get some-

CHAPTER TWENTY

thing like that, you sell it a week later for less than you got it for. Not worth it."

It seemed inconceivable, that someone could live in 2026 without a phone. But Tom had seen it before, with addicts.

"Tell us about the caravan," he said.

"You saw the place." Chelsea sniffed. "It's rubbish, but it's home."

"How come you're there? I understand you both moved up from Whitehaven."

Chelsea laughed, a low, bitter sound that took him by surprise with its depth. "My aunt died. Left it me. We thought it'd be good to get away from Whitehaven. The people we knew. Thought we might get off the B." She laughed again. "Needless to say, we didn't."

"So the caravan's yours, then?" asked Nina.

"Yeah. The other residents don't like it, but it's mine."

"The other residents," said Tom. "Tell us about them. This dislike. Is it merely verbal, or..."

"Well, they threatened us."

"Who did?"

"That Barry Joyce. Baz," she added, contempt dripping from her voice.

"What did he say?"

"Said he'd seen off the likes of us before and he'd do it again. Femi asked him what he meant by that, he's sensitive, you know, the race thing, and..."

Chelsea stopped, hiding her head in her hands, and shook.

They waited.

"Sorry," she said after a minute, her voice muffled by her hands. "I still can't believe he's gone."

"I understand," said Tom. He waited for another few

beats before pressing on. "And Barry Joyce, did he explain what he meant?"

Chelsea looked up, her face somehow even paler than it had been, her eyes ringed with circles so dark it was like she'd drawn them there. "He called us scum. He told us he'd see us off the caravan park soon enough. We didn't take it seriously, though. Thought he was just... Thought it was all talk. Now I think..."

She shook again, and Tom realised that this wasn't just grief. Whatever Chelsea was coming down from, she was approaching the bottom. 'B', she'd called it. 'B', for 'Brown'.

Heroin.

They weren't going to get much more out of Chelsea Bright.

"Are you familiar with the name Ethan Reid?" asked Nina.

Chelsea frowned and blinked. "Dunno. Think I've heard the name, but I can't remember."

It was a wonder she could remember her own name, let alone Ethan Reid's. Tom exchanged a brief look with Nina.

"How about we take a little break, Chelsea?" he said.

There was a tiny movement of her head. It might have been a nod. But he wasn't even sure she'd heard him.

CHAPTER TWENTY-ONE

"Whatever you want," James Kirby said.

Carl studied him with a measured gaze and waited.

Kirby shifted in his chair. "I mean it. You're PSD, right? You trump the rest."

"I do," Carl agreed.

"So I get this woman from the Hub saying put him in solitary, and I explain I can't do that. Then my boss tells me to do what she says, and I'm like, yeah, alright, and now you're here wanting to talk to him. That's about the size of it."

"That's about the size of it," Carl confirmed, noting Kirby's choice of words.

"Well, sod them. You want Streeting, you've got him." Kirby leaned forward. "Oh, and if you want a little private time, just let me know."

"Private time?"

"Let's just say, no one's going to be too upset if Mr Streeting ends the day with a head injury and broken arms. Want the cameras off? Just bang the table twice."

"You can do that?" Carl asked, his interest piqued despite himself.

"Those things break down all the time. A few more minutes today – well, that's just bad luck for Mr Streeting."

"Thanks," Carl said, making a mental note to investigate inmate injuries at the unit.

Five minutes later, he was sitting opposite Ralph Streeting in a small room. Carl looked at the man, careful not to show surprise.

The last time he'd seen Streeting, he'd been cool and relaxed. A healthy forty-something, unbothered by his likely life sentence, unbothered that his former employer wanted him dead.

Something had changed. Streeting looked ill, or sixty, or both – but he couldn't be sixty. Carl had checked.

"Are you unwell, Ralph?"

Streeting offered a weak smile. "Let's just say the place doesn't agree with me. I don't sleep well."

"Have you been attacked?"

"Not yet. But it's coming."

"Do you need to see a doctor?"

"They brought one when I lost the first two stone. Apparently I'm fine. Just... older."

The swagger was gone, along with the weight. The arrogance had vanished. And this was just remand. Decades stretched ahead. By the time parole was possible – if ever – nothing would remain of the man.

"You've heard about Kaciaryna Ilinich?"

Streeting nodded. "It's all over the unit. I presume that's why I'm in here?" He gestured at the three-metre cube room with its bed, table, chair and cameras. Nothing wrong with it – just isolated.

CHAPTER TWENTY-ONE

"Yes," Carl lied, holding back about Olivia Bagsby's disappearance. If Streeting knew anything, it would surface.

"They think I was involved? In the incident outside court?" Streeting leaned forward, eyes bright. "Were you there, Carl? Did you see it?"

Carl nodded.

"How did she look? Was she scared?"

"Surprised, maybe. Possibly not even that. Not scared."

"It would take more than men with semi-automatics to frighten Kat. One of a kind, that woman." Admiration tinged his voice.

"And you don't know anything about it?"

"Nothing except that it happened."

"And nothing else? Nothing connected to the trial?"

Streeting's eyebrows lifted. "Why? What else has happened?"

Carl waited. Usually, men like Streeting – men who thought they were cleverer than everyone else – gave themselves away. But this warier version of Streeting held back.

"Nothing," Carl said finally. He glanced at the cameras, considering Kirby's offer. Even the best liar might crack facing broken arms and worse.

"I don't believe you," Streeting said.

"The feeling's mutual." Carl dropped his arm once on the table. Streeting frowned, understanding dawning slowly.

Two bangs meant two broken arms and a head injury. Not exactly subtle code – probably common knowledge throughout the unit.

Carl raised his arm again, watching Streeting's eyes.

He saw only fear and resignation.

Standing, Carl walked to the door and knocked on that instead.

CHAPTER TWENTY-TWO

"You still think it's drugs?" Nina asked.

"I thought you'd changed your mind." Tom raised an eyebrow. "You wanted to cancel the bet, remember?"

"That was before we sat down and spoke to her." Nina closed her eyes, picturing the young woman – the cut over her eye, the pale face, the trembling. "She doesn't know anything."

"What about her reaction when you mentioned Ethan Reid?"

Nina kept her eyes closed, replaying the scene. Chelsea Bright, frowning, then blinking.

"She didn't *have* a reaction. Thought she might have heard the name, wasn't sure."

"You don't think that was a bit too cool?" he asked.

Nina's eyes snapped open, fixing Tom with a hard stare. "Really?"

"You're doing it again," he said.

"Doing what?"

CHAPTER TWENTY-TWO

"That look. DI Keyes told you. Now you're a DS, you're not supposed to—"

"Yeah, I know, I know."

"To sneer like that."

"I know," she repeated.

"How was it he put it?" Tom tapped his chin. "Oh, yes. Like you're talking to something you just wiped off your shoe."

"OK, I get the—"

"And you know, that look, used on an officer who's junior in rank to you, it could be taken as bullying, DS Kapoor."

Tom sat back with an earnest expression, though the effect was ruined by the smirk that broke into full laughter seconds later.

"I still think she's genuine," Nina said. "This is about the neighbours. Or maybe something domestic."

Tom shrugged. "Maybe you're right. But I don't think so. And the thing about the cut on her head. Not remembering it. I'm not sure I buy that."

"Let's go and ask her about it, shall we?"

Back in the interview room, Chelsea Bright showed no signs of sudden recollection.

"Look," she said. "I told you. I don't remember."

Nina studied the woman's face. Was she being evasive? Or was she just strung out?

Strung out, she decided.

"We have a forensic medical examiner here," Tom said.

Chelsea turned towards him with glacial slowness. "A what?"

"Like a special doctor. They can take a look at you, make sure you're ok, and at the same time they can see if maybe there's any physical evidence on you that—"

"I just want to go home." Chelsea bent over the table, hiding her face behind her hands.

It was possible she was being evasive. But she was definitely strung out.

CHAPTER TWENTY-THREE

Nina leaned forward in her chair. "Humour me, will you?"

"You're the sarge, Sarge." Tom couldn't help enjoying the scowl she shot in his direction.

DI Keyes glanced up briefly, then remembered and looked back down again. He hadn't been 'Sarge' for a while now, but old habits die hard.

"The neighbours," Nina continued. "See what you can find out."

"You're really determined to win this bet, aren't you?" Tom turned to his screen and started the search.

Nothing would come of it. But it wasn't just humouring Nina – it was doing the job properly. Following up every lead until it went cold.

Within five minutes, his eyes widened. "Barry Joyce."

"What about him?"

"Take a look."

Nina wheeled her chair over beside him, scanning his screen. She gave a low whistle. "Nasty piece of work."

Tom nodded. "And that's his friends talking about him."

Barry Joyce hadn't seemed pleasant during their brief encounters at the caravan park. But at least they hadn't been on the wrong end of a baseball bat.

Joyce was an armed robber. *Had been* an armed robber, Tom corrected himself mentally, though he wasn't sure if being an armed robber was like being white or short or alcoholic – always with you. He'd served twelve years for robbing a jeweller, nearly two decades earlier. His precise role in the gang had never been established.

From what little Tom knew of the man, he suspected it hadn't involved charm.

Nina tapped the desk. "Maybe Chelsea has a point."

"Maybe. I'll see what else I can dig up on the neighbours."

The rest was disappointing after Barry Joyce. Speeding fines, affray, drunk and disorderly. One possession charge – ironic, given how Chelsea and Femi had been received, but it was just a small amount of Class C from years back.

Hypocrisy wasn't a crime.

Tom sat up straighter. "Archie Stern."

DI Keyes looked up with interest.

"Who's Archie Stern?" asked Nina.

"The neighbour – well, the neighbour's husband. His wife was there when we went to see Chelsea."

"Thin woman. Blonde."

"That's the one. She was staring out the window when we left, but half the park was doing that."

"What about her husband?" Nina asked.

"Went missing. Two years ago."

"I remember it," DI Keyes said. "Nothing serious suspected though, was there?"

CHAPTER TWENTY-THREE

Tom shook his head. "He travelled a lot. Assumed he'd done a runner. They were short on cash. It's probably nothing."

"Everything's worth knowing," Nina said. "But there's no doubt where the more interesting avenue leads."

"Barry Joyce," Tom agreed.

He returned to his research while Nina made calls and DI Keyes reviewed the forensics report. A message hit all their screens simultaneously – Chris Robertson would conduct the post-mortem later this evening.

Bash on the head, followed by drowning, the message read. *That's what I'll be telling you tomorrow. That, and signs of advanced heroin addiction.*

"There were drugs at the caravan, then?" DI Keyes asked rhetorically. No one answered.

After a minute, he spoke again. "Fishhead."

"I beg your pardon?" Nina asked.

"Fishhead. The kid who mentioned Ethan Reid. Stupid haircut."

"Stupid name," Tom said.

"It's not his real... Oh." DI Keyes realised Tom was joking. "Reckon you can find him for me? Can't be the most popular street name round here."

Tom had the information within two minutes. "Robert Mulaney. Lives in Abbeytown, just a few minutes from Silloth. Been arrested for burglary. Oh, and possession."

"Assuming everything else runs dry," DI Keyes said, "it might be worth paying Robert Mulaney a little visit."

CHAPTER TWENTY-FOUR

"You know she'll be using as soon as she's out, don't you?" Zoe crossed her arms, leaning against the desk.

"There's nothing in her caravan," Tom replied. "Keisha's pretty thorough. She won't have left anything behind."

"She'll find what she needs, one way or another." Nina's voice was flat with certainty.

Tom opened his mouth, then closed it again with a shrug. "Probably. But we can't really keep her here, can we?"

"Any grounds to arrest?" Zoe looked between her team members. Aaron had phoned with an update, and she'd decided to make the walk down to the team room.

They exchanged glances, searching for a better answer than the ones they had.

"No," Aaron said at last.

"You'll have to let her go, then," Zoe said. "Assuming she wants to."

The afternoon had been an exercise in frustration. Lesley had called twice more, until Zoe had texted her to stop and

CHAPTER TWENTY-FOUR

wait for an answer. Carl had managed to override David Cohen's instructions to see Streeting, which had left her annoyed at both James Kirby for defying orders and Carl for going behind her back. The guilt at being cross with Carl had triggered memories of her own lies to him, and his secrets from her. She'd pushed it all aside to focus on Streeting's interview.

But Streeting had nothing useful to say. Zoe had thanked Carl with forced politeness and ended the call, her mood darker than ever. When she'd video-called Nicholas five minutes later, he'd noticed immediately.

"Everything OK? You look even angrier than usual," he'd said.

She'd swallowed her irritation and chatted with her son until the anger subsided. He was buzzing about his move to Exeter. Though his master's wouldn't start for months, he'd already sorted accommodation and was planning how to earn money while studying.

It struck her that Nicholas always seemed to choose universities half a country away from her work. Or perhaps she was the one who kept moving away. Maybe if she wanted to see more of him, she needed to find work somewhere more convenient.

Exeter wasn't that far from Dorset, after all.

The conversation had improved her mood, but back in the team room, reality crashed in. Two witnesses missing, likely kidnapped, with at least one probably dead. She couldn't spare any guilt for Olivia Bagsby. On top of that, she had a murder she'd fought DCI Carnegie to investigate, with no solid leads.

"I'll drive Chelsea home," Aaron said. "Want to see what the place is like. And what she's like in person. Might pop round to see Ethan Reid, too, depending on what our friend Fishhead has to say."

"Fishhead?" Zoe frowned. The name was new to her.

"Robert Mulaney. The lad who mentioned Reid. Want to see what he says without his mates around to shut him up."

"Watch yourself with Ethan Reid," Nina said. "He might be young, but he's not one to take lightly. If you go, take some protection with you."

Aaron raised an eyebrow, unflustered. "You don't want to come with?"

She shook her head. "I've met Ethan Reid. It's not an experience I'd care to repeat."

"Sort it out amongst yourselves." Zoe pushed away from the desk. "And that includes the post-mortem, although Chris says he already knows what he'll be telling us. We've all got plenty to do, and I've got to be in court tomorrow. I can't miss Streeting's evidence."

"Good luck, boss," Aaron said, echoed by the others.

Two and a half years of work had led to this point. Tomorrow, they'd take a huge step towards securing Myron Carter's conviction, provided nothing else went wrong.

Provided nothing else went wrong.

As if that ever happened.

CHAPTER TWENTY-FIVE

AARON HAD BEEN in some awkward situations in his time.

The club night in Kendal twenty years ago still made his face burn – trying to chat up the best-looking bloke there, only to discover he wasn't gay. Then there was that endless lift journey with a detective superintendent right after police college, attempting small talk while pretending he knew what he was on about. And two and a half years ago, stopping DI Finch at Whitehaven Marina's entrance, mistaking her for some wealthy boat owner.

But none of those compared to driving Chelsea Bright back from the Hub to Silloth. She sat beside him, pale and quiet, barely responding to his attempts at conversation.

She climbed into the passenger seat, and her face fell when she saw him. "Oh," she said.

"Oh?" He hadn't met her before, and he knew he wasn't that hard to look at.

"I just thought... I thought it would be one of the others."

"DS Kapoor and DC Willis?"

"They were nice," she said.

"I'm nice," he replied with a smile, but she just looked frightened. He sighed and pulled his Skoda out of the car park.

The next forty-five minutes passed in near silence. Chelsea stared at the headlight beams cutting through the darkness, answering his questions with single words or nothing at all. She only showed interest when he mentioned Ethan Reid.

"What?" She turned to face him.

"Ethan Reid. Do you know him?"

"I don't know what you're talking about." She clammed up after that, staying silent until they reached North Cumbria Caravan Park.

The park was mostly dark, its streetlights broken and most caravans empty until summer. But it wasn't deserted. Aaron spotted faces pressed against windows as he drove past. A stocky, bald man stood outside one caravan, smoking and watching Aaron's car.

Aaron recognised him from the mugshot he'd seen earlier. Barry Joyce looked much the same as when he'd started his sentence.

He parked behind a white Honda near Chelsea's caravan. Before he could speak, she'd unbuckled and opened the door.

She paused halfway out and gave him a shy smile. "Thank you," she said, then hurried to her door, fumbling with the key before disappearing inside.

He'd wanted to get a sense of Chelsea Bright in person. He wasn't sure he had.

A flash of white caught his eye from the neighbouring caravan – someone standing in a doorway with light behind them, quickly closing the door before he could see them properly.

That would be Erica Stern, wife of the missing Archie Stern.

He felt eyes on him as he drove away – watchers from half a dozen caravans and a couple of the bigger lodges. The place had an eerie feel that went beyond the darkness and cold. As he passed Barry Joyce's caravan, Joyce raised one arm. Aaron couldn't tell if it was meant as a greeting or a threat, but he wasn't staying to find out.

Only when he reached the road past the golf club did he start breathing normally again.

CHAPTER TWENTY-SIX

It took longer than it should have done to select an outfit.

Elena held up a short skirt and a top that ended above the navel. "This one."

Nina eyed it suspiciously. "I don't know. I'm not eighteen anymore. And this isn't Ibiza. It's Cumbria. In February."

"These clothes are in your wardrobe, not mine," Elena said. "If you don't like them..."

She put them down and moved onto the next option. By the time Nina left the house wearing tight black jeans and an orange jumper she'd bought in one of her 'sophisticated' phases, the taxi had been waiting outside for fifteen minutes. Skip would probably have been waiting in the bar for twenty.

Nothing wrong with keeping people waiting. Especially not when it came to a third date.

Potatoes Tomatoes was a new bar just off Tangier Street that had attracted quite a crowd in its opening weeks. Nina waded her way through, trying not to think about how many of them she'd arrested at one time or another.

"Alright, Nina," said a voice beside her.

CHAPTER TWENTY-SIX

She turned to see a familiar face grinning at her under a mop of blonde hair.

"Davey Grant," she said. "When did you get back?"

Davey Grant was someone she hadn't arrested in a couple of years. He'd been useful when it came to finding the man who'd murdered Elena's friend Daria. And now he was with...

"Hello love." A tall woman with hair so dark it almost shone stepped forward. "Yeah, we've been back about a week. How's tricks?"

Davey had hooked up with Abigail Holinshed, and they'd been travelling Europe together while her mum Kay, a former employee of Cumbria Police, had played host to two women they'd rescued from Myron Carter's trafficking network. Abigail was wearing an outfit almost identical to the one Nina had rejected. Nina knew she'd made the right choice.

She was convinced of it when she finally found Skip, who'd managed to grab a rare table near the bar. His eyes widened as she approached, but it was a respectful widening, she thought. He stood to slide out a chair. A tall, mysterious-looking violet-coloured cocktail with a wide straw and enough ice to sink the Titanic sat in front of her place.

"What's this?" She gestured at the drink as she sat down.

"I took a guess."

She lifted it and sipped. She couldn't tell what was in it, but it was good. She nodded approvingly.

They chatted about Elena, who Skip had met during the fire at Nina's house, about his work, about her mum, who was still dating Abed from her art classes – the first man she'd seen in the ten years since Nina's father had died.

"And he seems OK, this Abed?"

Nina frowned. "Not really, no."

Skip leaned forward, concern in his eyes. "What's wrong?"

"Nothing's wrong. That's the problem. Abed isn't OK, he's lovely, and I haven't seen my mum so happy in as long as I can remember."

"So why are you frowning?"

"Because my role here is to pretend to be disgusted and complain about the things my middle-aged mum's getting up to with her middle-aged boyfriend, and I can't really do that if I'm really happy for them both, can I?"

Skip laughed and took a sip from his own drink, a shorter green concoction with less ice and more fruit. She reached out a hand, and he passed it to her. She sipped and passed it back with a grimace.

"At least I don't have to pretend to be disgusted now."

Skip frowned as he reached into his pocket and pulled out his phone. "Shit."

He turned the display to her. A callout from the fire station. All hands required. Skip's crew would all be receiving the same message, dropping everything they were doing.

"It's OK," she told him.

He flashed her a regretful smile before tapping out a quick reply and standing. "To be continued."

She sat alone at the table for a minute, sipping her cocktail, before pulling out her own phone and texting Tom. Maybe he'd be able to come out and join her. Shame to get all dressed up only to call it a night before the first drink was drunk.

The bar was nicer than she'd expected, although with Davey Grant and his friends in attendance, it wouldn't stay

CHAPTER TWENTY-SEVEN

Aaron looked up. "Hello, Fishhead."

"Bloody hell," Robert muttered.

"Watch your language," said the man, without turning to his son. He faced Aaron. "How can I help you, Detective Inspector?"

"George Mulaney?"

"That's me."

"I'd like a word with your son, if you don't mind," Aaron said.

"No," Robert called from the top of the glass-panelled staircase.

"Robert," George said firmly, "if the detective inspector wants you to talk to him, you'll talk to him."

"No," Robert pleaded.

A woman emerged from a room to Aaron's left. She was about George's age, taller, with bright blonde hair in a bob.

"What's going on?" she asked.

"Detective Inspector Aaron Keyes. I'd just like a few minutes with your son."

"Oh God," Robert groaned, his last hope of escape vanishing.

"I'm Linda." She turned to face her son. "Get down here now. Get in that room." She pointed to a doorway leading to the kitchen. "And tell the detective inspector everything he wants to know."

"But Mum—"

"Get. In. There." Linda gave Aaron a tight smile that promised trouble for Robert later.

The boy trudged down the stairs, sighing dramatically with each step, and slouched past Aaron into the kitchen.

"We'll leave you to it," George said as Aaron followed Robert.

Linda stepped forward. "I'll stick around, if that's alright with you. And I can make you a coffee if you want."

Aaron sat across from Robert at a round glass table. A coffee would be perfect, and having Linda there might make the boy more talkative – he seemed more afraid of his parents than the police.

"You mentioned the name Ethan Reid earlier," Aaron said.

The boy wrinkled his nose. "Gareth was right. I should've kept my mouth shut."

"Gareth?" Linda's head snapped up. "You've not been hanging around with that Gareth Burns again, have you?"

"Tell me about Ethan Reid," Aaron pressed.

"Look, I don't know anything, right?"

"This is a murder investigation. A man has been killed."

Linda leaned forward behind Aaron with a cold smile. "Robert, dearest. If you don't tell the lovely DI Keyes everything he wants to know, we'll be having a little chat about the things I found in your room this morning."

The boy paled. "OK. Look, I don't know much."

"Just tell me what you do know," Aaron said.

"I heard it, right? Don't remember who from, so don't ask. But the word is, they smashed in Ethan's Merc."

"They?"

"Dead guy and his bird."

"Bird?" Linda's tone was sharp.

"His girlfriend. Chelsea, isn't it? They smashed a window and nicked a box with a load of stuff in it."

Aaron eyed him. "What do you mean, stuff?"

Robert rolled his eyes. "What do you reckon? Ethan got well pissed off. And... Well, if Ethan Reid's pissed off with

CHAPTER TWENTY-SEVEN

you, you don't just go home and get off your face. You run for the hills. I guess the dead guy didn't know that."

"What else can you tell me?"

"Nothing," Robert said firmly.

Aaron finished his coffee, trying to get more information, but the boy had clammed up. Either that was all he knew, or even his mother's threats weren't enough to make him talk. But he'd said enough – Aaron had seen Keisha's preliminary report about the metal box with drug residue inside.

He thanked the Mulaneys and left, wondering what punishment awaited Fishhead, and hoping it would keep him out of the even worse trouble ahead. It hadn't been a waste of time after all. Tomorrow, he'd be paying a visit to Ethan Reid.

CHAPTER TWENTY-EIGHT

"You're sure you're OK?" Zoe leaned forward, concern etched on her face.

Carl closed his eyes and took a breath. "For the fifth time – yes. I didn't get shot. Nobody got shot, as it turns out, which is something of a miracle. So yes. I'm fine. Which is more than can be said for Kaciaryna Ilinich."

"There are people I care about a lot more than I care about her."

Carl set his beer down untouched, his heart quickening as he waited for her to continue.

"I'm worried about Olivia," she said.

He nodded, trying to mask his disappointment. Of course she was focused on Myron Carter's trial. When wasn't she?

"I don't think Streeting was involved." He'd already explained this earlier – their conversation, the change in the man.

"And you really think he didn't know anything?"

"He didn't." Carl took a drink of his beer.

CHAPTER TWENTY-EIGHT

Yoda slithered along the kitchen counter, past his arm, to investigate the empty fish and chips carton. The cat looked up at them, clearly unimpressed by the lack of leftovers.

"Look, Zoe, I—"

"I don't know how much longer I can do this, Carl." Her voice was barely above a whisper.

He turned to look at her, his previous thoughts forgotten. Her eyes glistened with unshed tears.

He felt a lump form deep in his stomach. "What do you mean?"

"I mean all of it. All the work I've done to get that man behind bars, and now two witnesses have disappeared, and I don't know if Streeting's going to play ball. It's such hard work. And I'm worried it's all going to be for nothing."

"I understand."

"I'm not sure you do." She shook her head. "It's everything. It's the place. It's the bloody weather, the incessant rain, the cold—"

"It's February, Zoe. Of course it's cold and wet."

A sad smile crossed her face. "Yes. But I could say the same thing any other month of the year, couldn't I?"

He couldn't argue with that. He just didn't really mind it.

"I'm still confident about the trial," he said.

"Maybe." She shrugged and picked up her drink, then put it down. "Even if..."

"Even if what?"

"Even if you're right. Even if we get the conviction. What happens after that, Carl?"

"You move on to the next one. That's the way it works. The criminals don't just stop being criminals."

"And the rain doesn't stop being wet." She fixed him with a penetrating stare. "What will you do, Carl?"

"What will *I* do?"

"If I go. If I decide that however lovely it is here, however much I like and respect my team, Cumbria just isn't for me. Wasn't for me, after all. What will you do?"

He nodded, considering. "I'll..." He stopped, frowning.

So much had changed since they'd arrived just over two years ago. They'd been through a lot, both of them. And he'd learned important things.

Cumbria was home now. That was one thing he knew for certain. The other was that he couldn't fully trust her – not after she'd lied about David Randle for two years. Even with Randle dead, that kind of deception left its mark.

But he loved her. Despite the trust issues, despite sometimes not understanding her, he loved her. That's what made this so difficult.

She watched him, waiting.

"I don't know," he said finally. "I wish I did, but I just don't know."

CHAPTER TWENTY-NINE

Nina's text came as something of a relief.

Tom wasn't lazy, and he wasn't unwilling to help with the decorating. He'd even enjoyed smashing up one particularly annoying wall with a hammer. But he was rubbish at it.

Harriett knew what she was doing, and he was just getting in her way. It was obvious to both of them, but he had to keep offering his assistance, and she had to keep accepting it, because neither could admit it out loud.

He put down his brush and picked up his phone, frowning as he read the text. He showed it to Harriett.

"You need to go," she said. "Your friend needs you."

"How do you figure that?" The text said simply *New tmto place.*

"She's on a date, right?"

"Is she?"

"Yes, Tom. Didn't she mention it?"

She hadn't. They'd been too busy trying to work out who'd killed Femi Moorhouse. And then Tom had attended the post-mortem, which had provided no surprises at all. Not really much opportunity to discuss Nina's love life. He opened his mouth to point this out, then thought better of it.

"No."

"Well, she's seeing Skip."

"The fireman," Tom said.

"That's the one. And they've gone to that new bar off Tangier Street."

"Oh." Of course. That was what she'd meant by *New tmto place*. The bar that had opened the other week. *Potatoes Tomatoes*. Stupid name.

"So she's gone there on a date?"

"Looks like it."

"And you think she wants me there?"

"Yes." Harriett waved a brush threateningly in his direction. "Or she wouldn't have texted you. Skip's probably had a callout, and she's all dressed up with no one to embarrass. I'm guessing she thought you were a good second choice."

"But what about the—"

"I can manage without you for a bit. Let me know where you end up. I might even join you."

He was changed in five minutes and walking into *Potatoes Tomatoes* twenty minutes after that. Nina sat at a table by herself, surrounded by glasses containing drinks of differing sizes and hues.

"Taste test," she said when he sat down opposite her.

"What?"

"Marks out of ten. So far I've tried these." She gestured at the empty glasses dotted between the full ones. There were five of them. "Nothing's managed more than two out of ten."

"But you still managed to drink them, I see."

CHAPTER TWENTY-NINE

She grinned. "All in the name of science, Tom. All in the name of science."

Four drinks later – four for Tom, he wasn't sure how many Nina had got through – there had been no great scientific breakthroughs. Just a decision.

"This place is shit," Nina said.

"Don't you want to—?"

"Look." She pointed to the corner of the bar where Abigail Holinshed sat surrounded by Davey Grant and his friends, Jay Whitwell and Mal McDonald. The last time he'd seen those three together, they'd been helping to piece together a murder.

"Just because they're here..." he began, but Nina was shaking her head.

"I need to sing," she said.

When Harriett finally found them two hours later, Tom was leaning against the bar at the Miner's Yard, nursing a pint of something nice and normal, watching Nina belt out *Heartbreak Hotel* to the usual crowd, all of them drunker than she was, and most of them three decades older.

"How's she doing?" Harriett asked.

"I think she's forgotten about the date." Tom passed her his drink and signalled for another. "I think she— Oh."

Nina had spotted Harriett and was waving at her, gesturing for her to join her on stage.

"Look after this." Harriett shrugged off her coat to reveal a sparkly top and a black leather miniskirt. He'd never seen her in those clothes before.

"What?" Tom said.

"Watch my coat and my bag."

"You're not going up there, are you?"

"Girl needs backup," Harriett told him.

He shook his head and watched as his best friend and his girlfriend moved seamlessly onto *Suspicious Minds*. For two people who worked in PSD and Major Crimes, they might have picked a song with a title that wasn't quite so reminiscent of the day job. But neither of them seemed to care, and that, Tom thought, was the important thing.

CHAPTER THIRTY

"Here?" Roddy leaned against the wall.

"Perfect," Aaron confirmed, watching as PC Chen attempted to look inconspicuous.

The police uniform didn't help with blending in. But it hardly mattered – at six feet ten inches tall, with legs and arms like tree trunks, Roddy Chen would stand out regardless of what he wore.

Aaron had been hesitant about bringing Roddy, but Nina's warning from yesterday echoed in his mind. *Take some protection with you.* Coming from Nina, who'd tackled an armed murderer last year and faced down a riot the year before, it carried weight. So here was Roddy, along with Tom, who kept rubbing his eyes and insisting he wasn't tired or hungover despite clear evidence to the contrary.

They stood on the top floor of Pears House, the upscale apartment complex overlooking Whitehaven Marina. Ethan Reid's flat took up most of the western side, which meant few neighbours would pass by where Roddy waited.

Aaron checked that Tom was ready, then knocked twice on Reid's door.

"Can I help you?" called a male voice from inside.

"It's the police, Mr Reid. I'd like a word, if you don't mind."

"Bear with me." The response came quickly, and the door opened just thirty seconds later. A young man appeared, wearing designer jeans and a white t-shirt that somehow looked expensive.

"Come in." Ethan Reid gestured them inside.

Aaron showed his ID and made introductions.

"Sit down." Reid pointed to two sofas arranged by a massive window overlooking the marina.

Aaron found himself drawn to the view of Bulwark Quay below. The memory hit him – two and a half years ago, standing there with Nina, Stella Berry and Dr Robertson around Daria Petrescu's body, when DI Finch had first arrived. His life had changed dramatically since then. He turned away and sat beside Tom.

Reid settled opposite them, arms folded, a relaxed smile playing on his lips.

"Thanks for this," Aaron said. "I was hoping you could help us with some loose ends in our investigation."

"Always willing to help the constabulary." Reid's smile widened, reminding Aaron of a shark.

"There was a murder, the night before last, up at Grune Point."

"Grune Point?"

"Just north of Skinburness." Aaron watched him carefully.

"Yeah, I know where you mean. Murder, though. Bit out of my league."

CHAPTER THIRTY

That smile again – the one that said nothing he said could be trusted, and he didn't care if Aaron knew it.

Most telling was that Reid hadn't asked who'd died.

"The young man who died was called Femi Moorhouse," Aaron said.

"Yeah?"

"He lives with his girlfriend, Chelsea Bright. Lived, I should say. They're in Silloth. That's your old stamping ground, isn't it?"

"I was there a year or two, true. But I don't know those names, I'm afraid."

That threatening smile appeared again. Aaron felt grateful for Roddy's presence outside.

"They lived in Whitehaven, too. Until recently."

"Did they?" Reid cocked his head. "Isn't that a coincidence?"

Reid stood abruptly, his meaning clear. Aaron and Tom rose too. At the door, Aaron paused.

"I don't suppose you'd be willing to come with us back to the station? Continue this discussion there?"

"I'd rather not," Reid replied.

Aaron took a final look around. Nothing flashy – just slightly better versions of normal things. Larger sofas, shinier appliances, sparkling granite worktops. Like the clothes – ordinary but expensive. *Money bought from fear*, Aaron thought.

"One last question," he said, hand on the doorknob.

Reid checked his expensive watch. "Yes?"

"Have you recently had a break-in? Items stolen, possibly from a vehicle?"

The smile dropped. Aaron met Reid's eyes and saw nothing there. Complete emptiness.

"No." Reid took a step forward.

Aaron opened the door and followed Tom out.

"Thanks," he called, but Reid had already shut the door. Roddy stood nearby like a stone giant, and Aaron had never been more relieved to see a fellow officer.

CHAPTER THIRTY-ONE

"So this is where it happened, is it?" Zoe asked, her curiosity getting the better of her professional demeanour.

"Right here," Carl confirmed.

They stood outside the court building in Earl Street, Carlisle. Less than twenty-four hours ago, shots had been fired here, even if no one had been hurt. Today, the cold blue sky stretched overhead as people went about their business – some finishing late breakfasts before heading inside, others emerging to light desperate cigarettes. The outside forensics team had already come and gone, much to Stella's annoyance, leaving no trace of their thorough examination.

Zoe's phone buzzed. She checked the display and answered to the familiar face and voice of DS Mo Uddin, her former colleague in Birmingham.

"Bloody hell," Mo said. "It's not raining."

"Says the man in Scotland." Zoe laughed. "Listen, I'm about to step into court. Can't chat. How are things?"

"Fine for me. I was just wondering if you'd—"

"Speak later, Mo." Zoe ended the call, not wanting Carl

to overhear any discussion about Lesley's offer. Things were already tense between them after last night – after months, really. Their stilted conversation had only highlighted the brewing conflict they'd both been ignoring.

Her phone buzzed again, displaying Zhang Chen's name – the forensic accountant who'd helped with Carter's case and testified last week. But Zhang could wait. The only person she wanted to hear from was Morris Keane, whom she'd already spoken to that morning from the car.

Olivia Bagsby was still missing. So was Kaciaryna Ilinich, though she wasn't Zoe's priority.

Zoe entered the building, emptied her pockets and switched off her phone. She passed through the metal detectors twice, forgetting her keys the first time – unusual for her. Her earlier thought nagged at her: *even if no one had been hurt*. But Kaciaryna Ilinich had surely suffered since her kidnapping.

Her breath caught as she entered the courtroom. There he was.

Myron Carter stood in the dock, behind bulletproof glass with two officers flanking him. Despite expecting him to be there, the sight shocked her. But it was satisfying – this was her work.

"May I approach the bench?" The lead prosecution counsel looked too young for his role, but his record spoke for itself.

The ensuing conversation, though hushed, carried clearly. Counsel requested a delay.

"Why?" asked the judge.

"Our witness, Olivia Bagsby, is unable to give evidence this morning."

"Unable?"

CHAPTER THIRTY-ONE

"Yes, Your Honour."

"I'm not happy about this," the judge said. "You've had months to prepare. Unless there are extreme circumstances, I'm minded to decline your request."

When the barrister asked to continue privately, the judge refused. This would have to be made public.

Zoe kept her eyes fixed on Carter as the lawyer spoke.

"Olivia Bagsby has disappeared from the safe house she was being kept in, Your Honour. Yesterday."

"Why wasn't I informed about this?"

"We believe it happened at the same time as the attack outside court. Things have been a little chaotic over the last twenty-four hours."

"That," said the judge, "is the understatement of the year. I need a moment to consider this."

While others watched the judge, Zoe studied Carter. She'd expected smugness, the usual unruffled demeanour she'd spent two years trying to crack. Instead, she saw shock, then confusion, before his smooth mask returned. So he didn't know. That was almost as shocking as Olivia's disappearance itself.

CHAPTER THIRTY-TWO

They took the stairs down. Tom appreciated having Roddy Chen's reassuring bulk between himself and Ethan Reid as he processed what had just happened.

"He's lying, Sarge," Tom said.

Aaron stopped and met his gaze. "What?"

"Sorry, DI Keyes. Force of habit." The title change still felt strange after so long.

"But yes." DI Keyes nodded. "He is lying. And he—"

Voices approached from below – male and female.

"Up here," the woman said. "Top floor, he said."

"Don't drop the bloody case," the man growled.

"Don't talk—"

They rounded the corner – a man and woman, both heavily tattooed, in ripped jeans and vest tops displaying impressive muscles. The woman fell silent at the sight of the officers.

She clutched a briefcase to her chest. "Morning," she said, smiling nervously as she sidled past.

"Morning," DI Keyes replied.

CHAPTER THIRTY-TWO

Tom waited until they were half a floor down. "They're buying drugs."

DI Keyes raised an eyebrow. "Probably."

"And there's cash in that case."

"Maybe."

"This is our chance." Tom's words were garbled. "We can go up there and search. We've got grounds to, now."

"I agree, we have grounds, but Ethan Reid's not stupid. He won't have drugs in the flat, and the cash isn't his, it's theirs, so we'll be back where we started."

They reached the ground floor. Tom stopped, frowning. He hadn't taken to Reid – the man was playing games when someone had died – but the DI was right.

"I don't like it," he said.

"Nor do I, Tom. But let's take a look downstairs, shall we?"

"Downstairs?"

"Underground car park." DI Keyes pushed on, Tom and Roddy following.

Darkness greeted them in the car park until sensors triggered the lights. Rows of luxury vehicles worth more than Tom's annual salary lined up between concrete pillars – Range Rovers, Teslas, Jaguars, Bentleys, and even a Rolls Royce.

DI Keyes let out a long, satisfied sigh. "Look."

He stood beside a grey Mercedes van, pointing to the front passenger side. Tom moved past Roddy and spotted the broken window.

"Oh." He grinned. "He said he hadn't had a break-in. I take it this is his van?"

"I checked before we came. It is." DI Keyes crouched down, examining the ground.

"What are you doing?"

"Checking for glass. There's hardly any here. And I can't see any inside the vehicle, either. Which means it's been cleaned up."

"Which means this hasn't just happened."

"Exactly." DI Keyes straightened up, matching Tom's grin. "Fancy another little chat with Ethan Reid?"

CHAPTER THIRTY-THREE

THE SECURITY around Ralph Streeting was double what it had been around Kaciaryna Ilinich. Even inside the courtroom, where everyone had been searched until they'd barely kept their belts and shoes, the guards were on edge. Carl watched one in particular – a woman with greying hair and a nose that had seen its share of fights. Her eyes swept the gallery, lingering on faces until she was satisfied they posed no threat.

He couldn't blame her. Not after yesterday.

Streeting shuffled in, looking even more aged than the day before. A chair waited in the witness box.

Carl had asked if he was ill. Streeting had denied it, but the lie was obvious now. Ralph Streeting was the sort of man who'd want to stand while he was giving evidence. He wouldn't sit without good reason.

The questions nagged at Carl: *had Streeting lied about Olivia Bagsby, too? Did he know what had happened to her? Was he involved?*

The prosecution led Streeting through his evidence. He

spoke with clarity, confirming the evidence from the recordings, the people-trafficking operation, and the orders for Victor Parlick's murder. His voice only wavered when he mentioned Bobby Silver.

That killing had been personal – Streeting had pulled the trigger himself. Perhaps guilt was catching up with him. Or more likely, he was remembering how that murder had led to his downfall: ballistics, fingerprints on the gun, prints on Bobby Silver's door handle. A trail of evidence that had sealed his fate.

Carl glanced at Carter in the dock. The defendant looked almost bored, as if he were contesting a speeding ticket rather than facing life imprisonment.

The cross-examination began, and Carl leaned forward.

"You're lying, aren't you?" The defence counsel – a middle-aged woman with short blonde hair – spoke with the casual air of someone chatting at a pub.

"No," Streeting said.

"You're trying to get yourself a lighter sentence. What have they offered you to lie about my client?"

"I'm not expecting to get out of prison before I die."

"Why's that?" The lawyer's tone suggested she was ready to pounce.

"Because everyone in this room knows that Myron Carter isn't going to forgive me for this, whether he gets convicted or not."

"What are you suggesting?"

"I'm not suggesting anything." Streeting's lips curved into a smile. "I'm making a statement of fact. My old friend Myron will try to have me killed, and whilst I hope he doesn't succeed, he probably will. If I'm somehow still alive

CHAPTER THIRTY-THREE

in twenty years' time, it'll be a miracle, whether I'm inside or not."

The lawyer froze, mouth open. She turned towards Carter, who remained expressionless in the dock, unmoved by Streeting's evidence.

"No further questions," she said.

Whether Streeting knew about Olivia's disappearance or not, it hadn't affected his evidence.

CHAPTER THIRTY-FOUR

NINA TOOK one look at the empty team room, pulled on her coat, and headed out. She'd had to beg a lift in, and now she needed one back out again.

Her head was pounding.

In the past, she'd have wondered what she'd drunk to feel this rough the next morning. But thanks to payment apps, she knew exactly what – the itemised bills on her phone had told the whole story during her ride in with PC Martinez.

Martinez was on shift now, though. Nina needed someone else. She spotted a familiar face in the canteen and walked over.

"Alright, Rob?"

PC Rob Collins looked up. "Better than you."

He was upright without support, so that was probably correct.

"Don't suppose you could do me a favour?"

Rob's eyes narrowed. "Maybe. What kind?"

This was where staying friends with uniformed

CHAPTER THIRTY-FOUR

colleagues paid off. Some CID officers thought the job made them too important for their old workmates.

Not Nina. She was equally impatient with everyone, junior or senior. It had caused plenty of trouble over the years, but today it was earning her a lift from Rob Collins to North Cumbria Caravan Park.

Or it was meant to. They'd almost reached Silloth when Caroline Deane called. Nina listened carefully, thanked her, then turned to Rob.

"Change of plan. We're heading to Grune Point."

The sun glared off the plastic and metal in the caravan graveyard as they drove past. The machinery's bone-shaking crashes pierced through the throbbing in her head. Something about it felt unsettling – all those holiday memories, those temporary homes, now being crushed to nothing in steel jaws...

"Mind opening it?" Rob asked.

Nina realised they'd stopped at the first gate leading to Grune Point. She climbed out carefully, hoping fresh air would help. It just made her cold.

Three more gates and a rocky path led them to Grune Point. Rob chatted beside her as they walked, seemingly unbothered by her silence.

Caroline waited at the end of fresh boards leading down to the creek. She appeared to be ankle-deep in water.

"Careful on your way down," she called.

"Do you think there's evidence here?" Nina pointed to the boards.

"No. But the ground's not safe. You'll sink otherwise."

Rob hung back. "Think I'll wait here."

Halfway down, Nina wished she'd done the same. The boards shifted under her feet. She fixed her gaze on the horizon, on the hills and the strange masts of Anthorn Radio Station, where atomic clocks broadcast the UK's official time.

If only they'd paused those clocks overnight. She could have used the extra sleep.

Caroline pointed downwards when Nina reached her.

"Is that it?" Nina asked

"That's it," Caroline said. "Thought you might want to see it in place before I moved it."

Nina crouched to examine the wooden beam. It was smooth and around four feet long, roughly an inch by two in cross section.

"Looks like a bit of batten."

"I thought so, too. It's odd – you don't get much driftwood here. And not this regular in shape. Look." Caroline pointed.

Near one end was a darker patch among the water staining.

"Blood?" Nina asked.

"Maybe. Probably. I think I see hair, too. We'll know once it's in the lab."

Nina stood carefully, her stomach lurching at the shifting ground. Without moving her head, she scanned the landscape. Sand, mud, patches of land amid water.

"I can't tell how far this is from where the body was found," she said.

"Nothing looks familiar because nothing stays put. The dunes move. This isn't solid land – it changes shape daily. But the body was about fifty yards from here."

"Could it have moved in the current?"

"Yes," Caroline replied. "Or whoever used it moved away before dumping it. There's more water here, closer to the main creek. Maybe they thought it would wash out to sea."

CHAPTER THIRTY-FOUR

Nina thanked Caroline and made her slow way back up the boards.

"Feeling any better?" Rob asked cheerfully.

She shook her head, watching Caroline carefully recover the beam.

"No," she said. "But at least I'm on dry land. Come on, let's go to the caravan park."

CHAPTER THIRTY-FIVE

Aaron, Tom and Roddy took the stairs again. The man and woman they'd seen earlier were gone, but they passed a different pair in the corridor outside Reid's flat. This man wore an anonymous suit and burgundy tie, his thin face hairless. The woman with him had a sharp-creased grey skirt and white shirt, shoulder-length blonde hair and glasses perched on her nose.

Aaron smiled as they passed. The pair returned his smile, but their expressions faltered when they noticed Roddy behind him. It could have been the uniform, but Aaron doubted it.

These visitors were a stark contrast to Reid's earlier ones, and more surprising.

"Hang on," Reid called when they knocked. He likely thought it was the pair who'd just left.

The door opened a crack and Reid's face appeared. "What do you... Oh. It's you, is it?"

"It is, Mr Reid. Mind if we have a quick word?" Aaron kept his smile fixed in place.

"I'm busy."

"It won't take long, Mr Reid."

Aaron felt his facial muscles fighting to relax. His husband Serge had always said his smile was infectious, and while Aaron couldn't see it himself, it had proven useful over the years.

But this wasn't his usual friendly smile. This was the one he used to unsettle people, to crack their confidence. Knowing Roddy was nearby, unseen by Reid, only added to the effect.

Reid frowned briefly before shaking his head. "Don't think so." He moved to shut the door.

"Where were you the night before last?" Aaron asked.

"Not sure."

"You said you hadn't had a break-in, Mr Reid."

"I just told you, I'm busy."

"What happened to, 'Always willing to help the constabulary'?"

Reid's lip curled as he examined Aaron, as if seeing him anew. "No. I haven't had a break-in."

"We've just seen your van, Mr Reid. The window's smashed."

"It wasn't when I parked it there an hour ago."

Aaron wanted to punch the air in triumph. He'd caught Reid in a lie. The CCTV would show when the van arrived, and Aaron was certain it would show a broken window.

"Are you sure about that?" he said.

"I am. And I'm beginning to think you bastards have been down there and smashed up my car to see what you can find in it."

Reid pulled the door wider and stepped into the corridor, inches from Aaron's face. Though only slightly taller and reasonably built, there was something in Reid's eyes – an emptiness – that made Aaron want to step back and apologise.

But he held his ground. Reid had lied and was refusing to cooperate in a murder investigation. The lie alone was enough.

"Ethan Reid, I'm arresting you for attempting to pervert the course of justice."

"I don't think so." Reid moved forward until they were nose to nose.

There was movement at the corner of Aaron's eye. Roddy. He smiled as Reid took a step backwards.

CHAPTER THIRTY-SIX

"Back, are you?"

Nina hadn't made it out of the car when Barry Joyce appeared, jabbing a finger in her direction. She squeezed her eyes shut and reminded herself that things could be worse. She could still be on those boards, slowly sinking into the sand as she wobbled her way back to dry land.

"Yes." The word came out weary.

The driver's door opened. Nina opened her eyes to see Rob Collins looking across the top of the car, offering Barry Joyce his usual pleasant smile.

"Everything OK?" Rob asked.

"I don't know. How about you tell me?" Joyce's tone dripped with hostility.

The exchange made little sense to Nina, and her head was still pounding with what felt like the drumbeat from *Jailhouse Rock*. She swung her legs out of the car.

"I mean it," Joyce said.

"Mean what?"

"You lot. We don't want you here. We don't want the police here."

Nina sighed. "People usually don't want the police around when they've got something to hide. Do you have something to hide, Mr Joyce?"

"How d'you know my name?"

"You told me your name," she reminded him.

He frowned. "I told you I was called Baz. I didn't tell you anything... Oh. Right. It was her, was it? The junkie scum?"

Nina started to walk past him.

"Seriously," he called after her. "We don't want you here. Puts people on edge."

Nina turned. "Can you tell me where you were the night before last, Mr Joyce?"

"Oh no you don't." He jabbed his finger again.

Nina wasn't sure what she disliked more – Joyce's face, his voice, or that bloody finger. But the voice had the edge. It had a whining quality mixed with naked aggression, like someone who'd punch you in the face and then blame you for hurting his knuckles.

"If you won't tell me where you were," she said. "I'll have to ask you to come with me to the station."

"Bloody hell. Fine. I was at the pub."

"Which pub?"

"Golf Hotel. On—"

"I know where the Golf Hotel is, Mr Joyce. Thanks for your cooperation."

She walked away, leaving Joyce scowling. Rob Collins maintained his pleasant smile, as if he'd just watched entertainment staged purely for his benefit. Rob Collins always seemed to smile, whatever the situation. If anyone was the very opposite of Barry Joyce, it was Rob.

CHAPTER THIRTY-SIX

There was no answer when Nina tapped on Chelsea's door. She knocked louder and called out Chelsea's name.

When silence persisted, she pushed the door. It opened easily.

Chelsea lay on the bed, staring at the roof. Tears glistened on her cheeks as she turned slowly towards the door.

"Go away." Her eyes finally focused on Nina.

"Are you OK, Chelsea?"

The girl laughed, the noise catching in her throat. "Do I look OK? Just leave me alone."

"Tell me about Ethan Reid."

"Go away."

"Tell me about the box. The tin we found here. Was it his?"

Chelsea shook her head, though Nina sensed it was more a general gesture than an answer. The young woman turned away, curling up to face the wall.

"Chelsea?" Nina tried one last time.

Silence.

"Chelsea?"

Still nothing.

Chelsea Bright didn't want her around any more than Barry Joyce did. Nina had been in less welcoming places than the North Cumbria Caravan Park.

But not many of them.

CHAPTER THIRTY-SEVEN

Zoe and Carl stood in silence in the shadow of the statue on Earl Street, watching people come and go from the court building. No one noticed them.

Zoe knew why she'd come – to watch Streeting give his evidence. She'd always planned to attend, but Olivia's disappearance made it crucial. Aaron would be giving his own evidence later, but she needed to ensure Streeting stuck to his story, even though she couldn't control what he said in the witness box.

He had done his part. Carter might have looked composed, but he had to know he was cornered.

She started to turn to Carl but stopped as four figures approached – two humans and two animals. Miles and Stacey from the Port of Workington, along with Freddie the parrot and Taylor the dachshund.

"Hello," said Zoe.

"Alright." Miles nodded.

"Hi," Stacey offered.

CHAPTER THIRTY-SEVEN

"Bugger off," squawked Freddie.

These two had worked under Bobby Silver before Streeting killed her on Carter's orders. Before that, they'd worked for Victor Parlick, who'd met a similar end. Taylor barked at some pigeons fighting over a sandwich nearby.

"That went OK," said Miles.

"You watched that?" Zoe hadn't spotted them in the gallery.

"Oh yes." Stacey's grim smile reflected the loss of her close friend. "Wouldn't have missed it for the world."

The gates to the court building ground open. Carl stared at the vans beyond, his face pale.

"It's OK," Zoe reassured him. "It won't happen again."

Three uniformed officers emerged, followed by Streeting, who scanned the area, his movements tense and jerky.

"I've done my bit," he called when he spotted them.

"I saw," replied Zoe.

"You'll bear that in mind."

Carl laughed. "What are you expecting?"

Streeting folded his arms. "A bit of leniency."

Zoe stepped forward, positioning herself between Streeting and her angry companions. The armed police moved to protect him.

"Ralph," she said, "you killed a lot of people. You murdered Bobby Silver in cold blood, and we've got overwhelming evidence. So no. I'm pleased you told the truth, but we promised you nothing."

"But you—"

"But we what?" Carl said. "You turned on Carter because he killed Mulligan. You didn't do it out of conscience. No one owes you anything."

The guards ushered Streeting into the van. He glared at them as the door slid shut. The convoy pulled away onto Warwick Road.

"Hope he rots," said Miles.

"He will," Stacey replied, her grim smile unchanged.

"Bugger off," said Freddie.

CHAPTER THIRTY-EIGHT

On the way back to the station, DI Keyes kept glancing at his watch. The first few times, Tom ignored it, but eventually he had to ask.

"Court," DI Keyes replied.

Tom nodded. Carter's trial.

DI Keyes would be giving evidence this afternoon. Nothing else mattered compared to that, but the world didn't agree. Stella's team had half a dozen crime scenes plus Grune Point to examine. Tom's request to check Ethan Reid's flat had earned him a stream of colourful language that might have startled anyone who didn't know Stella Berry.

Tom was used to Stella's outbursts. But it meant waiting for Roddy's colleagues to secure the scene. Then, at the Hub, Reid spent twenty minutes with his lawyer.

Now, finally, they could interview him. Tom followed DI Keyes into the room and sat beside him. He looked across the table and blinked in surprise.

Ethan Reid's lawyer was Trevor Singleton – a serene-looking man with white hair and an unlined face that seemed ready to smile at any moment. Tom knew him from previous cases.

"What are—?" Tom caught himself and went through the interview formalities instead.

It made no sense for Singleton to represent someone like Reid. The man's previous clients had all been high-ranking members of Myron Carter's organisation.

Either Carter's empire was crumbling, making work scarce for criminal lawyers of Singleton's calibre, or Reid was more significant than they'd thought. Tom remembered the professional-looking couple leaving Reid's flat earlier.

"What's your relationship with Femi Moorhouse and Chelsea Bright?" DI Keyes asked.

"I don't have one," Reid replied.

"What about the broken window on your van?" Tom leaned forward. "Did they do it?"

"I don't know anything about a broken window." Reid turned to Tom with empty eyes – more unsettling than any anger or hatred.

DI Keyes had the next question. "Where were you the night before last, after eight o'clock?"

Reid's forehead creased. "With Hannah."

"Who?"

"Hannah Field. She's my girlfriend."

"And where exactly were you and Hannah?"

"At her place."

"You'll need to be more precise, Mr Reid."

"Dalton Street, Cockermouth." Reid shrugged. "You want her phone number?"

"We'd be grateful," DI Keyes said dryly.

Reid rattled off the number without checking his phone. Tom watched him.

CHAPTER THIRTY-EIGHT

He was too calm for someone under arrest, being questioned about murder, with CSI about to search his flat. His alibi would be thoroughly investigated, yet he showed no concern.

Tom didn't like that at all.

CHAPTER THIRTY-NINE

Nina tried to console herself with the thought that she'd at least made an effort. If Chelsea Bright wouldn't help herself, there wasn't much more Nina could do.

Rob Collins waited in the patrol car by the patch of green near the caravan park entrance. A white Honda Jazz she recognised from Grune Point had joined him, along with an elderly woman Nina thought she'd seen before.

"You want to watch him," the woman called out as Nina walked past with a polite smile.

Nina stopped. "Watch who?"

"Him." The woman pointed towards the row of park homes behind Nina.

Nina turned, but saw no one there.

She studied the woman more closely. Unlike the usual troubled souls Nina encountered, this one appeared well-groomed and smartly dressed.

"Who?" Nina pressed.

"Barry Joyce," the woman said.

Nina realised the woman wasn't confused at all – she'd

been indicating the spot where Joyce had confronted Nina minutes earlier. This was the same woman Nina had spotted on their first visit to find Chelsea, standing on the green with an elderly man, both casting nervous glances at Barry Joyce.

"Why?" Nina asked.

The woman stepped closer, her voice dropping to barely above a whisper. "You can't trust him."

"No?"

"No." The woman shook her head. "Do you know about him? About his past?"

"Can I ask your name?" Nina said.

"Mrs Gaines. Veronica."

"Right. Well, yes, we're aware of Mr Joyce's—"

"I'm telling you," Mrs Gaines cut in, "if anyone here's causing trouble, it's him. Femi Moorhouse wasn't what you'd really want in a neighbour. But he wouldn't have done anyone any harm. No one except himself, at least. But Barry Joyce..." She shook her head, her expression grim.

Nina remembered Barry Joyce wasn't their only person of interest. "Can you tell me anything about Erica Stern?"

Mrs Gaines frowned. "Erica Stern?" she asked.

"She's in the park home opposite Femi and Chelsea's caravan. I believe her husband—"

"You don't need to worry about Erica Stern."

"No?" Nina hadn't been worried exactly. She just hadn't seen her. And the woman's husband had vanished two years ago.

Probably nothing significant. But 'probably' was never quite enough.

"Oh no." Mrs Gaines smiled. "She's a lovely girl, is Erica, poor lass."

"You know her well?"

"Us widows have to stick together."

Nina's attention sharpened. "Widows?"

Mrs Gaines's mouth fell open. "Oh, no. I didn't mean it like—"

"I understand Archie Stern's been missing for two years. Are you telling me he's dead?"

"No, no. I don't… I didn't…"

Seeing the woman's growing distress, Nina softened her approach. "It's OK."

"I just meant it figuratively. Not literally. You understand?"

"Of course."

This had all been pointless. Joyce had an alibi that would need checking, but he wouldn't have offered it if it weren't solid. Chelsea wouldn't talk, and Veronica Gaines had nothing useful to share. Nina's gaze drifted past the woman to Rob's car, then caught on the Honda.

"Do you know Simon Miller?" she asked.

"The birdwatcher?"

"That's the one."

"Oh, yes," Mrs Gaines said. "We all know Simon. Bit of a character, isn't he?"

Nina smiled. "That's one way of putting it." But she didn't have anything specific to ask about Simon Miller. Not yet.

"Thank you, Mrs Gaines," she said.

The woman nodded. "Don't tell him I was talking about him."

"Barry Joyce?"

Another nod.

What had he done to make his neighbours so wary of him?

CHAPTER THIRTY-NINE

"Don't worry, Mrs Gaines. Thank you."

Nina walked back to the patrol car. She could think of other ways to describe Simon Miller, less charitable ones than 'bit of a character', but it took all sorts.

CHAPTER FORTY

HANNAH FIELD PICKED up on the first ring. "Hello?"

Tom introduced himself and explained why he was calling.

"Oh, right." Reid's girlfriend's tone suggested that receiving police calls about murder alibis was routine. "Yeah, that's true."

"It is?"

"Yeah. He came over to mine around half seven."

"And when did he leave?"

"Not till next morning."

"What sort of time next morning?"

"Early."

Tom waited for elaboration. When none came, he pressed further. "Any idea of an actual time?"

"Nah."

As witnesses went, Hannah Field wasn't the best he'd come across. "I don't suppose anyone else can vouch for this?"

"What do you mean?"

CHAPTER FORTY

"Did anyone else see him at yours? Both of you, together?"

"I bloody well hope not." She gave a nervous laugh.

Of course not. An alibi he could verify would be too much to hope for. Tom was about to end the call when a thought struck him.

"Did Mr Reid drive to yours," he said, "the night before last?"

"Course."

Hannah Field was certainly economical with words.

"And can you tell me what vehicle he was driving?"

"The Bentley."

Tom's fingers moved across his keyboard, checking the registration before ending the call. "Thank you."

The records confirmed it – Ethan Reid owned a Bentley Continental GT in Moroccan Blue. Tom thought back to the car park beneath Pears House, trying to recall if he'd seen it there.

What mattered more were the cameras. Cockermouth had plenty, plus more on the A595 towards Whitehaven, and northbound and eastbound, as well as the A66 heading south. He began entering requests when his phone rang.

"Hello?" His gaze remained fixed on the screen.

"Just checking up on you," Harriett said.

Tom smiled. That was what he loved about her – her directness. No pretence, just honest communication.

"I'm fine," he said, then remembered to ask after her. "What about you?"

She groaned about confidential long-term investigations, but he was used to that. Her passion for the job was evident – she'd mentioned it enough times for him to believe it.

Once he'd ended the call, the team room felt oddly quiet.

DI Keyes was at court, the boss was returning, and Nina was still interviewing Chelsea Bright. He needed someone to bounce ideas off.

"Do you think Ethan Reid did it?" he asked the empty room.

Reid's relaxed demeanour in custody made it hard to believe he was guilty.

"No," Tom answered himself. "But I don't trust him."

He made two final calls before his coffee break. Inspector Keane had no updates on Olivia Bagsby or Kaciaryna Ilinich. "Sorry, Tom. Whoever's got them, they're hiding them well."

His last call was to track down Archie Stern's mother, Millicent. The number connected him to a care home.

"Briggs Hutchinson Care," a woman answered in a strong north-eastern accent. "How can I help you?"

"I was wondering if I could talk to Millicent Stern."

"'Fraid not, pet."

"Oh." Tom's heart sank. "I'm sorry—"

"She's on her nap," the woman continued. "And when she wakes up, well, I dunno if you'll get much sense out of her. Could it wait till tomorrow?"

"Yes," Tom replied, relieved. "Yes, it can."

After exchanging contact details and receiving assurance about tomorrow's call, Tom ended the conversation.

"That went pretty well," he told himself, and headed out for his coffee.

CHAPTER FORTY-ONE

"And you knew the deceased how, precisely?" The barrister's voice echoed through the courtroom.

Aaron drew in a breath and scanned the room before answering. "I first came across Victor Parlick when he was one of a group of potential witnesses to a fight that got out of hand at a Workington pub."

"And was he involved?" The barrister leaned forward. "In the fight, I mean?"

"No. He wasn't even a witness, as it turned out. But he was helpful."

"Helpful how, precisely?"

Aaron shifted from one leg to the other. The barrister's repeated use of 'precisely' grated on his nerves. How could he explain the instinct that told him someone had more to say? The careful cultivation of trust that led to quiet meetings away from watchful eyes? The delicate dance between the detective and the potential informant?

The young barrister smiled encouragingly. Despite a heavy build that made him look more like a boxer than a lawyer, his demeanour was friendly. He waited patiently for Aaron to explain how Carter and Streeting had stolen decades of life from Victor – now just a barely recognisable body pulled from the sea.

Aaron looked up at the public gallery. Ryan Tobin sat there, fresh from his own mauling by the defence barrister. It hadn't been difficult to discredit someone who'd admitted to stealing emails from Carter's company servers. But those emails still existed, still told their damning story.

Behind the row of strangers, Aaron spotted a familiar face. Blond hair, handsome features. His heart quickened as he met Serge's eyes, forcing himself to maintain his composure.

His husband had come, despite Aaron never telling him how difficult this would be. He hadn't known himself it would be so different from his previous court appearances.

But Serge had understood. He'd witnessed Aaron's mental spiral after Victor's death.

Miles and Stacey sat beside Serge. They'd known Victor, just as they'd known Bobby Silver. If he couldn't do this for the dead, he could do it for those left behind.

Aaron closed his eyes and conjured Victor's image. The nose ring, pierced eyebrow, that characteristic smile. When he opened them again, the barrister was still waiting.

"Well," Aaron began. "I suppose it all began the first time I suggested to Victor we meet for a drink."

CHAPTER FORTY-TWO

THE THING about driving a Bentley Continental GT in Moroccan Blue with personalised plates was that people noticed it. Luckily for Ethan Reid, it had been one of those cold, wet days where people stayed warm indoors and avoided looking out their windows.

He was less lucky that ANPR cameras didn't mind the rain.

Tom narrowed his eyes at the notification on his screen, then blinked and read it again.

At half past nine, Reid's Bentley had been captured on the A594 heading north from Cockermouth through Papcastle. The cameras on the major roads heading east and south were down for maintenance, but this one was new and had received its software update without going offline.

Tom scanned through his notes from the call with Hannah Field, Reid's girlfriend. She was lying. They both were, and that was after Reid's lie about the broken window on his van. This one, Tom could prove.

There were many places Reid might have gone after

leaving Hannah Field's. A big chunk of Cumbria lay in that direction, plus road networks leading everywhere else. With the other cameras down, there was no way to know where he'd headed after the A594.

But one destination made sense – Grune Point. The same car appeared again hours later, which would have given him enough time to do… whatever he might have done to Femi Moorhouse.

Tom reached for his phone to call DI Keyes, then remembered he'd be in Carlisle giving evidence. He tried Nina next.

She answered immediately. "What's up?"

"You nearby?"

"Half an hour, give or take. Everything OK?"

"Yes. We've got Ethan Reid here. Caught him out in a lie."

"You have?"

"His second of the morning, he's on a roll. I want to interview him."

"Go on, then," Nina said.

"I'm on my own here."

"So? Find a PC or something. You don't need me there to hold your hand."

He wanted to object, but she'd already hung up, leaving him staring at the phone wondering if she was right.

Of course she was.

He stood. He could do this himself. Find someone available, brief them, bring them in while he grilled Reid and stripped Trevor Singleton's pleasant veneer. He could…

He hesitated, still standing. It wasn't just Ethan Reid he was up against.

It was Reid and Trevor Singleton – one hell of a pairing.

CHAPTER FORTY-TWO

He'd completed the latest interview course months ago and knew the rules and tactics, but theory wasn't practice.

They'd have him for breakfast if he wasn't prepared. But they couldn't keep Reid much longer, not with the evidence they had – or more importantly, didn't have.

What should I do?

He stood there, looking around the room as if waiting for an answer, when the door opened and DI Finch walked in.

She frowned at him, half-standing, half-crouched by his desk. "What are you doing?"

He swallowed. "Just off to interview Ethan Reid, boss. Care to join me?"

CHAPTER FORTY-THREE

Zoe wasn't sure what she'd expected, but it wasn't this.

Tom briefed her on their way downstairs, almost breathless with excitement. Reid's name had come up in connection with the dead man. He had a record, a history of violence. And he'd lied about his van being broken into as well as about his alibi.

She'd met plenty of liars in her career. Some were criminals, but most weren't murderers. Ethan Reid would likely be another junior gangster hoping to progress but unlikely to make it. His record and photo hadn't changed her mind about that.

Then she saw Trevor Singleton sitting next to Ethan Reid in Interview Room Four. Tom hadn't said who his lawyer was.

This was Zoe's first encounter with Singleton since Carter's arrest. She'd seen him with Mick Halfpenny and beside Ralph Streeting in the custody suite. She studied Ethan Reid again, reconsidering her assessment.

Either Singleton had lowered his standards, or Reid was more significant than she'd thought.

Tom handled the formalities without fuss or mind games. Just facts and the obvious approach.

"Mr Reid," Tom said, "we've spoken to Hannah Field, who confirmed you were with her during the hours we've asked about."

"Good." Reid's voice was empty, like he was crossing a name off a list. Hannah Field's name. It wasn't a list anyone would want to be on.

Zoe felt what her team had described – the man's menace.

"She also told us you drove over in your Bentley, and unfortunately for you, that Bentley appears on ANPR heading north, away from Hannah Field's residence in Cockermouth, during the time you both claim you were at hers."

Reid remained silent.

Singleton watched with a faint smile, more like someone viewing mild entertainment than a lawyer in a murder inquiry.

"Can you explain this?" Tom kept his tone measured, avoiding accusation.

"Can I have five minutes with my lawyer?" Reid asked.

Zoe nodded.

They waited outside in the custody suite, checking emails and discussing Carlisle quietly. Aaron would be there now with Serge. She'd wanted to stay for him, but they couldn't have two DIs away.

A small cough made her turn. Singleton stood there, calm as ever. "We're ready."

Back in the room, Zoe decided to change tack. "You should be aware that we've found the object we believe was used to murder Femi Moorhouse. It's currently being examined by our colleagues."

"Fine," Reid said, somehow even calmer than his lawyer.

"What about your car?" Tom asked.

"Look, I lied." Reid shrugged with an easy smile.

"Why?"

"Because I was somewhere I wasn't supposed to be. Nothing to do with Femi Moorhouse, though."

He was making them work for every detail, Zoe realised. They'd have to beg for each morsel of information.

"Where were you, then?"

"Wigton. Visiting Vanessa Peters."

"Wigton's where you used to live, isn't it?" Tom asked.

"It is," Reid confirmed.

Zoe's patience snapped. "It's been a long day already, and you've admitted lying in a murder investigation. So why don't you just tell us what you were doing in Wigton, and we'll see if we believe you, rather than spinning this out all day."

Reid seemed pleased at breaking her patience. He leaned back, palms up. "Fine. Look, I haven't always been a pillar of the community like I am now."

Tom watched intently as Reid continued.

"When I lived in Wigton, I was what you might call an antisocial neighbour. I caused trouble, and when people complained about me, I didn't make their lives easy. Vanessa was one of those people."

"What did you do to her?" Tom asked.

"She complained about me, I threatened her, she went to the courts and got an anti-harassment order against me."

"And you've just admitted to breaching that order," Zoe pointed out.

CHAPTER FORTY-THREE

"Yes. That, and lying about it, but the only reason I lied is that I didn't want grief over the breach."

"Why did you want to see her?"

"I'm a changed man, DI Finch."

Reid's use of her name made Zoe blink. It showed unusual confidence for someone his age, with his record.

Singleton maintained his pleasant smile, still silent.

"How so?" Tom asked.

"I wanted to apologise. I made Vanessa's life hell. She got an injunction, I moved away, grew up, learned a few things. I wasn't visiting her to harass her. I was visiting her to say sorry."

"We'll be checking this with her," Zoe said.

Reid nodded.

Zoe knew Vanessa Peters would confirm everything. But that didn't make it true.

CHAPTER FORTY-FOUR

If Ethan Reid had hoped they'd accept his word and release him, he masked any disappointment well when they returned him to his cell pending confirmation.

Tom headed upstairs with the DI, where they parted company. She had calls to make in her office, and he had his own to handle.

"Keep your bloody hair on," Nina snapped when he called her. "I'm nearly back."

"Don't bother parking. Boss wants you to head out to Wigton. Check Reid's latest alibi."

He could hear conversation in Nina's car and remembered she wasn't alone. She'd been too hungover to drive and had grabbed a lift from Rob Collins.

"Rob's about to finish his shift," she said. "But he's sorted a lift with Martinez. She's waiting for me in the car park. And I've got a job for you."

"You have?"

"I had another run-in with Barry Joyce at the caravan park. And a chat with one of the other neighbours. Oh, and

CHAPTER FORTY-FOUR

Simon Miller, that birdwatcher who hates humans and somehow found a dead body in the dark?"

"What about him?"

"His car was there, too."

"He was the one who told us Femi lived there," Tom said.

"True. But he was also dead keen to convince us that Femi had been killed over drugs, and that they were all decent, law-abiding citizens at the caravan park."

"And we know that's not true."

"Exactly. So it might be worth doing some digging. See what you can find out about the residents. And whether there's any connection with Miller."

Fifteen minutes into his research, Tom wasn't sure who unsettled him more – Ethan Reid or Barry Joyce. Reid had an air about him, with whispers from competitors and victims, but his record wasn't particularly alarming.

Barry Joyce, however, had serious history.

His gang had favoured baseball bats, using them without hesitation. They'd gone on a spree – four robberies over three days. In two raids, they'd beaten staff unconscious just to make a point to others.

Their final job had gone wrong. Someone spotted them from outside, police arrived, and the ensuing chase ended with their car in a ditch.

Joyce had been the only survivor.

He'd never admitted his role in the beatings, and the prosecution couldn't prove it was him, though it matched his profile. He was convicted anyway under joint enterprise. Even if he hadn't wielded the bat himself, he'd been willingly involved.

Joyce's twelve-year sentence could have been shorter, but

his temper followed him inside. Tom read through his prison offences – attacks on inmates and officers alike – with growing unease. This seemed like exactly the sort of man who might murder again, years later, up at Grune Point.

The main lesson was clear: crossing Barry Joyce was dangerous. His victims usually ended up in the infirmary with stab wounds from makeshift weapons, broken bones from gym equipment, and in one case, severe burns from a massive vat of boiling soup.

Tom set aside Joyce's file and turned to Archie Stern's disappearance.

Archie's wife, Erica, had reported him missing two years ago. She'd told officers he'd packed and vanished overnight. Though distraught, she hadn't been completely surprised, admitting she'd suspected an affair.

As a travelling salesman, Archie had spent most of his time away. Erica had worried he might be leading a double life – other wives, other families. They'd never had children themselves; eight years before his disappearance, he'd suddenly decided against it.

"He said he was past that stage of his life," Erica had told police. "I wouldn't have minded a family myself, but it takes two to tango. And we never really had the money to make it easy."

The financial angle had interested police. The Sterns had lived in North Cumbria Caravan Park for years, but four months before Archie vanished, they'd ordered an upgraded park home, delivered just after his disappearance.

"I'm not going to pretend we weren't stretched," Erica had said. "But we could manage it, just. I thought we could, anyway. Archie seemed more worried than I was."

Archie's disappearance had been complete – no sightings

CHAPTER FORTY-FOUR

since. Tom still needed to speak with the man's mother, Millicent, but that would have to wait if she was still napping.

The neighbours' interviews had yielded little. Barry Joyce hadn't been there then, but Veronica Gaines had backed up Erica's story, adding her own suspicions about Archie.

"Always looking past you when he spoke to you," she'd said. "Shifty type, he was. I hope nothing bad's happened to him, of course, but she's better off without him."

Other neighbours had nothing useful to add. Neither did the few friends police had interviewed.

One of those friends was Simon Miller. He'd claimed no special knowledge, expressing sympathy for Erica, but having no idea of Archie's whereabouts.

Tom struggled to reconcile this with the Miller he'd met at Grune Point. That Miller seemed incapable of friendship or normal human empathy.

But perhaps Miller had changed in two years. People did change. Barry Joyce hadn't committed armed robbery in years. And Ethan Reid, if his claims were true, was now a pillar of the community.

CHAPTER FORTY-FIVE

NINA HAD EXPECTED an elderly woman with white hair and a yapping dog, but Vanessa Peters wasn't much older than herself. The white hair was clearly dyed, and there was no dog in sight.

Vanessa Peters eyed Nina with suspicion. "What d'ya want?"

"I was hoping I could come in and talk to you about a case we're working on." Nina mustered her friendliest smile.

Vanessa glanced back into the house before turning back with narrowed eyes. "What case? I've not done anything."

"No, of course not. It's just... I understand you had a visit from one of your old neighbours the other night. We're just trying to confirm that, and work out when it might have been."

Vanessa nodded but remained silent, keeping the door partially closed.

"I'm talking about Tuesday night. The night before last."

Another nod, another glance inside.

"Were you in?"

CHAPTER FORTY-FIVE

"Yes," Vanessa said finally. "And yes, Ethan Reid was here."

"When?"

"Not sure I remember." She looked back into the house again.

Nina waited, listening. "Are you OK, Miss Peters?"

"Mrs," the woman corrected.

"Are you OK? Is there someone here?"

"Yes."

Nina's smile vanished. "Has Reid sent someone? How many of them are there?"

Vanessa's lip curled in bewilderment and contempt. "What the bloody hell are you talking about?"

Nina stepped closer, lowering her voice. "If you can't speak freely, just nod. If you can tell me how many there are, I can get you out of here and get backup."

"My son," Vanessa said, her expression clearing slightly.

"What?"

"My son. He's three. He's in the kitchen. That's what I'm listening out for. Toddlers are a right menace."

"I don't—"

"And yes. Ethan Reid was here. About half nine, ten. Stayed for an hour, hour and a half."

"Seems a long time. Why did he come?"

"Said he wanted to apologise. For all the trouble he'd caused."

"And that took an hour and a half?"

"We drank tea."

A bang echoed from inside, followed by a wail.

"Got to run." Vanessa shut the door.

Nina raised her hand to knock again, but let it drop. She walked back to the patrol car where Martinez waited.

She wouldn't learn anything else from Vanessa Peters. The woman might be telling the truth, but Ethan Reid had had time to arrange things. His lawyer could make calls, set up an alibi, ensure everything was properly documented.

And if Ethan Reid told Vanessa to say something, she'd say it. No one would want to cross him. Not if he knew where they lived. And especially not with a toddler in the house.

CHAPTER FORTY-SIX

"How did it go?" asked Zoe.

Nina and Aaron started talking simultaneously. Tom remained quiet, though his lips twitched with suppressed laughter.

"Sorry, Nina. I meant Aaron."

"Right." Nina's tone was clipped. "Yeah. Course."

Zoe glanced at the large screen where Aaron's face dominated the top box. Nina's box remained empty – she was heading back with Martinez driving, the signal too weak for video.

"Good, boss." Behind Aaron, the statue loomed. The sky had darkened where Zoe sat, but in Carlisle, the setting sun still caught fragments of the giant figure.

"Good?"

"Well, I don't know how much difference it'll make. Can't say I saw Carter killing Victor."

"No," Zoe said. "But it all adds up. Whatever evidence we have against Carter, we still need a motive. You're the only one who can give it to us. You know why he died."

"Yes." Aaron's single word hung in the air.

"I'm sorry. I know it's a sore—"

"It's OK, boss. But it's about to rain and I want to head back. Speak later." He disconnected before Zoe could respond.

He'd looked fine. He was past all that now. She hoped.

"Boss." Nina's voice cut through Zoe's thoughts. "I spoke to Vanessa Peters. Reid's alibi checks out."

"Oh." A familiar weight settled in Zoe's stomach. *Another dead end.* "That's annoying. I really thought—"

"But I don't know if I believe her. She seemed scared, wouldn't let me in. Nothing obvious, just..."

"If Reid asked her to lie for him, she probably would," Tom said from his desk.

"You've met the man," Nina replied.

"And he's already lied to us once," Zoe added.

"Twice. About being at his girlfriend's, and about the van window."

Zoe considered their options. They could hold Reid, question him again. But would he break?

"You'll have seen the post-mortem report from Chris Robertson," she said. "Exactly as predicted."

"Banged on the head, left to drown," Tom summarised, no doubt echoing the words Chris had used during the post-mortem itself.

"The actual report has more detail than that—"

"Bloody hell," Tom interrupted, staring at his screen.

"What?"

"The flat. Reid's flat."

"What about it?"

"Look." He brought up the report on the main screen.

"I can't see anything," Nina said.

CHAPTER FORTY-SIX

"Stella couldn't get anyone to Reid's place while her team was at the crime scene and Chelsea's caravan. We left two PCs watching."

"Yes," Zoe said, having read ahead.

"Incident report just came in. Someone lured them away. Screaming from the stairwell."

"And?" Nina asked.

"They're in hospital. Been beaten up." Tom scanned the report. "Nothing too serious, apparently." He met Zoe's gaze.

"But whatever was in Reid's flat," she said, "it won't be there now."

CHAPTER FORTY-SEVEN

"You want to do it?" DI Finch asked.

Tom felt the word 'no' forming in his throat. He smiled, pushing it back down.

Did he want to tell Ethan Reid, a man who terrified him without even trying, that despite his verified alibi, he wasn't going home? Did he want to face Trevor Singleton, the kind of lawyer who represented the most dangerous killers, and explain his client would spend the night in the cells instead of his posh marina flat?

It was like being a lion tamer. You never wanted to walk into the cage. But it was part of the job. When the opportunity came, you took it.

"Absolutely," Tom said, forcing confidence into his voice.

DI Finch frowned. "You sure?"

"Yes, boss." He turned away to hide his uncertainty.

"Because I'm happy to do it. And if you want to—"

"I can do it, boss." Tom strode out towards the stairwell.

He had to wait while Singleton finished a call, pacing the

CHAPTER FORTY-SEVEN

corridor outside Interview Room Four for fifteen minutes before the lawyer appeared with an apologetic smile.

Reid's empty gaze fixed on Tom as he entered with Singleton. The suspect showed zero emotion.

Tom started the formalities, but Reid cut in. "On your own?"

His sympathetic smile and neutral tone left the question open to interpretation. None of the possibilities running through Tom's mind ended well.

"Yes," Tom said, glancing down at his blank notepad.

"Have you spoken to Vanessa Peters?" Singleton asked.

"We have."

"And has she confirmed my client was with her at the times we discussed?"

"She told my colleague Mr Reid was there, yes." The careful phrasing landed heavily in the silent room.

After a long pause, Tom continued. "We left some colleagues to keep an eye on your flat, Mr Reid."

Reid shrugged.

"They've been attacked. They're both in hospital."

Singleton leaned forward. "I hope they're going to be OK."

"Nothing too serious, I understand. But in the circumstances, I don't think we'll be releasing Mr Reid until morning."

Singleton just looked at his client with resignation. Reid's face remained blank.

"Nothing we can say to change your mind?" Singleton asked.

Tom shook his head. "Not unless your client's prepared to be more forthcoming about his van, his relationship with

Femi Moorhouse and Chelsea Bright, or his whereabouts on Tuesday night."

Reid shrugged again. "I've already told you all that."

"Right," Tom said. "Well, I'll... I'm sure we'll talk later."

"I look forward to it." Reid smiled.

Tom bolted from the room, only later realising he'd left his blank notepad behind.

CHAPTER FORTY-EIGHT

The text came in just as Zoe was about to leave.

Anchor Vaults. After seven.

A glance at her watch showed it was already past seven. She was bone-weary after bringing in both Streeting and Carter – the latter now likely facing life in prison. All those hours, the danger, the people lost.

Now Ethan Reid had emerged like an unwanted virus. At twenty-one, he had no empire, no complex web of companies or accounts. Just attitude. That, and Trevor Singleton sitting beside him in interviews. Anyone who hired Singleton was worth watching.

She'd considered ignoring the text. Let Jake have his lemonade alone. But she remembered hanging up on him yesterday, and another thought struck her – how many more meetings would they have? Would she be here long enough to spend time with the people who mattered?

Twenty-five minutes later, she slid onto the stool opposite Jake. The green drink before her would be non-alcoholic

– neither of them drank. They'd taken to surprising each other with new mocktails.

She took a sip and grimaced. "Sorry. Aniseed and orange isn't a good combination."

"Agreed." Jake passed her the backup lemonade.

She smiled and sipped it gratefully. "How are you?"

"OK, I suppose." He updated her on his father's dementia, which had stabilised. "He knows who I am more often than not," he added with a smile.

When it was her turn, she shared what she could about the case. Jake's steady gaze suggested he knew she was holding back.

"What?" she asked.

"Olivia Bagsby."

Her mouth fell open. *How could he know?*

"She didn't appear to give evidence," he said. "I did some digging. Found an incident at a location I've chosen to forget. I won't publish anything about her. It's you I'm worried about."

"Me?"

"Olivia's gone missing."

"Yes."

"And you're blaming yourself."

"No, I'm not," she protested, raising her drink.

But as she lowered it, she considered it properly for the first time since Olivia's disappearance. She'd pushed aside the guilt, but it had lingered.

"Maybe I am," she admitted.

"It's not your fault," Jake said.

"That's easy for—"

"You didn't make her take those photos or run. Didn't make her hide with David Randle."

CHAPTER FORTY-EIGHT

"If I'd never met her—"

"She'd have shared those photos anyway. Posted everything online. They'd have found her within days."

Zoe closed her mouth, processing his words. She'd never considered that angle.

"You can't keep everyone safe," Jake said. "But you do better than anyone else I know."

The conversation could have ended there, but Jake wasn't finished.

"Kiki Carnegie," he said.

"What about her?"

"I've been hearing rumours."

They both sipped their drinks, eyes locked. Zoe was determined not to fall for such an obvious prompt.

"What sort of rumours?" she asked.

"You've not heard anything?"

She considered lying, but shook her head. "No. She wanted the Grune Point case. Was angry when we took it. But something was off. Like she knew it wouldn't matter long term. Anyone else, I'd say they'd gained perspective. But Kiki Carnegie?"

"No," Jake agreed. "She's on her own side. No room for others."

"What sort of rumours?" Zoe repeated.

"I want to check my sources first," he replied, changing the subject.

But it was too late. The Olivia-shaped hole in her mind now held Kiki Carnegie, and her guilt had transformed into a persistent unease that wouldn't let go.

CHAPTER FORTY-NINE

NINA TOOK A STEP BACK, looking expectantly at Martinez. "I'd really appreciate it."

"I remember offering you a lift in this morning." Martinez crossed her arms. "I don't remember telling you I'd drive you all over Cumbria this afternoon, offering you a lift home after work, or agreeing to stop off in bloody Silloth."

Nina flashed her a grin. "But you're going to do it anyway, right?"

Martinez gave a rueful smile. "Get in."

They passed the journey north in companionable silence. Martinez was good like that. She let Nina get on with her own thinking, unlike Rob Collins, to whom a minute without conversation was a minute wasted. She didn't let her play Elvis, or sing Elvis, or talk about Elvis, as Nina had discovered in the past. But she couldn't have everything.

The idea was to stop off at the North Cumbria Caravan Park and make one last attempt to get Chelsea Bright talking.

CHAPTER FORTY-NINE

Nina wasn't confident. But at least she'd get to see the woman again. To make sure she was safe.

It didn't feel particularly safe as they drove in. The rain had eased up, but the air was still heavy with it, a low mist hanging in the darkness. Once again, the external lighting didn't seem to be working.

"It's like something out of a horror movie," Martinez said as they passed a third park home with a face pressed to a window.

Nina didn't reply, but she couldn't disagree. The quiet didn't help. They parked right by Chelsea's caravan.

"You OK waiting here?" Nina asked.

"Not got a lot of choice." Martinez smiled again.

The quiet lasted as long as it took for Nina to get out of the car, and then it was shattered by a voice.

"Get out here, you cow!"

A male voice, shouting. Nina turned her head, trying to work out which direction it was coming from, but the mist and the damp weren't helping.

It might have been next door. It might have been half a mile away.

She got back in the car. Martinez had heard the shout and already had the engine running.

"Any idea?" Martinez asked.

"No." Nina pointed ahead. "But go that way."

Moving slowly, windows open, they made their way through the caravan park. The shouting got louder as they progressed.

"I want to talk to you!" they heard.

Most of the park homes and caravans were in darkness, and the ones that weren't tended to have thick drapes blocking out all but the edges of the light. Every now and then they drove past a scene of domestic normality – lights on, curtains open, an elderly couple sitting on a sofa with tea and biscuits, a man alone at a wooden table with a radio and a book – incongruous and eerie, like moments from a stage play.

"Get out here, you bitch!" The voice was closer now, followed by the sound of banging. Nina pointed to the right, where another row of park homes sprang from the darkness, but Martinez was already making the turn.

"Who do you think you are, talking to the police?" they heard, as the headlights from Martinez's car fell on the final park home.

The man standing by the door turned to them, shielded his eyes, and turned back to the door and thumped it.

"I know you're in there, Veronica!" he shouted.

Nina had the door open before the car had come to a complete stop.

"Want me to wait in the car again?" Martinez asked.

"Not this time."

They approached Barry Joyce together, but he didn't turn to face them until they were just a few feet away.

Nina cleared her throat. "Evening, Mr Joyce."

"This doesn't concern you." He turned back to the door and banged again. "Get out here!"

"I don't think Mrs Gaines wants to talk to you," Nina said.

"I don't think it's any of your bloody business."

Martinez had left the headlights on, illuminating the patch of ground outside Veronica Gaines' park home, and Nina could see an anger in his eyes that she'd seen in men like him before.

CHAPTER FORTY-NINE

Things hadn't ended well when she'd seen it in the past.

"I think you need to calm down," she said.

Joyce turned away from the door and took a step towards them. "I told you, it's none of your business."

Nina shook her head and carried on walking towards him. "It is, I'm afraid. This isn't—"

"Get out here now, you bitch!" Joyce smashed his fist against the door, the heaviest blow yet. Nina winced at the pain he had to be feeling, but he just stood there, staring at the unyielding wood.

"Why don't we have a little chat?" she suggested. "Maybe calm down a little, see if—"

Wrong thing to say. He turned, the rage in his eyes now magnified tenfold. Barry Joyce was getting nowhere with a solid wooden door, but there were people made of soft human tissue right in front of him.

He took a step towards them. "Want a little chat, do you?"

"You need to calm down," she replied.

"I'll give you a little bloody chat." Nina could smell the alcohol on his breath from several feet away.

"Mr Joyce," she said, just as he lunged at her and fell flat on his face, his legs trapped quietly and expertly by Martinez, who he hadn't noticed slipping behind him as he approached.

Nina checked Joyce's handcuffs and pushed him into the back of the car.

"What's the plan?" Martinez looked pointedly at her watch.

"Sorry," Nina replied. "But we're going to have to take this one back to the Hub."

Martinez muttered something inaudible.

"What was that?" Nina asked.
"Ancient Cumbrian proverb."
"Yeah? What is it?"
"Never do Nina Kapoor a favour." Martinez started the engine, and they began the journey back.

CHAPTER FIFTY

"Sit down," Zoe said. "Please."

Carl frowned and sat at the kitchen counter opposite her.

"Don't you need to be heading in?"

"I can go later. They'll manage without me for a bit. But you..."

"But I what?"

Zoe lifted her coffee to her lips, trying to figure out what to say. "But we need to talk. You and me. We need to have a proper—"

Her phone buzzed on the counter beside her. Nina's name flashed on the screen.

"You can get that, if you want," Carl said.

Zoe shook her head as the phone stopped buzzing. "If it's important, she'll try again."

They sat in silence, both waiting for the phone to buzz again. Nothing happened.

"Have you decided?" Carl asked.

Zoe shook her head.

"Why not?" His jaw was clenched. Zoe hated doing this to him. "I mean it, Zoe. What's holding you back?"

She swallowed. "You are."

Carl nodded, as if he'd expected this. "You're blaming me for your inability to decide whether to move to Dorset?"

"It's not blame, Carl. I just don't know how you feel about it. I don't know if you want me to stay. I don't know if you'd consider coming with me. I don't know any of it, because we haven't been able to speak to each other properly since—"

Her phone buzzed again.

"I'm sorry." Zoe picked up.

"Boss," Nina said. "I got your message, I know you'll be in late, but I wanted to let you know where we are with Barry Joyce."

Zoe turned away to face the door, unable to meet Carl's eyes. "I don't suppose he's admitted to murdering Femi Moorhouse?"

"No. He admitted he didn't like the bloke, but says he had nothing to do with his death. Speaks like one of those racists from the seventies you read about. He actually referred to Femi as a 'darkie'. I don't think I've ever heard anyone say that in real life."

"I have," Zoe said, "but then, I'm older than you. What do you think?"

"I mean, he's got the temper, boss. You should have seen him last night. Went for me, too. And you've seen his record, what he got up to inside. He's dangerous and he's violent. But..."

Zoe risked a glance around to see Carl studying his phone. "But what?"

"I don't know. I just don't see him following someone out

to the middle of nowhere and attacking them. He doesn't have the patience for something like that."

"People can surprise you."

"And he has an alibi, boss," Nina reminded her.

"Aaron's checking that this morning, right?"

"He is," Nina confirmed. "Bloody hell!"

"What?"

"Just seen the time, boss. I've got to get to court soon. Elena will be in there now, and I'm giving evidence after her."

"Right. Good luck. I'll be in soon. I just need..." Zoe glanced towards Carl. "I've got a few things to sort out."

She ended the call and turned back to Carl, who put down his phone and looked at her.

"Since Randle died," he said.

"What?"

"You were saying. We haven't been able to speak to each other properly since... I'm finishing the sentence."

"Right," Zoe agreed, waiting for him to say more.

"And yes, that's true. I know it was work, it wasn't anything personal. But I'm struggling, Zoe."

"I'm not the only one who kept things to themselves, Carl. I asked you not to follow Randle back to where he was staying, and you did it anyway."

His eyes narrowed. "And if I hadn't, you'd never have found Olivia Bagsby. And that was only after everything you'd done. You lied to me, Zoe. For more than a year. You were talking to David Randle when you said you hadn't heard from him. I don't know if I can ever..."

They looked at one another in silence until Zoe's phone buzzed again. Tom this time.

"Yes?" she snapped.

"Morning, boss. Just wanted to update you on where we are with Archie Stern."

"Who?"

"The man with the park home opposite Chelsea's. He disappeared two years ago."

"Right." Why was he calling her about a man who'd been missing for two years?

"That new park home, the one that got delivered just after he went missing."

"What about it?" she said, dragging her hand through her long hair.

"It would have cost an arm and a leg. I can see someone realising he'd messed up ordering it, doing a runner before he had to face the music."

"So how did the wife... what's her name?"

"Erica, boss."

"How did Erica manage?"

"The notes from the disappearance say their friends were rallying round," Tom replied. "I guess if she got enough people to help a little, it would have added up."

Archie and Erica Stern were a dead end. Zoe was sure of it.

"Where are we with Ethan Reid?" she asked.

"Same as last night, boss. Not enough to charge him. They haven't been able to search his flat yet, but hopefully they'll find something useful when they do."

She nodded. "We'll need to extend his custody. I'll speak to the super when I get in. And then you and I can have a little chat with Barry Joyce."

"Look forward to it," Tom said.

Zoe ended the call and turned to Carl. "Trust me," she said.

"What?"

"You don't know if you can ever trust me."

For a moment, he looked like he might deny it, but then he sat back, seeming to deflate.

Zoe glanced at her watch. "I'm sorry."

"I don't know if that's enough," he replied.

"I mean, I'm sorry, but I didn't realise how late it had got. If I don't get Ethan Reid's custody extended, we'll have to let him go. I've got to head in."

Carl said nothing, just watched as she gathered her things. She turned to speak as she left the room, to suggest continuing the conversation later. But there was something in his eyes, something raw and wounded, that told her now wasn't the time.

The trouble was, she wasn't sure there *would* be a time. Not unless she could go back a year or two and be honest with him. If she could do that...

If she could do that, it would have ruined everything she'd achieved, in all that time. And that was the problem.

It wasn't that she'd lied to him. It wasn't that she'd betrayed him.

It was that she wasn't entirely sure she regretted it.

CHAPTER FIFTY-ONE

"Carr Milton, how can I help you?" The woman's voice was crisp and professional.

"Hello," said Tom. "This is DC Tom Willis, from Cumbria Police. I was hoping I could speak to someone about a job you did a couple of years ago."

Silence stretched across the line for a moment.

"What sort of job?"

"A new park home. Installed in the North Cumbria Caravan Park, outside Silloth."

"Yeah, I know the place. But we've done a lot of work there. I'll need you to give me the details, and then I can check our records and get back to you."

Tom provided what little information he had – the names and approximate date. "The husband had just gone missing when you installed it. It would have been on the news."

The woman snorted. "We install park homes in caravan parks all over the country, mate. Our people have seen all sorts. Not gonna remember some fella who's gone on a wander."

"Right." Tom had hoped Archie Stern's disappearance might have stuck in someone's memory. That, and the Sterns' financial difficulties. Any payment issues would have been recorded.

"But I'll look into it for you," the woman's voice softened. "Can't promise anything, mind."

He thanked her and ended the call just as his phone rang again. The number seemed familiar.

"Tom Willis."

"Alright, pet?" The voice triggered recognition.

"Hi."

"She's awake now," said the woman from Briggs Hutchinson Care.

"Thanks. Can I speak to her?"

"She's here. I'll just pass you the phone, but I'll stay in the room with her if that's OK. Don't want her getting upset."

"Thank you."

"Who's this, then?" a gruff voice demanded.

"Hello, Mrs Stern. This is Tom Willis, from Cumbria Police."

"Police, is it? What you bothering an old lady for? I've not done anything."

"I'm just trying to find out what happened to your son."

"Archie?"

"Yes."

"What you want to know about him for?" Millicent's voice grew harsh. "You lot were useless then, always been useless. Never liked the police. I always said that bitch killed him, and I've not changed my mind. Now bugger off and leave me alone."

"I'm sorry." The care worker had taken the phone back.

"That's OK," Tom replied.

"I don't think you're getting anything more out of her today."

"I think you're right. But thanks."

Tom dismissed it as the angry ravings of a bitter woman and looked up one final number.

"Bloody hell," Simon Miller growled when he realised who was calling.

"No, just DC Tom Willis."

"What the hell do you want now?" Miller's voice was low, wind whistling in the background.

"You out, Mr Miller?"

"I'm on the marshes, if you must know. And I'll thank you to keep your voice down. I don't want you disturbing the birds any more than you already have."

Tom bit back his retort about Miller choosing to answer the phone. "I was wondering what you could tell me about the residents of the North Cumbria Caravan Park."

"Which residents?"

"Any of them. Barry Joyce, maybe."

"I have as little to do with Barry Joyce as possible," Miller said, "and if you're sensible, you'll do the same."

Tom thought of Joyce in his cell downstairs, face pale and eyes red, snarling during the welfare check earlier.

"Not an option, I'm afraid. Do you actually know anything about Barry Joyce, though?"

"Not really, no."

"And Erica Stern?"

"Poor woman, her husband leaving her like that."

CHAPTER FIFTY-ONE

"You knew them both?"

"Not well. Horrible, what happened to her. Is that all?"

"I understand your car has been seen around the North Cumbria Caravan Park since the body was found."

"Yes."

"What were you doing there?"

"I heard there was trouble, of course. Over the dead boy. I went round to make sure everyone was OK. Is that a crime?"

"No, Mr Miller."

Since when did Simon Miller show concern for other human beings?

"Good. Now leave me alone." The line went dead.

CHAPTER FIFTY-TWO

IF THERE WAS one thing Zoe hated more than people wasting her time, it was stupid, violent people wasting her time when she was already pressed.

Barry Joyce ticked every box.

She sat opposite him, beside Tom, and looked him in the eye. "Did you kill Femi Moorhouse?"

Joyce said nothing.

The lawyer sitting next to him leaned close. "We talked about this, Barry," she said, just loud enough for Zoe to hear. "I know you're annoyed, but you're not helping yourself sitting here saying nothing."

"What's the point?" He didn't bother keeping his voice down. "This lot have got it in for me, haven't they? Reckon I'm not Black or Asian enough for them."

The lawyer sighed. Tom had mentioned Sue Sharples before – he'd dealt with her during the Mulligan case last year, when she'd represented Gustavo Arroyo. Arroyo had been a liar and a timewaster, though not a murderer. Now here she was with Barry Joyce.

CHAPTER FIFTY-TWO

Tom spoke highly of her. Zoe supposed everyone needed representation.

"What have we talked about, Barry?" Sue's tone was firm but patient.

"Fine." Joyce turned to Zoe. "No. I didn't kill him. Didn't like him, him or his tart. But I didn't kill him."

"Tell them where you were, Barry."

"Pub. I told the other one. The queer one."

Zoe eyed him. *If you think you're going to rattle me...*

"You want to take a look at the people who've been bitching about me," he added.

Zoe doubted that. The person who'd complained about Barry Joyce was an elderly woman who'd have struggled to reach Grune Point, let alone kill someone there and find her way back in the dark. If Barry Joyce hadn't killed Femi Moorhouse, their other suspect probably had, and she'd just secured a twelve-hour custody extension for Ethan Reid.

"What people?" Tom asked.

Zoe resisted jumping in to wrap things up, despite being keen to get to court. These questions needed asking, even if they seemed pointless.

"Veronica bloody Gaines."

"This is Veronica Gaines, your neighbour, who you were shouting at last night when you were arrested?"

"She's got something to say to me, she can say it to my face, not go running to the cops."

"We've talked about this too, haven't we, Mr Joyce?" The lawyer's words fell on deaf ears.

"And Erica bloody Stern."

"I'm sorry," Sue Sharples addressed Zoe and Tom. "My client seems keen to ascribe unusual middle names to his neighbours."

Zoe couldn't hide her smile. She liked this lawyer. Maybe if Sue Sharples had been around instead of Stan Basham, Trevor Singleton and Clarissa Bexley – all deserving their own creative middle names – the last few years might have gone differently.

But Erica Stern and Veronica Gaines? Zoe had read the files. Whatever their middle names were, she couldn't see either of them killing Femi Moorhouse.

The trouble was, Nina was probably right. She didn't see Barry Joyce doing it, either.

CHAPTER FIFTY-THREE

The Golf Hotel overlooked the green at Silloth, not far from where Aaron had found the teenagers. Stepping inside from the drizzle felt like entering another world.

The bright interior featured a huge television showing what looked like an old football match, judging by the dated hairstyles and shorts. Despite the garish, green-patterned carpet, the atmosphere felt welcoming. A few people chatted quietly at tables while a friendly-looking barman stood behind the counter. Aaron felt a sudden urge to sit down and drink the day away.

He approached the bar, returning the barman's smile.

"What can I get you?"

Aaron explained who he was, watching the man's expression shift from friendly to understanding.

"Barry Joyce?" The barman nodded.

"That's the one."

"Big bloke, right? More muscles than brain cells, balder than an egg in a wind tunnel."

Aaron smiled. "You know him, then?"

"Can't help knowing him if you work in a pub round here, mate. Here, what you having?"

After ordering a non-alcoholic IPA, Aaron learned the barman was Will, an Australian who'd settled in Cumbria twenty years ago.

"William Moriarty, actually." Will leaned on the bar. "And before you ask, no, I'm not *that* Moriarty, and if I was, I wouldn't be working behind a bar, would I?"

"That, and you'd be fictional and about a hundred and fifty years old."

Will laughed, and Aaron felt his tension easing.

"So, what's Baz done now?" Will asked.

"I need to verify his whereabouts three nights ago, after eight o'clock."

Will checked his phone. "Yeah, Baz was in. From about five till at least ten, maybe later."

Aaron considered his next question carefully. The Grune Point body would be common knowledge by now. Will spoke before he had a chance to.

"So, what, you reckon Baz did Femi Moorhouse in? Don't think so, mate."

"You don't?" Aaron said, watching the man's expression.

"Nope."

"But if he left at ten, even eleven, he could have got there and done it long before the body was found."

"Not in the state he was in. Could hardly stand up, mate. Listen, you been up there? Grune Point?"

Aaron nodded.

"Imagine walking round there in the dark, when it's raining, and you can't see what's dry land and what's the bloody marsh."

True. "Someone managed it, though."

CHAPTER FIFTY-THREE

"Yeah, and whoever it was hadn't drunk more than ten pints of lager beforehand. Barry Joyce would never have made it out there. My guess is he spent an hour stumbling back to the caravan park. That, or he fell asleep on the way."

Aaron retreated to a quiet corner table with his drink. His thoughts drifted to his morning conversation with Serge.

"It's time," Serge had told him.

"Time for what?"

"Time to move on, Aaron. You're a DI now. You need to find a job instead of sitting around hoping one's going to land in your lap. You can put it all behind you. Everything you've been through."

"But what about your business? What about Annabel?"

"We do it now, before she starts school. And my business has a solid reputation now. I can set up anywhere. I can even travel. And you... You're so good at this. Don't waste your career waiting for something that's never going to happen."

Serge had given him that knowing grin, the one that said he was right even when Aaron couldn't see it.

But Aaron could see it. He loved Cumbria and the team, but Serge was right. He was a DI now. It was time to start acting like one.

CHAPTER FIFTY-FOUR

"And you witnessed this yourself?" asked Carter's barrister.

Nina nodded, then caught herself. "Yes."

For a moment, she'd almost forgotten where she was. This wasn't her first cross-examination, but she'd never found it quite so... relaxing.

The woman representing Carter wore what looked like a genuine smile, mirroring Nina's body language with such expertise it felt like chatting with a close friend.

It was pleasant. Easy. A lovely afternoon.

And Myron Carter was Gandhi.

The woman was skilled, attempting to lull Nina into comfort. Despite recognising the tactic, Nina had nearly fallen for it. Nearly.

"You saw Ralph Streeting, disgraced former Detective Inspector Ralph Streeting, pull a table apart with his bare hands?"

"I saw him separate two halves of a table designed to be

CHAPTER FIFTY-FOUR

separated that way, yes. With the assistance of a uniformed officer."

The barrister nodded, facing away from the jury. Only Nina and the judge could see her lips purse.

"And you saw him extract this device that supposedly held these recordings?"

"I saw him do that, and I was present when the recordings were played minutes later."

"OK." The woman turned to face the court, smiling as if everything was going to plan. "Would you mind going back a few minutes?"

"Of course."

"I understand that shortly before entering the building, you were present during an attempt on disgraced former Detective Inspector Ralph Streeting's life, is that correct?"

"It is."

"And you bravely put your own body between Mr Streeting and the woman attempting to kill him. You threw yourself onto Mr Streeting, and onto the ground, to ensure he wasn't injured."

"That's correct."

"You were willing to endanger your life to save that man?"

"I was willing to take a risk to ensure the evidence was preserved."

The barrister nodded. "And it was immediately after this that you entered the building and recovered this evidence, yes?"

Nina glanced up at movement in the gallery, spotting DI Finch taking her seat. "Yes."

"Had you been hurt, during the attempt on disgraced former Detective Inspector Ralph Streeting's life?"

The repetition was becoming tiresome. The jury must be sick of it by now.

"Not really," Nina said.

"What I'm wondering, is whether you might have been concussed, or had your hearing or eyesight or other senses compromised during the event."

Nina suppressed a laugh. "If you're suggesting that my recollection of the events that followed might lack credibility as a result of my senses being impaired, I can assure you that isn't the case."

"Can you?"

"I was checked out by medical on my return to the Hub. As is standard."

"That was some time later." The woman tilted her head. "Why don't you walk me through the events that followed the attempt on disgraced former Detective Inspector Ralph Streeting's life one more time, in detail?"

Nina sighed and glanced up at DI Finch, who smirked back at her. The boss knew Nina could recite details under pressure, even in the most uncomfortable situations.

"Fine," Nina said. "Like I said, it was Streeting at the front, followed by me. One foot behind me, to my right, was the first of the AFOs. Just behind her was the second, followed by two uniformed officers, then Blue, who was leading operations on the ground, and a third AFO bringing up the rear. The order was initially intended to be different, but following the attack on Streeting, I wasn't willing to let him out of my sight."

"That's very good, DS Kapoor. But can you—"

"The security guard was wearing a white shirt with an orange stain on the collar, and there were seven office workers – three men and four women – in the first office we

CHAPTER FIFTY-FOUR

walked through. One of the women asked if there had been an accident. One of the men asked if he could go home. A second man said, 'Shut up, Donald', when he said that."

"I think that's—"

"When we reached the final room, as we've already established, there was a table that Ralph Streeting pulled apart, with the assistance of one of the uniformed officers. I can take you through our trip back through the building to the car park, if you'd like." Nina smiled at the woman, who stared back with a stony expression.

"No further questions," the barrister said.

CHAPTER FIFTY-FIVE

It seemed a waste to come all this way and not drop in on the one person who clearly knew more than she was letting on.

Aaron stood outside Chelsea's caravan and knocked. He expected to wait, but the door opened immediately.

"Hello," she said, looking down at him.

"Hi. Can I come in?"

She turned and walked inside, leaving the door open. Aaron took that as an invitation.

The place had been tidied up. It took him a moment to realise that wouldn't have been Chelsea's doing.

Keisha Middleton might have a mouth like a sewer and an unprofessional attitude, but she knew her way round a crime scene. She knew how to leave one when she'd finished, even if the place had been a bombsite before.

But whatever magic Keisha had worked, she hadn't worked it on Chelsea Bright. That had been Chelsea's own doing.

The woman looked more alive than she'd been when

CHAPTER FIFTY-FIVE

Aaron had last seen her. Not quite happy – that would have been pushing it. But this might be what she was usually like, when she hadn't just heard her boyfriend had been murdered.

Chelsea crouched on the floor and gestured for him to take a seat on the bed. "Sorry about the mess."

"It's fine. I just wanted to see how you were doing."

"Better, I think." She wasn't shaking, and her colour had improved. Whatever she'd done to fix herself...

Fix herself.

That was it. She'd managed to get more heroin. It had lifted her from where she'd been to where she was now.

It wouldn't last.

"I also wanted to let you know that we've arrested Ethan Reid," Aaron said, watching her closely.

"What?" Her eyes were wide, deep pools of black at their centre. He couldn't tell if that was surprise or just the drugs.

"Ethan Reid," he repeated. "We've arrested him because he wouldn't cooperate with the investigation. We're questioning him over Femi's murder."

Chelsea closed her eyes, her lips moving in a silent prayer. When she stopped, her lips formed a smile.

Her eyes opened, serious and focused on his. "Really? You've really arrested Ethan Reid?"

Aaron nodded. Her entire body seemed to relax, easing into a gentler shape.

"We know he's lying to us, Chelsea. We know about the box and the van. We know you haven't told the truth about his involvement, or any of this."

He waited in silence while she stared at him, digesting his words.

"Yes," she said finally.

"Yes?"

"Yes, Ethan Reid did it."

"He killed Femi?"

"He was involved." She shook her head gently, as if that was as far as she would go.

It wasn't enough. Not enough to charge Reid, and certainly not enough for court, if she could even be persuaded to turn up.

And what did she mean by 'involved'?

"Why don't you come back to the Hub?" Aaron suggested.

Chelsea brushed the hair from her eyes, revealing the wound again. "I... I don't know about that."

"That cut over your eye looks nasty. It needs looking at, Chelsea. We can get someone there to help."

"Painkillers?" Her eyes suddenly brightened.

"What?"

"It hurts. Morphine might make me feel better."

In the short term, she was probably right.

"I don't know," he said. "Maybe. But if you come back with me, we can get it patched up, maybe get you some painkillers, and get to the bottom of what happened to poor Femi."

One mention of his name and all the brightness vanished, replaced with dull, sad acceptance.

"Fine." Chelsea got to her feet.

CHAPTER FIFTY-SIX

Some cops hated letting suspects walk free from custody without charges. Nina considered it a personal failure. Tom had never shared that view – working out who hadn't committed a crime was just as important as finding who had.

But today, escorting Barry Joyce to collect his belongings, Tom understood Nina's frustration.

Joyce was trouble. He might not have killed Femi Moorhouse, but given enough time, the team would likely have found something else to hold him on.

"If you continue harassing your neighbours," Tom said, "you'll be back here before—"

"Shut it," Joyce snapped, turning away.

"We'll be watching you."

Joyce flicked a dismissive hand gesture without looking back. Tom considered following him, but his phone buzzed in his pocket. He muttered under his breath as he answered.

"You wanted to talk to me?" The male voice was unfamiliar.

"Did I?"

"That's what Sheila said." The accent was northern – Lancashire or Yorkshire, Tom thought.

"Who's Sheila?"

"Sheila Carr. Said you spoke to her earlier."

The surname triggered something. Tom frowned as he climbed the stairs to the third floor.

"Milton Carr," the man added. "Park homes and lodges."

"Of course. I'm sorry, I didn't catch your name."

"Alex Worthing."

"Thanks for calling, Alex. I take it you were involved in installing the park home at North Cumbria Caravan Park?"

"I've done a dozen there. But Sheila said you were asking about Erica Stern's?"

"That's the one. Were there any issues around payment?"

"Not that I recall. Hang on." Papers rustled. "Yeah, there was an overdue amount, but that's normal. Got paid in cash by some old dear from round the corner."

Must have been Veronica Gaines, Tom thought.

"Funny one, though," Worthing continued.

"What was?"

"That job. We turn up expecting to dig holes, fill with concrete and hardcore, then put the pads in. But they'd already put most of the concrete down. Too much of it, too."

"I'm sorry?"

"It's a five-hundred-square-footer, right?"

"Right," Tom agreed, though he had no idea.

"They'd dug a foot deeper than needed and used twice the concrete required. Made our job easier. Hang on..." Worthing paused. "You're not... We didn't do anything wrong, OK? Just because they'd already done—"

CHAPTER FIFTY-SIX

"If you'd already bought the supplies, you were entitled to charge for them, Mr Worthing."

"Right. That's what I thought. So we turn up expecting a full job, and half's already done. Had a nice afternoon in the pub, as I remember."

"OK. Thanks." Tom ended the call and leaned back in his chair, mind rolling over what Worthing had told him.

Why would Erica Stern have paid to get her plot concreted when it was part of the package with the new caravan? And why so deep?

He picked up his phone. The sarge – the DI, he reminded himself – needed to know about this. As he brought it to his ear, it rang. DI Keyes.

"Sir, I've got—" Tom began.

"I'm with Chelsea. She's agreed to be interviewed."

"Sorry?" Tom scratched his chin.

"She's coming with me to the Hub. Can you meet us in about fifteen minutes?"

"Er... yeah. Yes, of course."

"Thanks, Tom. Sorry, I need to go." The DI hung up.

Tom pocketed his phone. The caravan could wait. He wasn't even sure why he'd pursued it. They should be focusing on Femi Moorhouse, not Erica Stern. He uploaded his notes to the team inbox and grabbed his jacket.

Chelsea was on her way, and that was the most important thing.

CHAPTER FIFTY-SEVEN

"Do you mind?" Chelsea asked.

"Mind what?" Aaron replied.

"I want to get changed. Can you...?"

"I'll wait outside," he told her.

The caravan reeked of unwashed clothes and sweat. Going outside wouldn't do him any harm.

The cold air hit him as he stepped out, though at least it wasn't raining. He walked to his car, then doubled back towards the caravan, crossing the narrow road to the park home opposite. He tapped lightly on the door.

Nothing.

He tapped again and shielded his eyes to peer through the little pane of glass, but darkness greeted him.

After a moment, he gave up. Erica Stern was never in.

He spent five minutes in his car reading team inbox updates before returning to the caravan.

"You OK?" he called through the door.

"Nearly ready," Chelsea replied.

CHAPTER FIFTY-SEVEN

"I'll be on the park. Just want to speak to one of your neighbours."

The door opened a few inches, and Chelsea's head appeared. "Which neighbour?"

"Veronica Gaines. You know her?"

"The old bag?" Chelsea's voice held no malice. "Yeah."

"Can you tell me where she lives?"

Following Chelsea's directions, he found another park home at the end of a row a few minutes away. Veronica Gaines interrogated him through the door about his identity before examining his warrant card through a crack with the chain still on.

Only then did she invite him in, her caution evident.

"Would you care for some tea?" She smoothed her cardigan. "Or coffee, maybe? That's what you youngsters like, isn't it? Coffee?"

Aaron declined politely and took a seat beside her at a square wooden table in the centre of a small, neat living room. A china cup sat on its saucer, perched on a slate coaster.

"We've had to release Barry Joyce," he said.

She nodded slowly, like someone receiving expected bad news. "He'll kill me."

"He's been warned to keep away from you. To stop harassing his neighbours."

Her gaze flicked towards the ceiling, before settling back on him.

Aaron pulled out a card. "My direct line is on there. For emergencies, call 999. But for anything else, you can call me."

"Thank you."

"And if it reassures you, we've established Barry Joyce wasn't involved in Femi Moorhouse's murder."

Veronica shook her head. "Thank you, but it's hardly reassuring. All that means is that we have one violent man on the park who we know about, and possibly a murderer, too."

Aaron leaned forward. "There's no reason to believe the killer lives here, Mrs Gaines."

"There's no reason to believe he doesn't. But thank you, anyway."

"I don't suppose you've seen Erica Stern?" he asked. "I've been trying to get hold of her since all this started. She's one of the few people we haven't been able to get a statement from."

Her eyebrows shot up. "Erica?"

"Erica Stern. Yes. Lives opposite—"

"I know who Erica Stern is, thank you. I'm sure she's just busy. Probably talking things over with Simon."

"Simon?"

"Yes. You know. Simon Miller. They're..." She lifted her cup to her lips.

"They're what?"

She frowned and shook her head. "Who?"

"Simon Miller. Erica Stern. You were talking about them."

"Was I?" Her eyebrows rose again.

"Yes. You said they were probably talking things over."

"What things?" Veronica asked.

Aaron frowned, wrong-footed. "I don't know. I think you were about to tell me."

She set down her cup. "Don't you pay any attention to me. I'm just a silly old dear who makes too many mistakes. I

CHAPTER FIFTY-SEVEN

was the one who told you Barry Joyce had killed that poor boy, wasn't I?"

"Well, yes. But—"

"Don't you pay any attention," she repeated, taking another sip from what Aaron suspected was an empty cup.

CHAPTER FIFTY-EIGHT

THREE PAINKILLERS THAT MORNING – one fewer than she'd been taking for the last couple of weeks – and Denise could feel the missing one more than she felt the benefit of the three.

She stretched her neck and looked back at the court clerk, doing her best to focus. The woman had her head cocked, waiting for Denise to speak.

Of course. "DS Denise Gaskill, Cumbria Police."

The clerk nodded and swore her in. Denise ran through the procedure on autopilot. She hadn't done this as often as DI Whaley, but she'd done it enough.

The prosecution barrister stood smiling at her with a hint of wariness. "You're here to set out the events that led to your injury last year. Are you able to recollect those events?"

She could still feel them – in her back, shoulders, neck, arms, and on bad days, even her legs and head. "Yes."

"Would you mind taking us through them?"

For five minutes, she laid it out. The murder of Bobby Silver. The chase after the killer's Jeep through snowy hills.

CHAPTER FIFTY-EIGHT

The discovery of that Jeep in a scrapyard near the crime scene, and her decision to assist in its recovery. The prosecution barrister let her talk without interruption, and the defence made no objections.

"There was a gun in the boot," she continued, "but you've already heard about all that."

"We have," the barrister agreed.

"I reached into the car, and then, well..."

"Well?"

"It blew up."

Suddenly, she was there again. Not *there* there – her eyes were open. She could see the court, the barristers and their juniors, the solicitors, guards, jury, and Myron Carter in the dock. But she was also on her side, with a car door handle sticking out of her – ice and fire, freezing and burning, floating away like a balloon before being dragged along steel teeth, until it all faded away.

"It blew up," she repeated.

The immediate sensations were fading, but the pain remained sharper than before. Her eyes darted to the clock as she thought of the blister pack in her bag.

"Are you feeling OK, DS Gaskill?" The barrister frowned at her.

"Fine, thank you." She sipped water from the glass before her. She'd been wondering if she might be getting addicted to those painkillers.

Now she had her answer.

She wasn't supposed to have them – not that many anyway – but Denise had friends everywhere, including Neville Warner, who had his own pharmacy.

"Would you mind taking us through the aftermath of

your injury, DS Gaskill? As much as you can recall, of course."

This was harder. She'd been in an induced coma initially, then on stronger painkillers than Neville's for weeks after. But she remembered enough to remind the jury what she'd been through. Enough to remind them what sort of man Myron Carter really was.

"Yes." She started with those final moments before losing consciousness, hearing Stella on the phone to Carl, Zoe Finch, and the rest of the team.

"And then everything just went black." Her gaze swept the gallery, past the strangers, past DI Finch, until they locked with another pair of eyes staring directly into hers.

Dark eyes beneath a mass of long, dark hair.

Sinead Conway nodded once, her gaze unwavering.

Denise stared back, time seeming to stop. The sounds around her fell away until there was just Denise, Sinead, and the space between them.

"DS Gaskill?" The barrister's voice cut through.

"I'm sorry. Where was I?"

CHAPTER FIFTY-NINE

"OK, Chelsea," DI Keyes leaned forward in his chair. "Are you feeling up to this?"

Chelsea Bright nodded. Tom reckoned she looked better than in their previous encounters – more alert, more present.

He went through the formalities, reminded her about the recording, and asked again about legal representation.

"No, you're alright," she said.

"Tell us about Ethan Reid." DI Keyes watched her carefully.

Chelsea closed her eyes, took a breath, then opened them. "The box."

"The metal box?" Tom shifted in his seat. "The one we found in your caravan?"

"Yeah. It was his. Ethan Reid's. But we didn't know that. If we'd known that..." She shook her head. "Christ, you think we'd steal from Ethan Reid deliberately? I'm not stupid, and Femi..." A fond smile crossed her face. "Femi *was* a bit stupid. In a nice way. But even he wasn't *that* stupid."

"This box, then," Tom prompted, wanting to keep her focused.

"Yeah. So, there's this van. Big grey Merc. New one, all shiny and everything. We're in Whitehaven, me and Femi—"

"What were you doing in Whitehaven?" DI Keyes interrupted.

Chelsea frowned at him. "Free country, isn't it? We used to live there, too."

Tom knew what that meant – they were visiting their local dealers.

"This van, then," he prompted again.

"Oh, yeah. We were walking past when we saw it, looked in the window, there's a box there, on the passenger seat. Didn't even think about it, really. Just smashed the window, grabbed it, legged it. Alarms going off and everything, but I reckon we were gone before anyone saw us."

"Was this you, or Femi?" asked the DI.

A shrug. "He smashed the window, I grabbed the box. Don't remember whose idea it was."

"Where was the van, Chelsea?" Tom asked.

"Parked on the street. Wasn't like we went on anyone's property or anything."

Tom suppressed an eye roll at her twisted logic. The smell of sweat and stale breath filled his nostrils.

"Which street?"

"Scotch Street. Near the chippie."

"And when was this, precisely?"

Chelsea laughed. "Precisely? I don't even know what day it was. Nighttime. Five days ago, I reckon. Maybe four. Maybe six. Does it matter?"

"Probably not," said the DI, though Tom knew this was a tactical lie.

CHAPTER FIFTY-NINE

"He found out, anyway," Chelsea said. "Ethan Reid. Figured out it was us, came after us. It was him that did this to me." She pointed to the cut over her eye.

"What sort of weapon did he use?" Tom asked, hoping they might find evidence in Reid's flat.

"His teeth."

Silence filled the room.

"His teeth?" The DI's voice was incredulous.

"Yeah. Bloody psycho, he is. Managed to get away, we both did. Legged it, but I knew he'd find us, so we kept on going."

"To Grune Point," Tom said, remembering the wet, sandy clothes from the caravan.

"Yeah."

"What happened there?"

"I don't know," Chelsea's voice grew quieter. "It was dark. We got separated, just a few minutes out of Skinburness."

The DI pulled up a map on his phone and handed it to her. She studied it before pointing.

"Ms Bright is indicating the western path," he said for the recording. "The one that leads north along the Solway Coast and meets Skinburness Creek at Grune Point. Tell us what happened, Chelsea. How did you get separated?"

"We were running. And then I couldn't see him. I remember shouting out for him, for Femi, but he didn't shout back. I don't know if he got lost or fell over or what, but I thought maybe he was ahead of me, and I kept going, and then... Well, I just gave up in the end, didn't I?"

"You gave up?"

"Walked back home. I'd had enough. I thought, if Reid

finds me, fair enough. I couldn't keep running. It was cold and it was dark, and I'd had enough."

"And after you lost Femi, you didn't see him again?"

"Nope."

Tom watched as the energy drained from her face. She shivered, growing paler by the second. Whatever she'd taken was wearing off.

"We have a doctor here," Tom said. "A forensic medical examiner. Would you be willing for them to take a look at you?"

"Why do I want a doctor?"

"Well," the DI interjected, "they can take a look at that wound, for a start. And maybe get you some painkillers."

"Nah." She shivered again, her eyes closing for several seconds. When they reopened, she seemed disoriented.

"Chelsea, I think—" Tom began.

"I want to go home."

"Why don't you let us take a look at—"

"Nah. Don't want anyone touching me."

Tom exchanged a glance with the DI. Earlier she'd agreed to treatment, but now she'd changed her mind.

"Chelsea," the DI tried again. "If we can get you some painkillers—"

"Just want to go home."

It took another ten minutes to convince her to stay, though she still refused examination. They left her in Interview Room Four with extra chairs for lying down and some blankets. She wasn't in custody, but Clive Moor, the Custody Sergeant, had agreed to check on her every fifteen minutes, quietly if possible, and post a PC or two outside to keep an eye.

CHAPTER FIFTY-NINE

They'd done what they could for now. Tom had other matters to discuss with the team.

CHAPTER SIXTY

Nina sat next to the boss in the small café near the court, adjusting the volume on her phone so they could hear Aaron and Tom without broadcasting to the other customers.

On screen, Tom's expression suggested he was bursting to speak. He kept leaning forward, opening his mouth, then stopping as others interrupted. With anyone else, Nina might have felt sympathetic. But Tom could do with learning when to keep quiet.

They began with Chelsea Bright.

Aaron cleared his throat. "She's in no fit state to be questioned further. And she isn't willing to be examined yet. Hopefully she'll feel better after some rest."

Nina imagined that rest wouldn't help unless it came with a small pack of brown powder.

"Is Clive looking in on her?" The boss leaned closer to the phone.

"He's been briefed, yes. In the meantime, you're aware we've had to release Barry Joyce. I'm hoping he keeps his nose clean for now, but there's no guarantees."

CHAPTER SIXTY

Nina leaned forward. "What about Ethan Reid?"

"No developments. Nothing back from forensics yet, so he's just kicking his heels downstairs, waiting for us to charge him or let him go."

"Or extend custody again, and given what Chelsea's just told you, that seems the right call," said the boss. "Can you sort that out, Aaron?"

"Will do."

In the brief pause that followed, Tom waved a hand, finally seizing his chance.

"Archie Stern," he blurted out.

The boss frowned. "The one who went missing two years ago?"

"That's him. There've been some developments."

Tom spent five minutes outlining his findings. The statement from Archie's mother seemed weak to Nina – just bitter ravings from an angry old woman. Erica Stern's repeated absence when they called was odd, but only mildly suspicious. People often avoided the police.

Nina's interest was piqued by the mention of the contractor, and she noticed the boss sitting straighter, too.

"So they dug the foundations out themselves?" DI Finch asked.

"Yeah. And they dug them deeper than needed. And then they filled them with concrete. All in the two days after Archie Stern disappeared."

Nina glanced at the boss, whose lips were parted.

"There's more," Aaron added. "I went to see Veronica Gaines. She's the old woman who complained about Barry Joyce. Looks like she probably gave Erica the money for the park home. They're close. And Simon Miller might be involved."

Nina frowned. "Simon Miller? The birdwatcher?"

"Yep. You'll have seen his car around the caravan park, right?"

Nina nodded as Aaron continued.

"Veronica Gaines implied there was something between Erica and Simon. She clammed up as soon as she realised she'd said too much."

Nina recalled their early meetings with the birdwatcher. He'd mentioned the caravan park initially, but only because Femi lived there. After that, he'd seemed keen to distance himself, muttering about law-abiding people and 'druggies'.

"It's not like we've got any actual evidence," Aaron said. "But..."

The boss broke the ensuing silence. "Is someone going to say it, then? What we're all thinking?"

Tom jumped in. "She killed him, boss. Erica Stern killed her husband and stuck him in the foundations of her new park home."

"I've already spoken to Stella Berry," Aaron said. "Asked her if the body would still be there, if there was one."

"And?" Nina asked.

"She said it depends."

The boss tutted. "It always depends."

"But concrete usually slows decomposition," Aaron added. "So it probably would."

The café was filling up. Nina moved the phone closer as the boss spoke quietly.

"OK. This one's for you, Aaron. I've got to get back in court."

"It is?" Aaron asked.

"Are you convinced enough of this to actually want to dig under the house?"

CHAPTER SIXTY

There was a pause before he replied.
"Yes. Yes, I am."

CHAPTER SIXTY-ONE

"It's all very well telling us about Olivia Bagsby," Carter's barrister said, tilting her head to one side, "but if she isn't here to back it up..."

Zoe knew the casual demeanour was calculated. Every gesture precise. She returned the barrister's smile.

"Are you implying that I'm making this up?"

"The defence accepts you met this woman. We accept she showed you photographs, and spent two years evading you, until she returned to Cumbria with your former colleague, who's sadly no longer able to provide evidence."

"He's dead, yes," Zoe said.

"But without questioning Olivia Bagsby herself," the barrister continued, "how can we challenge the authenticity of these photographs? For all we know, you and Mr Carter have both been victims of an elaborate hoax."

Zoe looked to the judge, who remained grim-faced.

"I would, therefore, argue that any evidence relating to Olivia Bagsby should be discounted entirely," the barrister said.

CHAPTER SIXTY-ONE

The prosecution barrister stood, but the judge waved him down.

"Agreed," he said.

One word. That's all it took for Zoe's work to crumble – all the hunting, coaxing and reassuring.

No, she reminded herself. Without Olivia, there'd have been no Streeting. Without Streeting, no recordings. Without those, no second arrest for Carter. The one that counted.

Everything had served its purpose.

She glanced at the gallery, seeking familiar faces. Carl had been there earlier – they'd had an awkward encounter by the café with Nina. Carl's boss, DCI Branthwaite, had broken the tension, muttering, "What is this, musical pigging statues?" as he passed.

"Stuff to do," Carl had said, heading back to Durranhill. "Oh, good luck."

With or without Olivia, Zoe had her own evidence about the investigation's conduct. She spent forty tedious minutes on Carter's finances, watching jurors stifle yawns while she detailed directors and bank accounts. She wished Zhang was there instead, though he'd already testified. She'd noticed his missed call during the café briefing. *Don't forget to ring him back.*

The defence challenged her about Ryan Tobin's stolen emails, but the prosecution had verified their authenticity. Every time Carter's team found a weakness, the prosecution reinforced it.

"And this Dean Somerville," the barrister said. "Why isn't he here?"

"Dean's in hospital," Zoe replied, "recovering from another attempt on his life."

"Another?"

"This will be the third since his sentencing."

The barrister fell silent. Zoe's gaze drifted to the gallery, remembering Denise Gaskill's evidence. Denise had frozen briefly – barely noticeable to strangers, but Zoe had caught it. The prosecution barrister had, too, checking if she was alright.

Something had rattled Denise. It wasn't just the pressure of giving evidence or reliving the explosion. Zoe was certain of that.

CHAPTER SIXTY-TWO

NINA HAD BEEN LOOKING FORWARD to seeing DI Finch give evidence, but here she was instead, dealing with a two-year-old missing persons case. She'd agreed to stop at North Cumbria Caravan Park on her way back to the Hub, though it was hardly on the way – a good thirty minutes in the wrong direction.

When she knocked on Erica Stern's door, there was no answer. She tried again and waited as grey clouds released a steady drizzle. Nothing. Perhaps Veronica Gaines would know where to find her.

"Sorry, I can't help you." Veronica stood in her doorway, offering a sympathetic smile.

Nina waited to be invited in, but Veronica gently closed the door instead. The message was clear enough.

Near the park entrance stood a converted office. Nina watched through the window as the man inside ignored her increasingly urgent knocks while he chatted on his phone.

"What?" He finally yanked open the door.

Nina pushed past him into the office.

"You can't just—"

"DS Nina Kapoor, Cumbria Police." She flashed her ID.

"So? You can't—"

"We need to dig the place up."

He shook his head. "I don't know what you think you're doing, but you can't barge in demanding to dig things up."

Nina circled his desk and settled into his chair, aware of the water dripping from her clothes onto the cheap carpet. She studied the desk – the laptop, photos and nameplate – while maintaining a steady smile until he sat down opposite her.

The nameplate read simply 'Mr Nelson'. He couldn't have been more than twenty-five.

"That's better," Nina said. "Mr Nelson, is it?"

He nodded mutely.

"Good. We intend to dig under Erica Stern's caravan."

"Why?"

"We're looking for something." She paused before adding, "A dead body."

"But... you found the body. At Skinburness."

"A different body."

"You think Archie's under there?"

"I can't say. Did you know Archie Stern?"

"No, I started after. But you'll need Erica's permission too."

"Yes, hers and yours. But we're applying for a warrant anyway, so this is happening one way or another."

Mr Nelson frowned and shook his head.

"Did you hear what I just said?" she asked.

"Yes. We don't have much choice. But we've got to be seen defending our residents, even when we know we'll lose."

"Defending them?"

"Against the police. Most of them don't really like the police," he said, as if that explained everything.

Nina pulled out her phone and typed a message to DI Keyes. "I'll wait here, if you don't mind."

CHAPTER SIXTY-THREE

"Why the bloody hell hasn't this happened already?" Superintendent Kendrick's sharp tone made Aaron's polite smile fade.

"Well, it's the—"

"Oh, don't tell me." She sighed. "Stella Berry's saying she doesn't have enough people, right?" A grin spread across her face. "She's probably right, too. So when is Reid's flat actually going to be searched? You can't keep him out of it forever, unless you've got enough to charge him."

Aaron shook his head. "Chelsea Bright claims she was bitten by him. We're hoping we can get some DNA off the wound, and hopefully that'll give us what we need. But if we don't, we'll be relying on whatever turns up in the flat."

"Better hope something does, then." The super raised her eyebrows and leaned back in her chair.

Something felt wrong.

"So, I think we'll need to apply for an extension," he said.

"Hmm." She stared past him through the window, her gaze unfocused.

CHAPTER SIXTY-THREE

"Is everything OK?"

"What? Oh, yes. Sorry. Extension, you said. Ethan Reid's custody. Fine. You do that." She waved a hand dismissively, still gazing out of the window.

Aaron's phone pinged. He glanced at the message from Nina – the one he'd been expecting.

"There's something else," he said.

"Is there?" She kept staring out the window.

That's when it hit him – what was different about the super.

She didn't seem to care.

He'd had his criticisms of Fiona Kendrick over the years. Working directly under her before DI Finch's arrival had shown him both her weaknesses and strengths.

But she'd always cared. About every aspect of the job. About her reputation, which made sense – you didn't become a detective superintendent without caring about your career. But she cared about the small stuff too. She knew case details inside out, knew everyone in the Hub. If there was anything she didn't know, she made it her business to find out.

She asked questions. Gathered information. Made decisions.

She never said things like, 'Fine. You do that.' Not without more debate and discussion.

"Since we need to talk to the magistrate anyway," he ventured.

"Yes?"

"We need to dig up under a park home at the North Cumbria Caravan Park."

She turned back to him, a spark returning to her eyes. "You do, do you? Tell me more."

He outlined what they'd learned, expecting her usual pushback. They had no actual evidence, after all.

"Fine," she said.

"Fine?"

"Yeah. While you're sorting out Reid's extension, get that taken care of, too. Two murders, no waiting. And another little job for Stella Berry and her team." She leaned forward. "Oh, and Aaron?"

"Yes?" A nervous feeling crept over him.

"What's the latest with you?"

"With me?"

"Don't play coy, Aaron Keyes. DI roles. Are you applying yet? I expected to be filling out dozens of reference forms for you, but no one's been in touch."

"Ah. I haven't got round to it yet. But I have sort of decided to start."

She nodded. "Well, don't do anything hasty. You never know what the future holds."

With that cryptic pronouncement, he was dismissed.

CHAPTER SIXTY-FOUR

THE CALL CAME in less than a minute after DI Keyes had gone upstairs to talk to the super, but Tom reckoned he could handle Chelsea Bright by himself. A piece of cake.

He took the stairs at speed. 'Climbing the walls' – that was how Clive Moor had described Chelsea. The sooner someone got in there and calmed her down, the better.

He nodded at the two officers outside the room – Will Parton and Marie Stones. He'd worked with both during the Mulligan case a few months back.

Marie's lips twisted. "Better you than me."

"She's that bad?"

Marie stayed silent while Will grimaced as Tom pushed the door open.

Chelsea Bright reclined in one of the chairs, eyes closed, hands in loose fists with fingers tapping a frantic rhythm on her palms. The smell of sweat hung thick in the air. She didn't stir as he entered or when he cleared his throat. For a moment, he thought she was asleep, or so deep in a heroin haze she might as well have been.

Then he said her name, quietly, just that one word, and three things happened.

Chelsea opened her eyes.

Chelsea's lips parted in an animal snarl.

And he realised his mistake.

He probably couldn't handle Chelsea Bright alone. And it definitely wouldn't be a piece of cake.

"Want... to... go... home," she said, pausing between each word as if struggling to form them.

"That's OK, Chelsea. If you really want to, that's fine. But I think—"

"You have to get them away from me," she said, her voice steadier now.

"Who?"

"You can't keep me here!" Her eyes went wide with fear.

"I know." Tom took a single step forward from his position by the door.

She shrank back into her chair.

"It's OK," he said. "If you really want to—"

"Yes," she whispered.

He nodded.

"Don't you understand?"

The shout made him step back until the door handle dug into his spine.

"Yes, I do. We'll organise that if—"

"I don't want you to *organise* it. I want you to *do* it. Just take me home. Just do it."

He nodded again.

"Do it now!" She lurched to her feet and advanced towards him with jerky but surprisingly quick movements. The door opened behind him as the officers outside reacted.

CHAPTER SIXTY-FOUR

"It's OK," he said, but Chelsea had frozen, terror masking her features as she stared over his shoulder.

"No," she breathed.

He turned. Just Parton and Stones.

"It's OK," he repeated.

"Get them away from me!" Chelsea screamed.

"Are you OK?" Marie asked Tom.

He nodded. "I think I can handle this."

"That's fine. Probably best if we stay in the room with you, though."

He turned back to Chelsea, who had collapsed into her chair, shaking, her gaze locked on the two officers.

"I reckon it'll work better with just me," he said.

Will shook his head. "I wouldn't advise it."

"Really. Just wait outside. You'll hear if I need you."

Once the PCs had left, Tom crossed to Chelsea's chair and crouched beside her.

"It'll be OK," he said, trying to sound convinced. To his surprise, she met his gaze and nodded.

"Will it really?" she whispered.

"Yes."

Her right hand clenched and unclenched, but her left reached out suddenly. Tom took it between both of his, holding it gently as tremors ran through her body.

They stayed like that in silence for what might have been five minutes or ten. His back started aching after seconds, his legs burning shortly after. He leaned carefully against one of the desk legs, moving slowly to maintain his grip on her hand.

Finally, the pain became too much. Tom released Chelsea's hand and stood to sit beside her.

Her eyes tracked his movement, but otherwise she remained still.

"Will you let us get the doctor to help you?" he asked.

She nodded.

"They can patch up that wound. See if there's anything on it we can use."

"What do you mean?"

"Evidence," he said.

Fear flickered across her face.

"Maybe give you some painkillers," he added.

Naked greed replaced the fear. "OK."

"So you'll stay a little longer?"

"Yes."

When he left five minutes later, Tom had to work hard not to strut. It hadn't been easy – definitely not a piece of cake. But it felt like a victory, possibly a big one.

If they could pick up foreign DNA in Chelsea's wound, they'd be taking a giant step towards charging Ethan Reid.

CHAPTER SIXTY-FIVE

IT HAD BEEN PREYING on Denise's mind since leaving court. From before that, even – from the moment she'd looked up from the witness box and seen Sinead Conway looking back at her.

Sinead persisted in haunting her. Though she hadn't turned up on Denise's doorstep since that night after Carter's arrest, she'd sent flowers to the house. Letters. Messages. With anyone else, Denise might have felt flattered, or maybe reported it as stalking.

But Sinead Conway wasn't just an ex. She was a criminal – a clever one who, like Carter, hid behind companies and bank accounts. Unlike Carter, no one had ever come close to charging her. She wasn't the sort to get her hands dirty, or even speak directly to those who did her dirty work.

Now, it seemed she wanted to rekindle things with Denise, who wasn't naïve enough to think this was romantic. With Carter gone, Sinead Conway was West Cumbria's closest thing to Al Capone. A police contact would be valuable.

Time to come clean.

Denise pulled off the road at Blencogo and headed north until she found a narrow lane to stop in. It was dark now, with the rain easing, but she could sense the landscape – the gentle rises and falls, less dramatic than further south but still noticeable on her motorbike. Traffic hummed along the A596 half a mile away, but otherwise there was just the soft patter of rain on tarmac.

She climbed off the bike and dialled. DCI Branthwaite answered immediately.

"You OK, Denise? Evidence went well?"

"All fine. How was your meeting?"

"Waste of time." His tone shifted. "Everything OK? Not that I don't welcome hearing your voice, but you don't usually call me."

"She's been in touch."

There was a long silence before he spoke. "I take it we're talking about Sinead Conway here."

"We are, sir. She sent flowers while I was in hospital, and again during recovery. Messages, too. A few months ago, she came round."

"You didn't let her in, did you?"

"I'm not stupid, sir."

"No. But smart people can do stupid things sometimes. Why didn't you tell me this before?"

Denise hesitated. She'd told the DCI about her former relationship with Sinead Conway years ago, when the property developer's true nature emerged. She'd assured him it was just a brief fling from long before any criminal suspicions arose.

He'd kept it private – hadn't told DI Whaley or Harriett

CHAPTER SIXTY-FIVE

Barnes, or anyone else as far as she knew. She'd trusted him then.

"I don't know, sir," she said, the only honest answer possible.

"Any more recent contact?"

"She was in court, watching me give evidence."

"She's an associate of Carter's. Couldn't she just have been watching her old friend's trial?"

"She could," Denise agreed, but didn't believe it.

"Well, I think we can continue to keep this between ourselves for now."

"Thank you, sir—"

"But I can't promise that'll always be the case."

Something shifted – the ground seemed less solid beneath her.

"What do you mean?"

"I mean, there may come a time when Carl has to be told, and he won't take kindly to being kept in the dark all this time."

"No," Denise said.

"I'm sorry?"

"No. This is a personal matter. I've informed a senior officer. I don't see what—"

"Don't quote the blooming regulations at me, Denise. I've known them since you were building sandcastles at the beach. Look, I'm happy to keep things as they are. But if it becomes necessary to widen the field, we'll be widening the field, and you'll have to live with it. We've all made mistakes. Yours just happens to have fingers and thumbs in half the organised crime in Cumbria. Now, tell me, how's the body?"

"The body?"

"*Your* body. The one that got blown up last year. Every time I ask if you're better, you say everything's fine, which is about as likely as me winning the Grand National. As the horse."

"I am fine, sir," Denise lied. "All in perfect working order."

"And the old brain?"

"I'm seeing the police psychiatrist next week."

"That'll be a waste of time."

"I couldn't agree more," she said, ending the call on a truth at last.

CHAPTER SIXTY-SIX

Nina sat behind Mr Nelson's desk for ten minutes before the silence became unbearable. The rain had eased, and she could have waited outside or in her car, but Mr Nelson had got under her skin. Sitting in his chair felt like the perfect petty revenge.

But ten minutes was her limit.

As she stepped outside, leaving the door open, headlights swept past. She turned just in time to catch the rest of the car.

White. Probably a Honda Jazz.

What's Simon Miller doing here at this hour?

She took a few steps after the car, but it had vanished before she reached the turning where the caravan park met the main road.

Back at her car, she sat as the rain returned – first in uncertain drops, then in a sharp burst that settled into a steady drizzle within a minute.

The sound against the car roof was soothing. Almost as calming as Elvis. After a few minutes, she stepped out into the rain and walked to Erica Stern's park home again. No surprise – no answer when she knocked, no lights on inside.

Dull work, this. But someone had to be here. DI Keyes would have spoken to the super by now, and he'd be on to the magistrate. Soon enough, the diggers would arrive, and whatever Erica Stern had hidden would be found.

There might be other evidence, too. If anyone planned to disappear with evidence, now was the time. Someone needed to keep watch.

But did it have to be Nina?

She pulled out her phone and dialled.

"Nina." Inspector Keane's voice carried a smile. "How's things?"

She could picture his round face. Morris Keane had put on weight this past year, but it suited him. He'd always been large – now he was properly substantial.

She explained her request.

"You do realise we're trying to track down two missing women?" he said. "And I've got two of my men in hospital after what happened at Pears House."

"I know. And I'm sorry. But if you can spare anyone, we need someone here making sure nothing happens before the digging starts."

"What about you?"

Nina sighed. "I can wait until someone turns up. But we'll need Uniform here later anyway. To keep people away from the site."

"Fine. I'll do what I can. Sit tight. You won't be on your own for long."

Nina ended the call and sat facing Erica's park home, though she could see nothing in the darkness. The rain continued its steady beat on the roof, and after a few minutes, her eyes began to close. She jerked upright.

Stay alert. There was no point in being here if she couldn't stay awake. And the best way to stay awake was with The King.

She sat back and closed her eyes. No chance of sleeping now. *From Elvis In Memphis* might only be thirty-six minutes long, but they were thirty-six minutes of pure joy.

Nina smiled and put it on repeat.

CHAPTER SIXTY-SEVEN

So this was the famous Chelsea Bright.

Zoe entered Interview Room Four, expecting someone barely holding it together. Tom's phone call had painted a picture of chaos – a woman who'd nearly attacked him, desperate to leave, unravelling at the seams.

But the young woman before her wasn't a mess at all. She wore clean custody suite clothes – jogging bottoms and a top several sizes too large, the kind of outfit someone might choose to disappear into.

Chelsea frowned as Zoe approached.

"I'm DI Zoe Finch. How are you feeling, Chelsea?"

Chelsea nodded from her perch on a chair against the wall. Another chair sat beside it, positioned to allow her to lie down if needed. Her complexion was pale, but fashionably so.

Zoe took a careful step forward. Chelsea remained still, watching.

"Are you OK?"

CHAPTER SIXTY-SEVEN

"Yes." Chelsea brushed her hair back, revealing what Tom had described.

The bite wound Ethan Reid had allegedly inflicted was now covered with a bumpy strip of bandage above her left eye. Stitches underneath, Zoe guessed. Despite Chelsea's earlier state, Tom had managed to get her seen by the forensic medical examiner.

Zoe had checked who was on FME duty with Clive Moor on her way in.

"Dr Manning," he'd told her. "She's good."

The room was surprisingly fresh. Tom had mentioned sweat and stale breath, but there was no trace now. A shower and clean clothes had worked wonders.

But Chelsea's eyes remained vacant.

"Did the doctor give you something?"

Chelsea blinked slowly.

"A sedative, maybe?"

Chelsea nodded, and Zoe allowed herself a small smile. She didn't usually approve of sedating witnesses, but sometimes needs must.

This Dr Manning warranted looking into. She'd managed to settle an important witness and prevent her from running. But more than that, any evidence she'd gathered while examining Chelsea's wound could prove invaluable.

That would be pure gold.

CHAPTER SIXTY-EIGHT

AARON HAD ONLY BEEN BACK in the team room for five minutes when DI Finch walked in.

"Good work," she said, dropping into the chair at the spare desk – the one that had belonged to Kay, then Harriett, and was now empty again. "Anything come from it?"

He frowned and turned to Tom, who looked equally confused. "Anything come from what?"

"Long day." She leaned back and closed her eyes.

Aaron frowned. The boss had still been at home during their morning briefing.

"Chelsea Bright," she added. "What did the doctor say?"

Aaron exchanged another look with Tom. "What do you mean?"

DI Finch opened her eyes. "Dr Manning. She's been in to see Chelsea Bright. Treated the wound. Did she find anything that might end up being viable?"

Aaron turned to his screen, searching for messages. Nothing. Tom was checking his own screen and shaking his head.

CHAPTER SIXTY-EIGHT

"We haven't heard from her, boss," Aaron said.

Tom reached for his phone. "I've got the number."

Aaron walked over and dialled it on speaker.

"Elizabeth Manning." The voice was deep and rich.

"Hello, this is DI Aaron Keyes. I understand you've just treated one of our witnesses. Chelsea Bright."

"Ah, yes. Unfortunate girl. Not sure how long the sedative's going to keep her calm, but she needed something."

A sick feeling crept into Aaron's stomach. "Did you find anything in her wound? Above her eyes?"

"I patched that up and started her on antibiotics. Should heal well enough."

"Yes, but did you recover any evidence?"

"I really don't know what you mean." Concern edged into her voice.

He felt his stomach clench. "Chelsea claims she was bitten by a murder suspect. We were hoping you'd have recovered some foreign DNA. Saliva or something. Or taken photographs for tooth analysis."

"I'm sorry." Her voice sharpened. "I didn't examine the wound at all. I wasn't instructed to."

Tom stood up, frowning. "But..."

"Who did you instruct, Tom?" asked the DI.

"I put it through the system. In the custody suite. Filled out the details there."

"Is everything OK?" Dr Manning asked.

"I don't know," Aaron said. "I assume you've sterilised the wound?"

"Yes, I'm afraid so. If there was any foreign DNA, there won't be now. And the stitching moved the skin around so much, you won't be able to compare the wound to your suspect's teeth. I'm so sorry. I wasn't told, or I'd have got photos taken."

Aaron ended the call with a quick thanks and immediately dialled Clive Moor.

After listening to Aaron's explanation, Clive went quiet. Papers shuffled and keys clicked slowly in the background.

"Yeah," Clive said. "I can't see Tom's request here, but I remember him submitting it."

Relief flickered across Tom's face before worry returned.

"So why wasn't it acted on?" Aaron asked.

"Not sure. Seems like it's just got lost. Some sort of mix-up. Systems here aren't as good as they should be. More paper, less electronic, easier for things to get lost."

"Why?"

"The shiny new building didn't get shiny new computers, unfortunately. Half the stuff we're working with was out of date before the Hub was completed."

"This is a bloody disaster, Clive."

"I get that, Aaron. DI Keyes," Clive corrected himself. "And I'm sorry, and I'll look into how it's been allowed to happen. But crying about it won't help anyone, will it?"

Aaron wanted to object, but Clive was right. They were very different people – Aaron would lie awake worrying about everything, while Clive wouldn't give it a second thought if he couldn't fix it.

The world needed both types, he supposed. And Clive was right. There really was nothing they could do about it.

CHAPTER SIXTY-NINE

From Elvis In Memphis finished its second play-through when Nina decided she'd had enough.

She'd surprised herself with her endurance. If she'd placed a bet on how long she could stand being out here in her cold car, staring into the darkness and mist, she'd have wagered on lasting one album play. Even the best music had its limits.

As the final notes of *I'm Movin' On* faded, Nina took Elvis's advice. Time to move.

She tried Erica Stern's door again. One tap. Nothing. A second tap. Still nothing. A third, harder knock. She walked away without waiting for a response.

What was the point?

She headed to Veronica Gaines' park home. Whether Erica was home or not, Veronica knew more than she was letting on. Nina paused at the door, hand raised.

There were voices inside. She lowered her hand and pressed her ear to the door.

"...head north," came a woman's voice she didn't recognise. "...obvious choice..."

"...last thing we should do," a man replied. The voice was familiar.

The voices dropped lower, as if someone had adjusted the volume.

"...better idea?" the woman asked.

Must be the radio, Nina thought. Veronica was elderly – probably still called it the wireless.

"Holyhead," the man said, before rain drowned out his words. When it eased, she caught something about Ireland.

Nina knocked on the door. The voices stopped.

"Hello?" Veronica called out.

"It's DS Kapoor. It's a bit wet out here."

The door opened a crack. Veronica's face appeared with a nervous smile. "What are you doing out there in all this rain?"

"I'm looking for Erica Stern."

"Still?"

Nina made an exaggerated show of looking behind herself before turning back. "Doesn't look like I've found her, does it?"

Veronica's smile vanished, replaced by tight lips. The sarcasm hadn't been lost on her.

"I was hoping we could talk about Erica," Nina said.

"I don't know what it is you expect from me."

"I just want to find her, Veronica. In an hour or two, this place is going to be..." Nina caught herself. Veronica didn't need to know that. Not yet.

"Can I just come in?" she said.

"You're not going to give up, are you?"

Nina smiled. "I don't have it in me."

CHAPTER SIXTY-NINE

Veronica glanced behind her before stepping back to let Nina enter.

"Thanks," Nina said.

She stepped into the semi-dark room. A window with drawn curtains. A bookcase beside it. No TV. Must have been a radio she'd heard. She started to turn, looking for it, when something hard struck the back of her head.

It took a moment to register the blow. By then, her eyes were closing, her legs giving way. As she hit the floor, everything went black.

CHAPTER SEVENTY

Zoe took the stairs two at a time. It wasn't until she reached the ground floor that she realised the rhythmic thumping wasn't in her head – it was Tom's footsteps as he raced to catch up.

"Sorry, boss." Tom panted as they headed into the custody area together.

They both stopped dead, frozen in place. The custody suite was in chaos.

In the middle of the waiting and processing area, four people knelt on the floor. Zoe recognised Will Parton and Marie Stones, the PCs she'd encountered during the Kieran Mulligan murder investigation last year. They were all hunched over piles of paper while Clive Moor strode about, muttering and occasionally shouting.

The officers on the floor must have heard their footsteps – they all looked up simultaneously. Clive hadn't noticed them yet.

"Find the bloody thing!" he bellowed.

The four officers bent back over their papers, frowning.

CHAPTER SEVENTY

"What's going on?" Zoe asked.

"I'm looking for the..." Clive stopped, took a breath, and gave a single nod, as if confirming something to himself. "I'm sorry."

Zoe had never heard Clive Moor apologise, nor seen him anything but completely calm. She wanted to tell him it wasn't his fault, but she wasn't sure that was true.

"What's going on?" she repeated.

"I've got this lot looking for the forms. The stuff Tom sent through. I want to know how this has been allowed to happen. I know things don't always work perfectly here, but this is..." He turned back to the group and bellowed, "Find it!"

Zoe watched the four officers leafing through separate sets of papers – loose sheets, stapled bundles, paper-clipped documents of various sizes, typed, printed, and handwritten, in colour and black and white.

Absolute chaos. She noticed Stones and Parton looking up simultaneously, exchanging glances with expressions she couldn't quite read. Hatred? Blame? Fear?

Whatever it was, it wouldn't help them discover what had happened. Standing here watching wouldn't achieve anything either. Zoe turned without a word and headed back the way she'd come.

She took the stairs slowly this time, but Tom was even slower. She stopped to wait, but there was no sign of him.

He'd be down there still, trying to get to the bottom of it. Zoe considered going back to grab him, remind him they had a live murder case – possibly two – and recall what Clive had told Aaron: it had happened now, nothing could change that, and crying about it wouldn't help anyone.

But even Clive didn't seem to believe that anymore. He was down there trying to get to the bottom of it.

This wasn't just chaos or a system flaw. She might have thought so before learning Ethan Reid's lawyer was Trevor Singleton. When people like Singleton got involved, the stakes were higher, and nobody could be trusted.

This wasn't a coincidence.

Back in the team room, Aaron was just ending a call.

"Diggers," he said as she walked in.

"When?"

"Stella can have them on site within the next couple of hours. And Morris Keane'll be sending Uniform to keep things calm."

"So the magistrate came through?" she asked, and he nodded.

"We've got permission to dig. We don't need the owners' consent."

When Zoe dialled Nina's number, there was no answer. She left a message: "Your diggers will be with you in the next couple of hours. If you can stick around until they get there, that would be great."

She ended the call and turned to Aaron. He hadn't asked how things had gone downstairs. He probably already knew.

This wasn't a coincidence. Not with Singleton involved.

CHAPTER SEVENTY-ONE

Ten minutes in the custody area confirmed what Tom already suspected.

The station was staffed by good people – dedicated officers and civilians doing their best. But they were human. They made mistakes.

This wasn't a mistake. The form Tom had filled out had vanished completely. Jefferson, the IT technician who seemed to permanently inhabit the space under people's desks, fixing cables, was behind the custody desk now. He tapped at Clive's keyboard, shaking his head and making tutting sounds.

Tom stepped into the stairwell and pulled out his phone.

Harriet answered on the first ring. "What's up?"

"We've got a problem."

For most couples, a problem meant domestic issues – cars, kids, houses. Their car worked fine, they had no children, and Tom's DIY disasters were best left unmentioned. His attempt at painting had proved particularly catastrophic.

But they weren't most couples.

"A PSD problem?" she asked.

He explained the situation – or rather, the aftermath, since the actual events remained unclear.

"We've got no forensic evidence on Chelsea herself," he said. "If nothing comes from the search of Reid's flat, then..."

"Then you'll have to break his alibi."

Tom considered Reid's multiple alibis, each one sprouting like snakes on the Hydra's head when another was cut down.

"I think we've got an issue in custody," he said. "Either that, or it's the FME. Dr Manning."

"Hang on." Keys clicked in the background. "Elizabeth Manning?"

"That's her. Has anything come up before?"

"You know I can't tell you that. But no. Leave it with me. We'll discuss it later. While we're sorting out the house."

Tom's heart sank. 'Sorting out the house' meant fixing his painting disaster.

His phone beeped.

"Hang on," he said. "It's Caroline Deane. I'd better take it."

"I've been trying to reach Nina," Caroline said.

He nodded. "You'll have to put up with me."

"Yes. Anyway, that beam of wood we found."

"The possible murder weapon," he said, climbing the stairs.

"You can upgrade 'possible' to 'likely'," she told him. "Initial tests show human tissue. We haven't identified whose yet, but I think it's likely Femi Moorhouse's."

"It was a joist, right?"

"A batten," she corrected.

CHAPTER SEVENTY-ONE

Tom remembered seeing dozens scattered near the crime scene in the caravan graveyard.

"There's more," Caroline said.

"Go on."

"The batten was smooth enough to hold prints. Partials, but enough for a clear match."

Tom stopped. "A match for who?"

"Chelsea Bright."

CHAPTER SEVENTY-TWO

"How are you feeling, Chelsea?" Aaron kept his voice low and calm.

The young woman looked up with glazed eyes.

"Chelsea?"

"Yeah?"

He heard the boss sighing beside him but resisted turning towards her. They needed to keep Chelsea calm. DI Finch knew that, too.

But after what had happened with the doctor, Aaron was struggling to maintain his composure. As for Tom...

Tom had wanted to conduct this interview alongside Aaron, but one look at the DC had made it clear that wasn't wise. He couldn't keep still.

Whatever Chelsea Bright had been given, Tom could have used a dose. DI Finch had made the call immediately, telling Tom to stay put while she accompanied Aaron.

"Chelsea." DI Finch's tone was low but less patient than Aaron's. "We need to talk to you under caution. Do you know what that means?"

CHAPTER SEVENTY-TWO

"Yeah," Chelsea replied, sounding like she neither knew nor cared.

Aaron exchanged a glance with DI Finch before explaining her rights, the use of evidence, and her option for legal representation – information she must have heard countless times.

"Nah," Chelsea said.

"You don't want a lawyer?" Aaron asked.

"Yeah."

"You do want a lawyer?"

"Nah."

That would suffice.

"Chelsea, we've found what we believe is the weapon used in Femi's murder."

"Femi." She nodded.

"It's a bit of wood. A beam. About four feet long. It turned up near where Femi was found, on Grune Point."

"Femi." Chelsea looked around the room, seeming puzzled, as if expecting to see him.

"Do you understand what we're saying?" DI Finch asked.

Chelsea nodded. "You've found it. Bit of wood."

"The piece of wood has your fingerprints on it, Chelsea," Aaron said.

She stared at him blankly.

"Can you explain that?" DI Finch asked.

Chelsea turned to her with painful slowness. "What?"

This was getting nowhere.

"Chelsea," Aaron said. "Your fingerprints have been found on the murder weapon. Can you tell us how they got there?"

"No." Her response could have meant anything.

"We'd like to get Dr Manning back in," DI Finch said suddenly. "She can have another look at you."

Aaron hadn't expected this suggestion. They hadn't discussed it, and the doctor had already sterilised the wound. Likely, nothing remained to be found.

"Nah," said Chelsea.

"No, you're not willing to be examined by the doctor?" DI Finch asked.

"Nah."

Despite her slow movements and single-word responses, Aaron detected intelligence in Chelsea's eyes, a hint of wariness suggesting she understood more than she let on.

He turned to the boss, who nodded.

"Chelsea Bright," he said. "I'm arresting you on suspicion of the murder of Femi Moorhouse."

CHAPTER SEVENTY-THREE

Nina woke shivering, gripped by an unsettling sense of déjà vu.

Her brain urged her to stay still even as her body yearned to pull the duvet closer. *We've been here before*, a voice in her head whispered.

Had they? Had she?

Not here, precisely. But in this exact situation.

She reached for what should have been her duvet, but her arms met resistance after just a few inches. Something solid yet slightly yielding blocked her movement.

Bloody hell.

The realisation hit her – she *had* been here before.

She twisted onto her side, gaining a fraction more space to move. The darkness pressed in around her, the cold seeping through whatever material contained her.

Fuck. She was in a bag. Again.

The absurdity struck her – how could anyone end up stuffed in a bag twice in less than three years?

Stretching her fingers outward, she explored the material surrounding her. This bag felt different – coarser, more industrial. There was more space than last time, and she knew she hadn't lost that much weight. This was the sort of bag used for construction materials – rubble, rocks, aggregate. At least she wasn't in Mick Halfpenny's basement this time.

But where was she?

As she twisted, searching for any weakness or opening, she found herself humming *Are You Lonesome Tonight?*, the steady rhythm helping to regulate her breathing, keeping panic at bay.

Through the material, she caught distant sounds – heavy crashes and smashing noises, muffled but distinct. A slight vibration accompanied each impact.

Her mind raced. The widow, Veronica Gaines. She had to be involved, along with Erica. And Simon Miller, too – she'd spotted that Honda Jazz at the caravan park. Those sounds... they must be demolition equipment. They'd started on Erica's park home.

Which meant help wasn't far away. Stella's team would be nearby – Tom, DI Keyes, maybe even the boss. Morris Keane would have sent uniformed officers.

"Help!"

The sound bounced back at her, trapped within the bag's confines.

The machinery would drown out her cries, but it would have to stop eventually.

She finished *Are You Lonesome Tonight?* and moved onto *Love Me Tender*, following the same sequence that had sustained her during her last bag imprisonment.

But this time was different. Her colleagues were close by.

When the machinery stopped, she'd shout until they found her – if she hadn't already freed herself by then.

If they couldn't hear her...

No. They would hear her. Until then, she had Elvis for company and a bag to escape from.

CHAPTER SEVENTY-FOUR

"I bloody well told you, didn't I?"

The voice came from close behind him, just inches from his ears. Aaron felt his shoulders tense but forced himself to turn slowly, keeping his feet planted.

Don't show fear. Don't back away.

Barry Joyce wore what passed for a smile, though it held no warmth. He looked like someone who'd rather smash a bottle than share one, and the smile suggested he'd enjoy it.

"Told me what, Mr Joyce?"

"I told you. Your lot. Not you. The tall bird. And the gormless one."

Aaron knew he meant DI Finch and Tom. A shout from nearby made him turn – just one of Stella's men confirming the brackets were in place and Erica Stern's park home was ready for lifting. He turned back to Joyce.

"What did you tell them, Mr Joyce?"

"I told you to look out for Erica bloody Stern. Her and Veronica Gaines and that pillock who spends all his time watching the birds."

"Right," said Aaron.

"The ones that fly, I mean. Not women."

"Thanks for the clarification." Aaron wondered if he'd pushed too far, but Joyce missed the sarcasm.

"I told you, anyway."

"You implied they had some connection with Mr Moorhouse's death, yes?" Aaron said carefully.

Joyce took a step back as the lifting equipment rumbled to life. "Yeah."

"What makes you think the others are involved? Simon Miller, I mean. And Veronica Gaines?"

Aaron watched the park home rise slowly into the air, debris falling from underneath. They'd spent ages sorting the utilities – especially the gas pipes connected to the blue canisters by the back porch. He was glad they'd taken the time. An explosion was the last thing they needed.

"Well, they're not here, are they?" Joyce said. "Can't keep the bloody pair of them away lately, and suddenly they're nowhere to be found."

Aaron nodded. Joyce might be a thug and a bigot, but he had a point. Simon Miller's Honda Jazz, usually a fixture at North Cumbria Caravan Park, was conspicuously absent.

Just like Veronica Gaines.

Other residents had been quick to share their thoughts about 'that Erica Stern' once the heavy machinery arrived. Beyond the usual comments – 'kept herself to herself', 'never trusted her', 'not from round here' – one theme kept emerging: Simon Miller.

"Shagging 'im, she were," one elderly resident had said.

"They thought no one knew," another added.

"Not for a while, mind," a third pointed out, earning nods of agreement.

The consensus was clear – Miller and Stern had been a couple, though it had ended some time ago.

So where were they all now? And Nina – Aaron hadn't seen her car either, though she'd definitely been here earlier. Wherever she was, she could handle herself.

Aaron thanked Joyce and stepped away to call Inspector Keane.

"Bloody hell. You're serious?" Keane asked when Aaron explained.

"I'm afraid so."

"You want me to run a search for three more people?"

"That's right. Erica Stern, Veronica Gaines, and Simon Miller."

"And is this before or after we find Olivia Bagsby and the ginger assassin?"

"I'm sorry, Morris. But it is a priority."

"They're always a priority," Keane grumbled. "But yes, we'll do what we can."

Aaron couldn't ask any more than that.

CHAPTER SEVENTY-FIVE

THE PLAN HAD BEEN an early night. A decent sleep, which was rare enough these days, and then maybe Carl would be in a better mood in the morning.

He'd got to bed early enough. That bit of the plan had worked out. As for the rest... not so much.

Zoe sat fully dressed on the bed beside him, propped against the wall, earphones in.

"Yes," she said into her phone. "No, Your Worship. I believe the suspect's continuing detention is necessary if we're to gather and preserve evidence."

A short pause followed.

"Mr Singleton might well disagree, sir. That's his job. But if you review the documentation, you'll see that our grounds for the initial arrest were entirely valid, and that—" She broke off, her mouth turning down at the corners.

"I appreciate that, Your Worship." She nodded.

Carl edged over to peek at her screen, then moved away when he realised it was a video call. He glanced at Zoe, catching the slight twitch of her mouth.

"Thank you," she said, ending the call with a long, slow breath.

"All OK?" Carl asked.

"That was a close one."

"Magistrate wasn't minded to extend Reid's custody?"

"Not that. I mean you. Sneaking into my video call without a top on."

Her grin reminded him of better times between them. Years of getting to know each other, finding common ground and surprising differences that made everything fascinating. All so recent, here in this house, in the hot tub just outside.

"Sinead Conway," Zoe said, jolting him back to the present.

"What about her?"

"What's the deal with her and Denise?"

He frowned.

"Don't tell me if you can't," she said. "If it's one of those PSD things."

"I don't know about it," he said honestly. "I really don't. Are you saying..."

"When Denise was giving evidence, she froze. It wasn't like her."

"No," Carl agreed. There were plenty of people he could imagine freezing on the witness box. Denise Gaskill wasn't one of them.

"I followed her gaze," Zoe continued, "and she was looking at Sinead Conway. What was Sinead Conway even doing there?"

"I don't know. She knows Carter. I suppose she could just be..." He shook his head. "I just don't know. It's probably nothing."

CHAPTER SEVENTY-FIVE

"Yeah." Zoe hadn't moved from her position, but her attention had shifted to her phone.

"Expecting something?" he asked.

"Aaron's at the caravan park. They should be lifting Erica Stern's park home soon. I'm hoping they find something quickly."

"They put concrete under it, didn't they?"

Zoe nodded.

If there was anything under Erica Stern's park home, they wouldn't be finding it quickly. This was going to be a long night.

CHAPTER SEVENTY-SIX

HARRIETT LEANED BACK, sipping her red wine as she watched Tom touch up the mess he'd made of the wall. Having a boyfriend who was clueless about DIY wasn't entirely bad. Not when he owned up to his mistakes and agreed to fix them.

She adjusted the dust sheet beneath her and shivered. Even with the heating on, lying on the floor in an unfurnished room was chilly. Her gaze drifted from the wall to her boyfriend and back again.

The wall was a disaster.

Perhaps she should have supervised more closely. Tom had admitted from the start that he didn't know what he was doing. He'd called himself an enthusiastic amateur, and she'd assumed that was false modesty.

Now she knew better. Tom was enthusiastic, but 'amateur' was generous. 'Beginner' would have been generous.

'Complete novice' was more accurate. She should have watched more carefully. Perhaps not quite as intently as she

CHAPTER SEVENTY-SIX

was watching now, but there were other attractions to her current view.

Tom wasn't stupid. He was a capable police officer who could unravel complex problems and juggle multiple thoughts at once.

Which made it baffling that he'd managed to misread the paint can label, ignore the colour displayed on the outside, and finish the living room wall she'd already painted in delicate eggshell blue with the ghastly neon green he'd chosen for the downstairs bathroom.

A green that had revealed its true horror only after it dried.

He'd admitted his mistake, at least. Agreed to fix it under her supervision and whatever other conditions she chose to impose.

Which explained why she was reclining on the floor, head on a cushion, body under a dust sheet, drinking wine while watching her boyfriend paint over his mistake, wearing nothing but an apron.

The ill-fitting apron was his problem.

"Missed a bit." She took another sip of wine.

"Sod off." He didn't turn around, but she heard the laugh in his voice.

"I don't want a multicoloured wall, Tom."

"You've made that clear. And you're probably right about the neon green."

"Good thing there isn't enough left to do the downstairs loo, then." She drew in a breath as he bent to the skirting board.

Harriett had long since realised he had no idea how attractive he was. She was lucky.

"Which leaves us with half a tin of neon green and

nothing to use it on." The tin lay at his feet, a painful reminder of his mistake.

He prised open the lid and peered inside.

"Shut that thing," she said. "We don't want you accidentally using it."

"Really?"

"Really."

"Because I had an idea." He turned, grinning, holding a brush coated in neon green. She remembered it had been his idea to bring in the sheets – the cheapest, roughest ones, he'd said, 'just to protect the floor' – and that she should wear as little as possible, 'in case of accidents'.

"Oh, bloody hell," she said as he flicked the brush, landing a dollop of neon green on her neck.

He dipped his brush back in the tin. "Just gonna sit there and let me cover you in neon green?"

"Not likely." Harriet jumped up and grabbed the spare brush before he could reach it. The neon green tin was out of reach unless she wanted to get completely covered.

But the eggshell blue was closer.

It would be cold, washing paint off each other outside with the hose in February. But as she flicked her brush towards Tom's back, watching him turn and catch a dollop right on his nose, she knew it would be worth it.

CHAPTER SEVENTY-SEVEN

The noise was closer than Nina had expected. She'd thought she was near Erica Stern's park home, where Stella's team would be working, but this sounded different.

The forensic team should have been making delicate sounds – the occasional drill through concrete, quiet voices, metal instruments clanking against stone. Instead, there was a relentless smashing that vibrated through her body, making her muscles twitch with the urge to move.

But she couldn't move. All she could do was feel around inside the bag, searching for any weakness – a zip, a seam, anything.

Her fingers brushed against something. A lump, but it felt odd, distant somehow.

Like a zip on the outside of the bag.

She let out a frustrated breath and went back to *Heartbreak Hotel*. It had worked before, when she'd been in a similar situation. At least this time she didn't have a gag in her mouth.

Nina wriggled down, making herself as small as possible,

manoeuvring until her face was closer to the lump. Still not close enough. The noise outside grew louder, more insistent.

This wasn't the sound of lifting equipment. This was breaking equipment.

The thought hit her like a punch to the gut. Why would they need breaking equipment if they were searching for human remains?

She shifted again, getting her mouth closer to the bump. As her lips closed around it and she tugged experimentally, realisation dawned.

She wasn't at the caravan park at all.

She was somewhere else. Somewhere remote enough that heavy machinery could operate through the night without complaints from neighbours.

Nausea rose in her throat. The plastic surrounding her and the metallic taste in her mouth weren't helping, but they weren't the cause. This was pure fear.

Now she knew where she was, the sounds made horrible sense.

The grinding of approaching vehicles. The smashing of glass being repeatedly crushed. The crunch of metal being torn apart.

She was in the caravan graveyard between Silloth and Skinburness. No one was nearby. No one could help her.

If she didn't get out soon, she'd be crushed along with the remains of this caravan.

CHAPTER SEVENTY-EIGHT

AARON GLANCED AT HIS PHONE. Three hours had passed since Serge's call telling him to be quiet when he got home. He'd hoped they might finish soon after that midnight call, but here he was at three in the morning.

The only interaction since had been with irate neighbours demanding they keep the noise down, and Keisha Middleton swearing back at them. She supervised the diggers, occasionally getting stuck in herself, but spent most of her time shouting "STOP!" every quarter hour or so, rushing to examine something, then walking away muttering.

Nina was nowhere to be found. Aaron felt let down – she was probably at some karaoke bar singing Elvis, not caring about what was happening at North Cumbria Caravan Park. He'd thought the promotion would have changed that attitude. Perhaps a chat was needed.

He leaned against his car, watching the drizzle fall over the concrete foundations of Erica Stern's home. A shout caught his attention as a figure approached.

"DI Keyes!" The voice was familiar, making Aaron's heart sink.

"Hello, Sammy."

DI Sammy Knight stopped in front of him, his face showing its usual mix of belligerence and contempt in the dim headlight glow.

"I heard this was going on. I couldn't really believe it."

Aaron waited, knowing there'd be more.

"But it's true, isn't it? You're really digging up some poor sod's home."

"We really are."

"It's bad enough you've invaded our patch. Bad enough you've taken this bloody case from people better equipped than you. But now you're just annoying the locals for no reason, aren't you?"

"Are we?" Aaron processed Knight's accusations. Better equipped? This case?

Then it clicked.

"Hang on. You think this is about the Femi Moorhouse murder, don't you?"

Knight blinked. "It isn't?"

A slow smile spread across Aaron's face. "It isn't. Something else entirely."

"Well, that's a bit unlikely." Knight turned to look at the excavation. "And people call you DI, do they?"

"I am a DI, Sammy."

"Not really, though. I mean, you're working for a DI, aren't you? Still reporting to Zoe Finch. Way I see it, you're... Well, you're not quite there yet, are you?" Knight tilted his head in mock sympathy.

Aaron clenched his jaw. *Don't let him rattle you.* "I'm very happy as I am. But thanks for your concern. In the

CHAPTER SEVENTY-EIGHT

meantime, I've got things to do, so whilst I'm grateful for the company..."

Knight gripped Aaron's arm. "Come on, Aaron. You're wasting your time. There's nothing here, and we both know it. Why don't you just—"

"Over here!" A technician's shout cut through the night. Keisha, who'd been bouncing on her feet with headphones on, was already crouching beside him.

"Aaron! You'll want to take a look at this!"

Aaron paused, savouring Knight's brief flash of disappointment before it vanished behind a smile.

"Thanks for coming," he said. "But you'd best be on your way. No point in two DIs wasting their time here."

CHAPTER SEVENTY-NINE

"STILL NO ANSWER?" Zoe drummed her fingers on the desk.

Tom set his phone down with a sigh. "Sorry, boss. She must be running late."

This wasn't like Nina. The new Nina had worked hard to move past her earlier slip-ups since her promotion. But now there was a new boyfriend in the picture. Someone to impress.

"Do you think she took the fireman to one of her karaoke bars?"

Tom refused to meet Zoe's eye. On the other end of her phone, Aaron was silent. When Nina finally showed up, she'd have some explaining to do.

"Fine. Tell me what we've got, Aaron."

"It's a body. Male, matches the age and height we're looking for. The concrete was poured fresh just before the park home arrived, so he's been under there about two years."

"Which matches how long Archie Stern's been missing. When can we confirm the ID?"

"Getting a DNA sample's proving tricky, boss. Nothing

CHAPTER SEVENTY-NINE

obvious in the park home. Local Uniforms are visiting Archie's mother in the morning. They'll be gentle – she's too frail for details. But she might have something of his we can test. In the meantime..."

"In the meantime, we treat our dead man as Archie Stern and work from there."

Tom glanced up from his screen. "Still no sign of the three wise monkeys, boss."

His nickname for the fugitives – Erica Stern, Veronica Gaines and Simon Miller – had stuck. Miller and Gaines refused to hear, see, or speak against Erica Stern. And Erica herself remained completely silent.

"What did the neighbours say, Aaron? Anything useful?"

"Not much. They all claim they knew about Erica and Simon's affair. Course, no one mentioned it when Erica's husband vanished."

"Do we think there's a connection with Femi Moorhouse?"

Silence.

"Right then. We've got the extension for Reid's custody, but without evidence, our hands are tied. Reid's not talking, and Trevor Singleton's already asking when his client will be released. Where are we with his flat search?"

"Still waiting, boss," Tom shifted in his seat. "It's just—"

"Just that Stella's team are swamped with other scenes. I know. You don't need to keep making excuses for everyone."

Zoe stopped, shaking her head. This wasn't like her.

"I'm sorry. There's... a lot happening. But for now, Chelsea Bright's fingerprints are on the murder weapon, whatever she says about Reid. Let's regroup in the morning and question her again. Meanwhile, you both have homes to go to."

CHAPTER EIGHTY

Nina had learned more than she'd ever wanted to know about the sounds of heavy machinery.

Six hours she'd been at it. Six hours of humming Elvis albums in her head while her teeth stayed clamped around the zip on the outside of the bag. The machines grew louder, closer with each passing minute.

She'd nearly given up several times when the zip got stuck. Like trying on clothes before a night out, when the zip always jammed at the worst moment. But unlike those times, she had no other options. She had to keep going.

And now, finally, there was a gap.

She thought she'd spotted one earlier, but in the darkness she couldn't risk shifting position to check. Losing the zip would be catastrophic.

So she'd persevered, working through Elvis album after Elvis album in her mind. Each tiny movement of the zip felt like scaling a mountain, but now she could make out a faint shape in the darkness.

Probably her own hand.

CHAPTER EIGHTY

But if she could see it, that meant light was getting in. There was definitely a gap now. Just a bit longer before she'd dare to move, to try finding that gap with her hand.

The machinery cut out suddenly. The world seemed to pause, holding its breath. A burst of birdsong broke through – it must be morning. Then the machines started up again, even closer than before.

Keep going, she told herself. The gap was there. She was almost free.

Just keep going.

CHAPTER EIGHTY-ONE

"Miss me?" The lawyer looked round as Aaron walked into Interview Room Four, bright and early, behind the boss.

Aaron stopped dead and stared at him, taking a moment to confirm it really was Stan Basham sitting beside Chelsea Bright on the opposite side of the table.

"Not really." Aaron sat down.

"Suit yourself, DS Keyes," replied Basham.

"It's DI Keyes," DI Finch pointed out. Even before the words were out, Aaron wished she hadn't.

Basham knew. Of course Basham knew. Aaron hadn't seen Stan Basham for months, and he hadn't missed the man at all, but Basham would have kept on top of local police news.

The lawyer turned to his client, speaking in affected tones that weren't fooling anyone. "Well, aren't we the lucky ones, Chelsea? Two DIs, all for you? We're truly spoiled."

Aaron ran through the formalities, and Chelsea jumped in before they could begin questioning.

"It wasn't me." She leaned forward, looking serious,

CHAPTER EIGHTY-ONE

almost angry. Aaron hadn't seen that expression on her before, but it made sense. She'd managed to drag herself away from Whitehaven, after all, with Femi in tow. There had to be some strength in her.

"What wasn't you?" asked DI Finch.

"That killed Femi. It wasn't me."

"How do you explain the fingerprints on the murder weapon, Chelsea?" Aaron asked.

"I don't know." She fixed him with a steady gaze. "Have you charged Ethan Reid yet?"

Aaron's eyes flicked towards the DI, and she gave a tiny nod.

"No," he said, "we haven't been able to."

"Bloody hell."

All that seriousness and anger seemed to drain from Chelsea in an instant. She sat back in her chair and blinked, tears welling in her eyes.

"Chelsea?" Aaron said.

"Fuck," she said and buried her face in her hands.

"My client needs some time," said Basham.

Chelsea removed her hands and shook her head. "No. No. I want to tell them everything."

"Yes?" prompted DI Finch.

"Shut up," Basham told his client.

"It was me," said Chelsea.

"I said shut up," Basham repeated.

Chelsea shook her head. "No. I'll tell you everything, but you have to understand, it wasn't my fault."

"We're listening," Aaron told her. "We'll take careful note of everything you say."

"She's not saying anything," said Basham.

"Yes I am." Chelsea's voice cracked. "I did it. I killed him.

I... But it wasn't my fault. It really wasn't. Ethan Reid, he... If I hadn't done it..."

Basham had his own head in his hands by this point. Chelsea fell apart completely, tears streaming from her eyes, her breath coming in big wet gasps. Aaron stood, walked around the table, and helped her take a sip from the cup of water in front of her.

"I'm sorry," she said.

DI Finch checked her phone. "We'll take a break."

Outside the interview room, she showed him the message she'd received. "I'm sorry. It's from the super. I've got to go."

"A development?"

"In the case," the boss said. "Carter."

"What sort of development?" Aaron caught himself. "Sorry. You don't know. Obviously you don't know. Think he's changed his plea?"

DI Finch shook her head. "No. It wouldn't be like Carter to make anyone else's life any easier. Whatever it is, it won't be good news."

"You want me to come with?"

"No. You stay here. Work with Tom to find out what the hell happened to Femi Moorhouse. See if you can get anything we can use against Ethan Reid. And when Nina shows her face, tell her..."

"Yes?"

"Tell her whatever you want, Aaron. I've got to go."

CHAPTER EIGHTY-TWO

"You got the same message?" Denise asked.

DI Whaley passed her his phone.

Get your pigging carcass over to Earl Street. There's news.

She'd received identical words.

"Any sign of him?" DI Whaley asked.

"DCI Branthwaite? No." She'd diverted to court after getting the message on her way in. "I've been waiting outside nearly half an hour. He hasn't come past. Could be inside already."

"Anyone else?"

She shook her head. DI Whaley stepped closer.

"What's the deal with you and Sinead Conway?" he muttered.

Denise cast around the empty street. They stood alone by the statue of Major Aglionby, metres from court. The gentle Cumbrian rain fell steadily, a constant February reminder of where they were.

"What?"

"You and Sinead Conway," he said. "What's going on there?"

Denise's mind raced. Had she let something slip? Had DCI Branthwaite said something? He'd promised to keep quiet, though he hadn't seemed happy about it.

Then she remembered – yesterday in court, seeing Sinead in the gallery. She'd frozen.

Zoe Finch had been watching, too.

Bloody hell.

She'd given herself away. Not the details Branthwaite knew, but enough to show she was hiding something.

"I'm sorry, DI Whaley."

"What?"

"I'm sorry, boss. But it's got nothing to do with you." She turned and walked away down Earl Street towards the main road.

"Denise!" DI Whaley shouted behind her. She tensed, expecting footsteps, a hand on her shoulder, but nothing came.

Keep walking.

"Denise!" His voice was fainter now, tinged with anger and hurt. Betrayal.

If anyone should be used to betrayal by now, it was Carl Whaley. The urge to turn back and explain everything nearly overwhelmed her, but she'd made her choice long ago.

She kept moving, reaching Warwick Road and turning right towards The Crescent. Her pace quickened past the Citadel, turning left and left again, barely aware of her direction, just letting the streets of Carlisle swallow her up.

CHAPTER EIGHTY-THREE

There.

The gap was wide enough now. Nina could see through to the white room inside, with its mix of grey, brown and green shapes. Enough space to fit her hand and pull. Enough to lose and find again if needed.

The machinery's vibrations pulsed through her entire body, as if they'd become part of her bloodstream, part of her very being.

She took a deep breath and relaxed her jaw. Only as she moved away from the lump did she notice how much her teeth ached. That was tomorrow's problem.

The machines roared so loud she could barely think.

She pushed her hand through the gap, feeling around until her fingers found the zip's metal bar.

It wouldn't budge.

"Fuck!" She yanked hard. The zip tore open with a ripping sound, creating a gap that went from an inch to three, then four, then a foot, then two.

Fighting to stay calm, she pulled it another foot before

wriggling to reposition herself. Just as she prepared to tumble out, she froze.

The bag wasn't on the ground. What would she land on?

She hung there, half in and half out, her eyes stinging from the sudden light. Before she could consider the drop, momentum carried her forward.

A moment later, she hit hard ground. But the grunt of pain she let out was nothing compared to last night's ordeal or the aches yet to come.

She jumped to her feet and took in her surroundings – an ancient caravan shell with half a roof. No furniture except a built-in table jutting from one wall.

The table where they'd left her. Where they'd put her in that bag to...

The noise grew deafening. No time to think. She spun in circles, searching frantically for an exit before spotting the boarded-up doorway. Fuck. No way through there.

Nina leapt onto the table and grabbed the roof's edge, pulling herself up despite her screaming muscles. Her head emerged first, then her shoulders. With one final push, she was out.

She tumbled from the roof onto soft grass – thank hell it wasn't concrete or glass – rolling away from the massive metal monster bearing down on her, its jaws snapping inches from her face before retreating.

She lay there panting for what felt like a full minute before realising the machine had stopped. The only sounds were rain and a nearby voice asking if she was OK.

Opening her eyes, she found a young man peering down at her, his face etched with concern and confusion.

"Nina Kapoor," she managed. "Cumbria Police. Have you got a phone?"

"No signal here."

"Have you got a car?"

"Are you alright?" He studied her, his eyes wide. "Do you need a doctor?"

"Have you got a car?" she repeated.

"My mum drops me off in the evening and picks me up next day."

Bloody stinking hell.

She blinked, properly looking at his face now. Of course he didn't have a car – he was barely old enough to drive.

"When?" The word came out with effort – speaking seemed to drain her energy.

"Not for an hour or... Hey, are you OK? Where are you going?"

She was already up and running, heading south through the caravan graveyard. It had better be south. And there'd better be a car to flag down – Silloth wasn't far, but she couldn't make it on foot.

A car sat at the field entrance – blue, sea-faded, unwashed for months. Her electric Nissan.

She reached for keys that weren't in her pocket.

The bastards. They'd knocked her out, bagged her up for crushing, and driven her to her own murder in her own bloody car.

The absolute bastards.

She glanced back at the car, then beyond to where the boy stood by the metal dragon of a breaking machine, his face twisted in confusion. Turning back to the road, she began to run.

CHAPTER EIGHTY-FOUR

A NAGGING FEELING tugged at the back of Tom's mind.

Something wasn't right. Nina had been late before, turning up tired and hungover, but recently she'd managed to be on time despite being tired and hungover. "'Two out of three ain't bad,'" she'd joked.

"Ready?" DI Keyes asked.

Tom nodded, pushing the worry aside as he steeled himself. Chelsea Bright waited behind that door. And Stan Basham.

"Good morning." Tom reintroduced himself, though it wasn't necessary after the hours he'd spent interviewing Chelsea, and dealing with Basham over the past couple of years. He completed the formalities and glanced at the DI, who nodded.

"Do you want to tell us what happened?" Tom kept his voice gentle.

"We robbed Ethan Reid's van. You know that, right?"

"We do," DI Keyes said.

"But we didn't realise it was his," Chelsea said. "If we

CHAPTER EIGHTY-FOUR

had, we'd never have... Well, like I said before, we're not stupid."

Chelsea paused to take a sip of her water. Tom glanced at Basham, who stared at the table with a bored expression.

"He found out," Chelsea said, meeting Tom's eyes. "I heard that when I was out the day after we took the box. Or the day after that. I'm not sure. But he knew it was us."

"How did he know?" DI Keyes asked.

Chelsea turned to him. "We weren't exactly subtle. There was gear in the box, but there was also money, and we spent most of the money on more gear."

She stopped, the implication clear.

"Go on," Tom prompted.

She pressed her lips together. "All the dealers round Silloth work for Ethan Reid. He used to live there. Everyone knows him, and if they're not actually working for him, they're scared of him."

"Who did you—?" Tom began.

"I don't even remember. Might have been that Gareth Burns. You know him, right?"

"I've come across him," DI Keyes said. "So you bought drugs from Gareth Burns, and Burns told Ethan Reid you suddenly had money, and Ethan Reid realised it must have been you and Femi that broke into his van."

"Maybe. Like I said, I'm not even sure it was Burns. Either way, I heard Reid wasn't happy. He was looking for us. I told Femi, and he didn't think it was a big deal."

Tom shook his head; how stupid was Femi? His brief encounter with Reid had been enough to know that crossing him would be dangerous.

"You disagreed?" DI Keyes asked.

"I did. We argued. I told him Reid would kill us. He said

Reid wouldn't even find us. I told him Reid already knew, and he just laughed it off. He was..."

She shrugged.

"He was high?" Tom suggested.

"Most of the time."

Basham remained silent, focused on the table.

"What happened after that?" Tom asked.

"I went to his flat."

Tom felt his pulse quicken. The DI leaned forward. Even Basham stirred briefly before returning to his examination of the table.

The flat. She'd been in Reid's flat. Maybe the search would uncover something after all.

"Go on," Tom said.

Chelsea shifted in her seat. "I took the money back with me. There wasn't a lot left. Eighty quid, maybe."

"How much had you taken?" The DI leaned forward.

"I don't remember. Maybe five hundred. Plus the heroin."

Tom considered this. Would Ethan Reid have killed for that amount? He knew plenty of dealers who would.

"And I took the last bit of the gear." Chelsea's expression softened. "Femi had hidden it in the cistern, like I wouldn't find it there. He spilled a load by the bed, and there was this bloody great trail of it leading to the bathroom. I thought... I thought if I brought it back, Reid might say it was OK. I'd made an effort, you know. Soon as I realised it was him."

"And did he say it was OK?"

She let out a short, bitter laugh. "No he didn't. He told me it wasn't enough. He didn't just want the money and the drugs. It was too late for that. If people found out, he said, it would be open season. So he had to send a message."

CHAPTER EIGHTY-FOUR

"A message?" Tom asked.

"To anyone thinking of stealing from him, or taking over his business, or anything, really. 'If you mess with me, you die.'"

"He said that?"

She nodded. "Those were his words. Said people had to know. But he said that because I'd made the effort and come back, he'd offer me a deal."

Tom waited, already knowing where this was heading after what she'd told the DI and the boss. After what he'd seen in her caravan, and the prints on the murder weapon.

"He said only one of us had to die," she continued. "Me or Femi. He said either I killed Femi, or Reid would kill me."

Tom glanced at DI Keyes, whose face remained stony except for a flicker of horror in his eyes that only someone who knew him would notice.

"And you chose the first option?" the DI asked.

Chelsea nodded.

Basham stirred. "Hang on—"

"Forget it," Chelsea said. He returned to staring at the table.

They had nothing on Reid. Chelsea Bright had killed Femi herself, even under coercion. Proving that coercion would be next to impossible.

"But he did bite me," she said.

"He did?" Tom asked.

"Yeah. That bit was true. I didn't know if he was just talking big, didn't think he really meant it, and he wanted to make sure I took it all seriously. So he bit me."

"There?" The DI gestured. "In his flat?"

"Yes."

Something fluttered in Tom's chest. "Was there much blood?" he asked.

She laughed again. "Yeah. Loads."

Her head dropped, and tears coursed down her cheeks.

"We'll take a break," Aaron said. They paused the interview and headed out of the room.

Reid had bitten Chelsea Bright in his flat. The wound had bled. And though the wound had been sterilised since then and Reid's DNA was gone, his flat was still being searched.

CHAPTER EIGHTY-FIVE

AARON HAD BARELY MADE it back to his desk when the call came. It was the third one that morning from the same number. He'd ignored the first two, which explained why the caller had gone straight to DI Finch afterwards.

But he couldn't ignore it forever.

"Hello," he said.

"DI Keyes." Trevor Singleton's voice was smooth and charming, with an easy affability. "I'm glad I caught you."

No mention of his earlier attempts to reach Aaron. That wasn't Singleton's style. Stan Basham would have made a point of it, but Singleton was different. Aaron couldn't stand Basham – a man of mediocre intelligence who thought he was cleverer than the police. Basham was merely annoying.

Trevor Singleton, on the other hand, was frightening.

"Mr Singleton," Aaron said. "How can I help you?"

"Well, first off, we haven't had the chance to speak outside the interview room, so I wanted to congratulate you on your promotion. Does this mean you'll be heading for greener pastures at some point?"

It was bad enough hearing it from Nina and Serge's constant reminders. But Trevor Singleton?

"Thank you." Aaron deliberately ignored the question.

Singleton paused in mock politeness before continuing. "I was hoping you could provide an update on my client's detention."

"Yes?"

"Well, you haven't actually questioned him this morning, have you? So it's difficult to see why he should be kicking his heels in your cells, however luxuriously appointed they might be."

"Ah," Aaron said.

"Am I to take it that you'll be releasing him shortly, then?"

Aaron closed his eyes. He pictured Reid back on the street, outside his flat, bearing down on him with that icy stare and menacing presence. The sort of person who'd have Trevor Singleton representing them.

Despite the lawyer's polite manner, his clients were always the most dangerous. That said something about Ethan Reid.

Though Reid was frightening and violent, it seemed odd that he could afford Trevor Singleton. Reid felt like small-fry for someone of Singleton's calibre. Which meant, of course, that he wasn't small-fry at all. Aaron remembered the man and woman he'd seen in the corridor outside the flat in Pears House – smartly dressed in suit and tie, grey skirt and pressed white shirt.

No. Whatever he was, Ethan Reid wasn't small-fry.

And he wasn't going home yet. Not while his flat was still being searched.

CHAPTER EIGHTY-FIVE

"We're just waiting to hear back on some potential evidence," Aaron said.

"Evidence? I don't believe I've heard anything about that."

Aaron glanced at his watch. The clock was ticking. If they didn't find Chelsea Bright's blood in Reid's flat, and find it soon, there would be nothing he could do to stop the man walking out of the Hub and heading straight back to Whitehaven.

"If anything comes of it, we'll be in touch." He hung up.

CHAPTER EIGHTY-SIX

"Can we get this over with?" Basham rocked in his chair.

DI Keyes' jaw tightened. "You have somewhere better to be?"

"Takeaway curry and an adult movie." Basham delivered the line with practiced indifference.

Tom watched the exchange, wondering what Basham's clients made of him – this lawyer who seemed interested only in antagonising the police and winning petty mind games no one else was playing. Perhaps they thought all lawyers behaved this way.

For some clients, such treatment was fitting. But Chelsea Bright...

"Tell us about that night," Tom said once the interview had formally begun.

Chelsea wiped her eyes and drew a steadying breath. "I was still bleeding when I got back to the caravan. I wanted to explain it to him. Tell him what had happened, how we had to go, immediately, as far as we could. But he wouldn't listen."

"You mean Femi?" DI Keyes leaned forward.

"Yes. He was standing at the door with the box in his hands, empty, and this look in his eyes like I'd betrayed him. Like a wounded dog. I was bleeding, and all he wanted to talk about was the money I'd returned."

"So he was angry with you?"

"Yeah. Angry and upset." Chelsea wrapped her arms around herself. "He just didn't understand how serious things were. He disappeared into the bathroom, where he'd hidden the B, and then he must have realised I'd found it and given that back, too, because when he came out again he was..." She briefly closed her eyes. "He lost it. Just lost it."

"He attacked you?"

"Not me, no. It was like he was attacking himself. He was screaming and banging his head against the wall. And I was trying to talk to him, but he just wouldn't get it. Trying to explain that we had to run. But he wouldn't. The only thing he cared about was the drugs."

Tom let the silence stretch, processing her words. Chelsea might have been describing herself before her latest fix – that desperate need, that inability to think rationally.

"That was when I realised what I had to do." Chelsea's voice dropped.

Basham looked up from the table. "We done now?"

"Not exactly," Tom said. "What did you do, Chelsea?"

She drew another deep breath and nodded. "I told him I knew where we could get a fix."

Tom understood. If fear wouldn't motivate Femi Moorhouse, perhaps addiction would.

"We walked," she said. "It took a while. It was dark, and he kept stopping and asking where we were heading, but I said not to worry. I picked up..." She stopped, eyes closing. Her hand found the water cup, trembling as she raised it to her lips. "I'm sorry."

"That's OK." DI Keyes kept his voice gentle. "Just tell us, Chelsea. In your own time."

"There's this place, just south of Skinburness, where they smash up all the old caravans."

"I've seen it," Tom said.

"We stopped there for a minute, so Femi could catch his breath, and I picked up a bit of wood. He didn't even ask me what it was for. He was that far gone. And then we just went on through Skinburness. He kept asking where we were going, and I kept telling him we were nearly there."

Chelsea held up her hand when Tom tried to speak. "No. I need to finish this. I led him onto the marshes. Up the path, right to the top. Grune Point. And then, I..." Her eyes squeezed shut. "I waited until we were by one of those ditches, full of mud and water. He was in front of me. I just lifted it up and brought it down on his head, and he went down."

"Into the ditch?"

She nodded. "Into the ditch. He drowned, didn't he?"

"He did, yes," Tom confirmed.

"I didn't wait. I didn't want to know. I just... I turned and ran. I made it back to the caravan park, and then I was sick."

Tom remembered the smell of vomit from the tiny bathroom in the caravan.

Chelsea opened her eyes, meeting his gaze. "I killed him. I loved him, but I killed him."

CHAPTER EIGHTY-SEVEN

Zoe navigated the outskirts of Carlisle, talking to Jake Frimpton on hands-free. "I don't know."

"Would you tell me if you did?" he asked.

She laughed. "Good point. I suppose it depends what it was. But yes, it's true, there's been some development with the trial, and I'm on my way in, and no, I haven't got a clue what that development is, but I doubt it'll be anything good."

"Do you think the judge could have declared a mistrial?"

"Why would that happen?" She slowed for a set of traffic lights and glanced at the phone. "Do you know something?"

She thought back through her own appearances at the court, trying to summon up images of the jurors. Had Carter got to them? Had someone said the wrong thing to the wrong person?

A horn blared behind her. The lights had turned green. Zoe's hands shook on the wheel as panic gripped her.

Keep it together.

"No," Jake said. "Just thinking aloud."

Her phone buzzed as she turned right into the centre of town, already searching for a parking space.

Zhang Chen. No doubt he wanted an update. Everyone was after news, no one actually telling her what she needed to know.

Zhang could wait.

"I'm sorry, Jake. I've got to go."

She ended the call and managed two more minutes' driving before it rang again. She cursed, ready to ignore it, then saw Morris Keane's name on the screen and hit the green button.

"Morris. Tell me you've got news."

"I think so." Inspector Keane's tone told her that whatever the news was, it wasn't good.

He hadn't found the three wise monkeys. Which meant this was about Olivia or Kaciaryna.

Was one of them dead? If so, Zoe knew which one she hoped it was.

She spotted a space ahead on Chiswick Street and could hardly believe her luck, then swore under her breath as the BMW in front nipped in and took it.

"It's about your Olivia Bagsby," Inspector Keane said.

Zoe's heart sank. "Go on." She manoeuvred the car in a three-point turn, ignoring the angry horns from both sides of the road.

"We think she's left the country."

"What?"

It had been a long time since Zoe had stalled a car, but now she was stuck with a dead engine right across the middle of a busy road.

Damn.

CHAPTER EIGHTY-SEVEN

"There's been a report," Keane said. "Someone matching her description."

Zoe got the engine started again and turned, waving a vague apology at the world outside. "Plenty of people match her description," she said.

"Yes," Keane agreed. "But most of them aren't travelling on false passports."

"Bloody hell."

"Indeed."

Seconds earlier, she'd been sure he was about to tell her Olivia was dead. Surely this was better?

"Where was she headed?"

"She boarded a flight from Heathrow to Brazil. Rio. Late last night. We've got people checking the footage, but the chances are..."

Could it be her? It might be.

It probably was.

But why?

Zoe spotted a space and slipped into it without incident. Just a two-minute walk from the court.

Whatever had happened with the trial, she'd find out soon enough. And in the meantime, what the hell was Olivia Bagsby up to?

CHAPTER EIGHTY-EIGHT

"We've got Chelsea Bright," Tom said as they walked back to the team room.

There was nothing positive about the statement. No hint of the usual celebration when someone confessed to murder.

Aaron pushed open the door to the team room. "We've got Chelsea Bright, but it's Ethan Reid we want."

Nina's absence weighed heavily. This wasn't like her recent behaviour at all.

"Let's just hope the search—" Tom stopped as Aaron's phone rang.

Aaron checked the display. "Stella Berry," he said, answering the call.

"It's been cleaned up," Stella said without preamble.

"What?"

"The flat you had my people looking over."

"What about it?"

"I've just spoken to Caroline. She tells me it's been cleaned up. Professionally. And by 'professionally', I don't

CHAPTER EIGHTY-EIGHT

mean a little old lady with a mop. I mean people who know what DNA is and how to remove every trace of it."

"Bloody hell." Aaron collapsed onto his chair and switched the phone to speaker, shaking his head at Tom's eager expression.

"Nothing," he mouthed as Stella continued.

"We did what we could, Aaron."

"I'm sure you did."

"What were you hoping to find?"

"We've just been talking to a woman who was bitten in that flat."

"No sign of any dogs there, but like I say, it was cleaned up."

"Not by a dog. By the owner of the flat. Lots of blood, she says. Coerced into murdering her partner. Her blood was pretty much our last hope of proving it."

"I'm sorry, Aaron. The flat's been disinfected so thoroughly, there isn't a chance of finding a thing."

"Bloody hell," Aaron repeated.

Reid had been in custody, but the officers watching his flat had been attacked. In normal circumstances others would have been available to take over, but half of Cumbria Police were still out there trying to find Kaciaryna Ilinich, which meant the place had been left unguarded for hours. And people with lawyers like Trevor Singleton probably had others who could handle various tasks, even from behind bars. All they needed was to get the word out.

And Singleton would have seen to that.

"Christ," he muttered, then apologised and thanked Stella just as Tom's phone rang.

Tom answered with a frown. "Hello?" His expression cleared. "About time."

He mouthed 'Nina' to Aaron.

"What?" Tom's mouth dropped open. "What do you mean?"

Another pause.

"You've flagged down a truck? What? In the..."

He waited, frowning. Aaron watched.

"In the caravan graveyard? That place by Skinburness?"

Aaron walked over, resisting the urge to tap the speaker button on Tom's phone.

"Whose phone is this?" Tom asked quickly. "You mean Erica Stern and the other two, right? They've disappeared."

He listened again.

"Holyhead? In Wales, isn't it? Ferry to Ireland?"

Tom shook his head at Aaron in disbelief.

"OK. I'll get onto the search teams. Call me when you're back at the caravan park."

He ended the call and turned to Aaron.

"You won't believe what's just happened."

Aaron raised an eyebrow. "Try me."

"Well, there's good news and bad news. The bad news is Nina's been knocked out and zipped into a bag again."

"Christ," Aaron breathed.

"The good news is that she's got herself free, she's on her way back, and she thinks she knows where they are."

Tom was right. Aaron wouldn't have believed it. Or at least, he wouldn't have believed it about anyone else.

But this was Nina. With Nina, anything was possible.

CHAPTER EIGHTY-NINE

Harriett Barnes sat at her desk in the brand new PSD team room at Durranhill and wondered what was going on.

Everyone else seemed to know something. Everyone except her. DI Whaley and DS Gaskill had received brief but urgent messages from the DCI, summoning them to court. By now, they'd probably have an idea why.

All three of them, on the spot, while the news was being made. Everyone except DC Harriett Barnes. The fact that she'd done more than the rest of them put together to bring Streeting in didn't seem to matter. Not when important things were happening.

Forget it.

She shook herself out, trying to throw off the lingering resentment, then turned back to her screen.

The Skeleton Key.

They'd been working on this one for ages, so long that she'd forgotten which of them had given their target the codename. But it had stuck.

The Skeleton Key was a cop. Or possibly not a cop, but

someone with access to one. They were senior. Or possibly not senior at all, just someone who could find out the sort of things that only someone with seniority usually knew.

There was a shortlist of names – police officers highly placed enough that they might have provided information and cover for organised crime over the years. And then a much longer list of names: civilian staff and associates, half of them in the assistant chief constable's office, the other half all over the country, and a handful of positions without names even attached to them.

The Skeleton Key knew things only someone highly placed was supposed to know, which should have made it easy to identify them, but they were remarkably elusive.

Her mind wasn't really here, but a couple of miles up the road in the court.

"You OK?"

Harriet looked up, startled. She'd completely forgotten she wasn't alone.

"Fine, thanks. Why?"

Phil from IT emerged from under the spare desk where he'd been connecting wires. "You look angry. I've never seen you looking angry."

He disappeared back under the desk before she could think of how to respond. Instead, she closed the window she was working on, opened another, and began scanning through the results from last night's searches.

Dr Elizabeth Manning was an easy start. She hadn't appeared anywhere. Not even a complaint from a patient, which was rare enough in her profession, particularly when many patients were in custody at the Hub. It didn't mean Dr Manning was clean, but she wasn't their first priority.

The custody suite at the Hub was different. Both Stones

CHAPTER EIGHTY-NINE

and Parton had faced complaints and disciplinary proceedings, but both had been exonerated or given warnings. If you didn't get complaints in the custody suite, you weren't doing your job right. Harriett had been complained about herself during her short undercover stint, and she hadn't even been on custody duty.

Stones and Parton were probably clean, but 'probably' wasn't definite. There were plenty of other candidates. Even Clive Moor had received his share of allegations. Another name for the growing list.

Harriett stood and threw on her coat. The list could wait. The worst of the traffic would have eased by now, and if she was lucky with parking, she'd be outside court in fifteen minutes.

Carter wasn't police. Technically, this trial had nothing to do with her, or with PSD at all. But the rest of the team was there, waiting, because even if Carter wasn't police himself, it was Carter who'd corrupted the worst of them.

And whatever had happened in his trial, Harriett Barnes wasn't going to be the last to find out.

CHAPTER NINETY

"It's been a pleasure," Ethan Reid said as Aaron led him and his lawyer through to the main custody area.

Aaron kept silent, glancing to his side. Trevor Singleton stood there, a bland smile on his face as he watched the comings and goings of police and suspects.

That relaxed, almost sleepy demeanour seemed at odds with the man's true nature. Aaron wondered if it was deliberate – a calculated approach to appear more approachable, to extract confidences from officers.

If that was his strategy, it wasn't working. Even with the smiles, Trevor Singleton wasn't someone any copper would trust. Aaron left the lawyer and his client by the doorway and approached the desk where Clive Moor stood watching.

Clive lowered his voice as Aaron drew near. "Listen, DI Keyes, I'm sorry, right? I don't know how it happened."

"How what happened?"

"The thing with the doctor. Last night."

Aaron could hardly believe it had only been last night. He'd been awake for most of it, supervising at the caravan

CHAPTER NINETY

park. Dr Manning and Chelsea Bright felt like ancient history, especially after what they'd just heard from Nina.

Tom was upstairs in the team room now, helping coordinate the search, trying to piece together what had happened and what came next.

"Forget it," Aaron said. "Or, don't forget it, exactly. We'll need to figure out how this happened. But I know you won't have messed up, Clive. Oh, and Clive?"

"Yup?"

"Don't call me DI Keyes. We've worked together too long for that."

Clive smiled and produced the release forms. Aaron was scanning them when he felt a tap on his shoulder.

He turned to find Reid smiling at him.

"No hard feelings," Reid said.

Aaron remained silent.

"But don't let it happen again," Reid added before walking out, not bothering with forms or personal possessions like a normal person would.

Singleton gave Aaron an apologetic smile and hurried after his client. Just like that, they were gone, as if they'd never been there.

Don't let it happen again.

Aaron had little doubt the man meant it.

If releasing Reid without charge was unpleasant, informing Chelsea Bright was worse. Basham sat there unmoved, like he was watching a dull film. Chelsea stared at Aaron, her mouth moving without sound.

"I'm sorry," Aaron said. "We did all we could."

The words echoed Clive's earlier apology.

"Is that it?" Chelsea asked after a pause. "Will I go to prison now?"

Aaron blinked in surprise.

"For murder, I mean?" she clarified. "If you can't prove Reid forced me, then... Is that murder? Is there nothing I can do about it?"

Aaron cleared his throat. Basham continued sitting there, silent and motionless.

"I think maybe your lawyer can advise you," Aaron said.

Chelsea turned to Basham, who seemed to finally notice their attention.

"What?" Basham said.

"I was just saying, your client's in trouble, maybe you can give her some legal advice."

Basham shrugged, and Aaron decided he preferred Singleton.

He probably preferred Ethan Reid.

"There are other lawyers available," Aaron told Chelsea.

"There are?"

"Better lawyers," he said.

"Hey." Basham's protest lacked conviction.

"Maybe I can recommend someone," Aaron said, thinking immediately of Sue Sharples. With Baz Joyce cleared, she'd be free to represent someone else.

"Mr Basham," Chelsea turned to her lawyer.

"Yeah?"

"You're fired," she said.

For the first time that morning, Aaron smiled.

CHAPTER NINETY-ONE

"Max, you're a legend." Nina jumped down from the truck and winced as she landed.

She hadn't realised the height, and with her exhaustion, she'd forgotten she wasn't invincible.

"Phone," said the Ukrainian driver, who'd spotted her running along the road and stopped to help.

"Phone?"

"You have my phone, Nina."

"Bloody hell." She reached up to pass it back, then moved away before he remembered the chocolate bar he'd offered to share.

Her stomach growled. She couldn't remember her last meal.

The driver had dropped her at the caravan park entrance. She ran past Mr Nelson's makeshift office, where he stood shielding a cigarette from the drizzle, his mouth agape as she passed. At the cordon a minute later, she found Rob Collins wearing a similar expression.

"What the hell happened to you?" Rob gestured at her arms and legs.

Nina looked down at herself. Her clothes were torn everywhere. Her hair must look worse.

"Ah, Nina, glad you're here."

Stella approached, then stopped, her eyes scanning Nina with disapproval. "I'm not sure who looks worse – you or the body we pulled from the concrete."

She pointed to the plot opposite Chelsea's caravan, where Erica Stern's park home had stood.

"You found something?" Nina said.

Stella gave her a nod. "A dead man. Expecting plenty of forensic evidence from him, too. Which is more than we got from Ethan Reid's flat."

"Ethan Reid's flat?" Nina had almost forgotten about him. "What... Hang on."

Another PC approached through the rain. Martinez. "Bloody hell."

"Yes?" Nina was tired of these reactions.

"You'll have to tell me all about it on the way back," Martinez said.

"What?"

"Got a car waiting. We're heading to the Hub. And I've got a phone for you."

"I want my car keys," Nina said. Everyone stared until she shook her head and followed Martinez to the waiting patrol car.

The keys would turn up eventually. She hoped so – she'd lost the spares.

In the back seat, someone handed her a phone. It rang immediately. Inspector Keane's voice came through, talking about a manhunt.

CHAPTER NINETY-ONE

"A what?"

"The manhunt, Nina. The one you and your colleagues wanted. For three fugitives. The three wise monkeys, Tom called them."

"Oh yeah. What about it?" Nina felt her body go heavy as the car pulled onto the main road.

"We've got them."

She blinked. *Stay awake.* "You have?"

"You were right. They were waiting to cross the Irish Sea. North Wales Police just arrested them in the queue at the Holyhead ferry terminal."

After everything, hearing it over the phone felt anti-climactic.

"They're being brought back up here," Inspector Keane continued.

He paused, waiting for her response, but her mind had gone blank.

Then one crucial question surfaced. Nina took a breath.

"I don't suppose any of the monkeys had a set of keys for an electric Nissan on them?"

CHAPTER NINETY-TWO

Tom was waiting with news when DI Keyes returned from the custody suite.

He looked up from his desk. "They've got them."

"Got who?"

"The three wise monkeys. Stern, Gaines, and Miller. Picked them up at Holyhead, just like Nina said. And we've got... Oh, hang on." Tom's attention shifted to his computer. "Boss is calling. I'll put it on the screen."

The large screen flickered to life, showing DI Finch standing outside Carlisle Crown Court, the familiar statue visible behind her.

"Any news?" Tom asked quickly.

"Nothing from here, no. Anything at your end?"

Tom let out a laugh. In the hour since the boss had left, they'd released one suspect, arrested three more, and then there was Nina's story...

"Bloody hell," DI Finch's eyes widened. "What happened to you?"

CHAPTER NINETY-TWO

Nina had just walked into the team room. Tom turned to look at her before facing the screen again.

"Nina was attacked by the three wise monkeys," DI Keyes said. "But she got away this morning and worked out where they were heading. North Wales Police have them in custody now, bringing them back here."

"Bloody hell," DI Finch repeated. "Are you OK, Nina?"

"Yup." Nina shrugged. "Bloody starving, and I've lost my car keys, but otherwise fine."

"And Reid?" DI Finch asked, moving the conversation along.

"We had to let him go." Tom watched disappointment cross the boss's face. "The search of his flat turned up nothing. He'd had the place cleaned while he was in custody."

"Bastard," DI Finch muttered, pacing between the statue and Warwick Road.

Tom spotted familiar faces in the background – DI Whaley with DS Gaskill and DCI Branthwaite. A flash of green caught his eye as Harriett approached the group.

"Hi," Tom said, but she couldn't hear him through the screen.

The boss turned, revealing the court exit behind her. DCI Kiki Carnegie stood there, looking unusually relaxed. DS Sharon Virgil and DC Nigel Shaw from Durranhill were there, too. Sharon had been helpful during the Mulligan investigation, while Nigel had been decidedly less so.

"You really don't know what's going on in there?" DI Keyes asked, gesturing at the court building.

"Not a clue," the boss admitted. "But—"

"Hang on." DI Keyes stepped closer to the screen, pointing. "Who's that?"

Tom squinted at where he was indicating.

"What?" Nina asked.

"Who?" echoed the boss.

"Behind you, standing by the exit. They're... Is that Sinead Conway?"

Tom moved closer, recognising the distinctive black hair. Next to Conway stood two well-dressed people he'd seen before – a man with small, rabbit-like eyes and a woman with shoulder-length blonde hair and glasses.

"I don't know," said the boss. "They've been here before. I've seen them with her."

"You remember them, Tom?" DI Keyes asked.

"Yes." He felt his heart rate pick up. "We saw them outside Reid's flat."

"Reid?" The boss's voice sharpened. "Ethan Reid?"

"Yes. In the corridor outside."

"Could they have been visiting someone else?"

"No." DI Keyes shook his head. "Nothing else up there. They'd just been visiting Ethan Reid."

"And they have an association with Sinead Conway," the boss said. "Which means Reid isn't just some low-life with a nice flat and a penchant for violence. He's connected."

Tom nodded slowly. It explained Trevor Singleton's involvement – only the best for Sinead Conway and her associates. And Ethan Reid, it seemed, was one of those associates.

CHAPTER NINETY-THREE

Detective Superintendent Fiona Kendrick had several habits that irritated Zoe. She'd stare out the window during conversations, had positioned her office plant to obscure visitors' view of who else was inside, and lately showed a defeatist attitude since the IOPC had questioned her leadership of the Hub.

But sometimes she was magnificent.

"Out of the way." Fiona strode through the crowd and into the court building.

Zoe followed a few steps behind as they passed security.

An official stood outside the courtroom. "They're not ready to speak to the police yet."

Fiona turned to Zoe with a smile. "You might want to step outside. You won't want to be associated with this."

"Right." Zoe backed away but stayed within view.

"Not ready to speak to the police?" Fiona's voice was sharp.

"I'm afraid not," the man replied.

"Do you know how many officers we have out there,

waiting for you and your chums to be ready, when they could be solving crimes and preventing other crimes from happening?"

"I'm sorry—"

Fiona closed the gap between them, getting right in his face. "I don't want your apology. I'm going in there, now." She pointed to the courtroom door. "I will speak to the lawyers and find out why we've all been summoned here and then told to sit on our arses until you're all ready for us. And then, when I come out again, I might be willing to hear you apologise. OK?"

The man nodded mutely as Fiona pushed past him into the courtroom.

Outside, Zoe turned her phone back on to find another missed call from Zhang Chen. She called him.

"Zhang," she said. "I'm sorry. I know you've been trying to reach me."

"I see you shut it down."

"Shut what down?"

Carl and the others approached, eager for updates. She could only shrug helplessly.

"The account. The main Jenson & Marley account. The one Carter had begun to empty when you took him in."

Zoe frowned. "What do you mean?"

"I still look into Jenson & Marley from time to time. That was interesting work. And when I logged in the other day, well, you've emptied it, haven't you? You, or the CPS, or someone else."

"We've what?"

"There was more than a million pounds in that account last time I checked," Zhang said, "so I'm assuming there was some sort of Proceeds of Crime confiscation order. But given the trial's still ongoing, I didn't expect it so soon."

"Hang on." Zoe wished she could see his familiar, calming smile rather than just hear his voice. "You need to slow down. Which account?"

"You know which account. The main operating account."

The account where Carter had funnelled all his criminal proceeds. The one he'd started emptying when he realised they were closing in.

"There's been no court order," she said. "Not as far as I'm aware. I don't know how this could have happened."

She shook her head uselessly. Carl stood beside her, with Denise Gaskill and Harriett Barnes nearby. DCI Branthwaite chatted with someone by the statue, and she could see DCI Carnegie and others.

"Bloody hell," she muttered.

"I'm sorry?" Zhang said.

"I have to go." She ended the call.

The realisation hit her. Besides Carter himself, only she and Zhang knew the details of his empire. Except for one other person.

David Randle.

Even before rescuing Olivia and getting shot, Randle had been fascinated by Carter's operation. He'd studied the parent companies, nominees and bank accounts. Zoe had shared Zhang's report with him, and they'd all discussed it together.

He'd been key to getting Streeting to talk, revealing six more companies they hadn't known about. Zoe had shared everything with him – not just what they'd learned from

Streeting and Zhang, but Alistair Freeburn's information, too.

"Zoe?" Carl approached, looking worried.

She shook her head, unable to speak.

After Carter's arrest... That was when it must have happened. Carter stalling and lying as expected. And Randle saying, "Let me talk to him, Zoe. I'll convince him, if anyone can."

No audio recording. Hands covering mouths to prevent lip-reading. What had really been discussed in that room while Zoe watched but couldn't hear? Had they talked about bank accounts and passwords?

She could see how Randle might have convinced Carter he needed someone trustworthy on the outside. Randle could be persuasive when he wanted to be. He'd certainly convinced Zoe.

But Randle was dead. So who had cleaned out Carter's account?

"Bloody hell," she said aloud.

Carl asked again if she was OK. She shook her head and dialled her phone.

"Zoe? I didn't think you were allowed your phone in court."

"Stella, there's something I need to ask you."

Zoe noticed heads turning towards the main door as silence spread through the crowd.

"What?" asked Stella.

"Hang on," Zoe replied.

Fiona Kendrick emerged, her expression unreadable. "OK, everyone." Her voice carried effortlessly across the hushed crowd. Even the rain seemed to pause.

CHAPTER NINETY-THREE

Zoe waited.
"I have news," said the super.

CHAPTER NINETY-FOUR

CLIVE MOOR's timing was terrible. The super had been about to deliver significant news when they'd been called downstairs.

"Can't it wait?" Aaron said, standing opposite him in the custody suite.

Clive shook his head. "I'm afraid not." Aaron shrugged at Tom.

They'd left Nina in the team room to figure things out, though Aaron doubted she'd manage to stay awake.

In Interview Room Four, Chelsea Bright sat across the table, looking more composed than during their last meeting. The woman beside her had made the difference.

Sue Sharples gave Aaron and Tom a brief nod as they took their seats.

"You know my client has an excellent chance of claiming duress," the lawyer said.

Tom leaned forward. "You know that duress isn't a defence to murder."

"That's true," Sue acknowledged. "And I also know the

CHAPTER NINETY-FOUR

evidence that might have supported my client's claim has disappeared. Her wound's been cleaned up, leaving no traces of who inflicted it. That person seems to have had the chance to clean up the scene, too."

Aaron watched Chelsea's face fall as her lawyer spoke, the hope draining away until she looked defeated.

"So that's it." Chelsea's voice was flat.

"I'm sorry?" Aaron said.

"That's it. I've lost Femi, and I'm going to prison for murder. That'll be most of my life, won't it?"

Sue cleared her throat. Aaron turned to meet her gaze, noting the subtle movement of her eyes, communicating something unspoken. Some lawyers caught on quicker than others, especially those who actually listened. Sue had only been with Chelsea briefly, but she understood the situation better than Basham had.

"DI Keyes," she said. "The evidence we just referred to – would you mind outlining how it was lost?"

"Ah." Aaron shifted in his seat. "Well, I'd be lying if I said there weren't errors on our side."

"To put it bluntly, there was potential evidence, and you've lost it. Is that right?"

Aaron was glad Sue wasn't a barrister; she'd be formidable in court. But right now, she was exactly where he wanted her.

"That's absolutely right," he said.

"And if this went to court, with my client facing murder charges, the police admitting to losing evidence supporting the defence... Well, it wouldn't play well for you, would it?"

Tom sighed softly beside Aaron, leaning back with a knowing nod. He'd caught on.

"It wouldn't play well at all, no," Aaron said.

"And that being the case, whatever the outcome, you won't be looking to charge my client with murder after all, will you?"

Aaron smiled. "That's right."

Tears rolled down Chelsea's cheeks, but the haunted desperation had vanished from her expression.

CHAPTER NINETY-FIVE

A CAR DOOR slammed on Warwick Street, shattering the silence.

The super stood before the group. "Myron Carter has changed his plea."

The weight of her words hung in the air.

"For what?" Zoe asked, cutting to the heart of the matter. With Carter facing multiple charges, a confession to financial crimes would mean wasted effort.

"Bobby Silver's murder," Fiona replied.

Zoe sagged against the wall, her legs unsteady. This couldn't be real.

"And Victor Parlick's," Fiona continued. "The hit on Iqbal, which predates all the rest. The hit on Kieran Mulligan, too."

Zoe glanced at DCI Kiki Carnegie and her two Durranhill officers. Mulligan had been one of theirs. The DCI's expression was grim but satisfied.

"And the trafficking charges," Fiona added. "All of them. He's admitting to it all."

"What about Daria Petrescu?" Zoe asked.

"Not that one, curiously. Not that it would have made much difference. He's admitted to bringing her into the country, but denies involvement in her death."

"So the trial's continuing?" someone asked.

Fiona shook her head. "No. CPS are happy with the pleas. They're dropping the rest."

Zoe stepped forward, then stopped. She wanted to protest. Daria Petrescu's murder demanded justice. But Mick Halfpenny was already serving life for it. Getting Carter would have been a bonus, but what they had was enough.

Still, why hadn't Carter admitted it? One more murder charge wouldn't change much.

"This is a brilliant result, everyone," Fiona said. "The culmination of years of outstanding work spearheaded by DI Finch and her team. There will be time to process it and hand round the praise in due course. But for now, I'm heading back to the Hub. And I suggest you all get back to work."

She strode down Earl Street as voices rose in celebration. Zoe found herself smiling and thanking people automatically.

A noise caught her attention – Stella was still on the call. She brought her phone up to her ear.

"Bloody hell," Stella said.

Zoe walked towards Warwick Street, aware of eyes following her. "Did you hear that?"

"Yes. And may I be the first to congratulate you on some outstanding spearheading."

Zoe laughed, then remembered why she'd called. The

CHAPTER NINETY-FIVE

laughter died in her throat. "There's something I need to ask you."

"Yeah?"

"Site Two. The DNA you used to confirm the victim was David Randle."

"Yes?"

"I remember you saying there wasn't much left intact to analyse. The victim's remains, I mean."

"That's right."

"But the remains you used. What were they?"

She already knew the answer.

"A finger," Stella replied. "Why do you ask?"

But Zoe was already heading back to the court building. People might try to stop her, but she'd seen how Fiona had handled them earlier. Time to follow her example.

CHAPTER NINETY-SIX

TEN MINUTES WAS ALL they had between leaving the interview with Chelsea and her lawyer and being summoned back. Tom spent nine of those minutes repeatedly dialling the boss without success. Each call went straight to voicemail.

Then Harriett called.

Tom rubbed his forehead. "Sorry, can't talk. Waiting to hear from the boss. Apparently there's news at the—"

"He's changed his plea," Harriett cut in.

"He's what?"

"Carter. He's changed his plea. Admitted it all. Well, most of it."

Tom put his phone on speaker. "Harriett, I'm with DI Keyes. Can you tell us exactly what's happened?"

"Sure," she replied. Tom felt his heart swell at the sound of her voice over the tinny speaker. The DI approached, looking puzzled.

"Myron Carter has changed his plea," Harriett said.

CHAPTER NINETY-SIX

"He's admitted to four murders, people trafficking and various lesser charges."

"Seriously?" the DI breathed.

"On my life."

Tom licked his lips. "What about Daria Petrescu? Is he admitting to killing her?"

"Not her, sorry. But..."

"But..." he echoed. *Bloody hell.*

The DI's phone rang, and he gestured towards the interview room. "Time to go back in."

"OK," Tom said. "Thanks, Harriett."

"No problem." She hung up as Tom followed DI Keyes back inside, his mind racing.

They sat down, placing drinks on the table. Tom was trying to keep calm. Myron Carter, pleading guilty?

He'd never have predicted that.

Sue Sharples cleared her throat, bringing him back to the present.

"We've had time to confer," she said.

"And?" DI Keyes leaned forward.

"And we need to reach an agreement. You and me."

"What do you mean?" asked Tom.

The lawyer's gaze stayed on the DI. "On what you're going to charge her with."

Tom glanced at the DI. They'd covered this ground already.

"We've agreed that a charge of murder is unlikely," said DI Keyes.

Sue Sharples shook her head slowly. "You say unlikely, I say impossible, that's fine. But we all need to be sensible here. Chelsea's not stupid. She knows she has to pay for what she's done."

Chelsea sat beside her lawyer, looking more alert than Tom had seen her since their first meeting. She gave a solemn nod of acknowledgement.

"And you know you're not charging her with murder." Sue Sharples paused, but neither officer contradicted her. There wasn't a chance in hell of a murder charge sticking.

"Manslaughter," said the DI.

"Maybe. But the duress defence might not work against murder, but it does work against manslaughter. And if Chelsea were to raise that defence, you'd have to explain what had happened to the evidence that would have supported it. Which means..."

Tom knew what it meant – no jury would convict when the police admitted losing evidence crucial to her defence.

"And anyway," Sue continued, "none of this is going to play out in front of a jury."

"Why not?" Tom blinked and turned to the DI, who looked equally confused.

"Because there's no way my client is going to stand there in the dock and point a finger at Ethan Reid."

Tom almost asked, 'Why not?' again, but kept quiet, waiting for the lawyer to continue.

"As I've already mentioned, Chelsea's not stupid. She knows that if she accuses Reid, she won't last more than a week inside."

Tom and Aaron exchanged looks. Was Ethan Reid really that powerful?

"It's not about Reid himself," the lawyer said, as if reading his thoughts. "It's about the people he's connected to."

Tom thought of the people in smart business-wear who'd been hanging around the court with Sinead Conway. But

Conway was just a property developer, wasn't she? She knew Myron Carter, but half of West Cumbria's business community knew Carter. She couldn't be involved with killers, could she?

"Which means," Sue Sharples concluded, "that we need to agree a charge my client is willing to plead guilty to. OK?"

"OK," agreed DI Keyes.

CHAPTER NINETY-SEVEN

THE SAME OFFICIAL who'd cowered before Fiona stood firm against Zoe's demands. She'd barely begun listing impossible threats when the courtroom door opened and a group emerged.

"You'll pay for this," Zoe snapped at the official before turning to follow them, knowing that nothing of the sort was true.

She trailed behind as they moved along the corridor towards the side entrance stairs, where armoured vehicles waited to transport the prisoner.

"Wait!" Her shout halted the procession before they reached the stairwell.

Among the prison guards, two police officers recognised her. After a brief discussion, they parted to let her through.

"Zoe Finch." Carter looked diminished compared to his appearance in the dock, dwarfed by the hulking guards surrounding him.

"Looking well," she said.

CHAPTER NINETY-SEVEN

"I try." His smile was inscrutable. She searched his face for any hint of remorse.

Questions burned in her mind, but the guards shifted restlessly. They whispered among themselves as the police officers who'd admitted her grew anxious. After the Kaciaryna Ilinich incident, everyone stuck rigidly to protocol.

She swallowed her questions about Daria Petrescu. "What did you talk about with David Randle?" she asked Carter.

"I'm not sure I need to tell you that." His smile returned, still believing he held some power.

She matched his expression. "I'll tell you what I think you discussed. I think David Randle claimed he'd convinced us to let him speak to you. He was meant to frighten you into confessing, but really offered to keep your operation running while you were inside."

Carter's smile faltered before he forced it back on again.

"I think he promised to protect your assets," she continued. "You knew that even beating the murder charges wouldn't save you from confiscation orders. All that money hidden away. The Jenson & Marley account. You'd lose everything unless you acted."

His silence stretched between them.

"I think he persuaded you to hand over your bank credentials. He said he'd look after it, and you had nothing to lose. Am I right?"

Carter shrugged. Zoe eyed him.

"He's a convincing man, is David Randle."

"Is?" Carter broke his silence.

Gotcha. "Oh, do you think 'was' is more appropriate? But he is convincing. He convinced me to let him speak to you, got you to give him your money, and lied to us both. He even convinced us he was dead."

"What do you mean?" The smile vanished, replaced by desperation.

"I mean, your bank account is empty. David Randle's likely enjoying your money somewhere without extradition to the UK."

"No," Carter whispered.

"Time to go," said a massive guard with a deceptively friendly smile.

"Wait," Carter pleaded as the group moved forward, his horrified expression fixed on Zoe.

His former power meant nothing now. The houses, the Petrus 1990, the Bentleys – none of it mattered. He was just another murderer, and that million pounds had been his last hope for a cushioned prison stay.

If there was any silver lining to Randle's deception, it was seeing Carter's face as he realised he'd been played, too.

CHAPTER NINETY-EIGHT

NINA LEANED against the wall in the custody suite, fighting to keep her eyes open. She'd worked plenty of full days on minimal sleep before, but this was different. Her impromptu Elvis concert performance had been to an audience of one – herself – while trapped in a bag. The fact that this wasn't the first time made it worse.

She waited for the current suspect to leave and the next batch to arrive, each minute stretching like an hour. Her eyes kept drifting shut before snapping open, forcing her to reorient herself.

Relief washed over her when Chelsea Bright emerged from the interview corridor, Sue Sharples guiding her with a gentle hand on her shoulder.

Tom approached, positioning himself close enough for Nina to subtly lean against him.

"What's the story?" she whispered.

"We've released her on bail," he murmured.

"You're not worried she'll do a runner?"

Tom glanced at Chelsea and her lawyer before turning

back. "We're going easy on her, and she knows it. She's not going to make it worse for herself. You're sure you're good for this?"

Before Nina could answer, Chelsea approached them, leaving Sue at the desk. "Thanks," she said.

"You're welcome," Nina replied, though she wasn't sure what the thanks were for. Chelsea was gone before she could ask.

"You're sure?" Tom pressed.

Nina straightened slightly. "Yeah. Those bastards put me in a bloody bag, Tom. I want to be there when they break."

"They're not going to make it easy. They've had long enough to get a story straight between them. We've just got to hope Stella's got enough evidence to break through that."

"Yeah," Nina agreed, concerned about their unity. The three wise monkeys had maintained their story for two years. Breaking that bond would be key.

"They're here," Tom said.

The doors opened, revealing three separate groups. Veronica Gaines entered first, flanked by officers, looking miserable. Simon Miller followed, handcuffed and shouting back at someone. That someone was Erica Stern.

Nina studied Erica – an ordinary-looking woman in jeans and a baggy jumper, her reddish-brown hair showing grey roots. Despite her exhaustion, anger radiated from her.

"I wish I'd never bloody met you, you freak," Erica spat at Miller.

"I wish I'd stuck to the birds," Miller shouted back.

"I wish you'd stuck to the birds. Would have been better for all of us."

Nina turned away when Veronica tried to catch her eye. Any apology now would be meaningless.

CHAPTER NINETY-EIGHT

"This is all your fault!" Miller's voice echoed through the room.

"You stupid piece of shit," Erica hissed venomously.

Tom returned from speaking with the officers by Veronica. "Apparently they've been arguing like this since they were arrested at the ferry terminal."

Nina grinned. Unity might not be such a problem after all.

CHAPTER NINETY-NINE

Zoe walked up the stairs and stopped in the corridor near the team room.

The updates had all been positive. Nina was safe, and they were interviewing the three wise monkeys separately.

"I think we've got a chance," Aaron had told her during her drive back to the Hub.

That brief statement meant everything. In their two years working together, she'd learned of Aaron's tendency to understate things. If he thought they had a chance, the three wise monkeys were likely spilling their guts across three separate interview rooms.

The team had taken Carter's guilty plea well. But she hadn't mentioned Randle to any of them.

She turned away from the team room, went to her office, and shut the door. The Randle situation wasn't certain anyway. But the evidence nagged at her – his shot hand, the months of complaints about his infected finger, that same finger being the only way to identify his remains. And then there was the missing money.

CHAPTER NINETY-NINE

She recalled her brief exchange with Carter outside the courtroom. He hadn't looked like someone whose plans were working out.

Sinking into her chair, Zoe closed her eyes. Following the money was key, but Randle – if he was alive – would be too clever to find. And tracing the money seemed impossible. Unless...

Her eyes snapped open and she grabbed her phone.

"Hello, Zoe." Zhang's face filled the screen. "Is everything OK?"

"I think so. Carter's pleaded guilty."

"Congratulations. You deserved this."

"I couldn't have done it without you," she said. "Listen, I don't suppose there's any way of tracing where the money went? The cash from the Jenson & Marley account?"

"I have an account number, but it's another locked box, Zoe. It could take years to trace it, and you and I both know that the money won't have sat in there more than a few minutes before it was moved on anyway."

She made a note as he read out the number. "You'll stay in touch?"

"You can count on it," she replied, meaning every word. Zhang Chen's Brummie accent and friendly face would be welcome even if she never needed his forensic accounting skills again – though she probably would.

She sat thinking for ten minutes. What do you give someone who has a million pounds? Ten more pounds, of course.

Opening her banking app, she added a new payee and entered her credentials. She typed in the amount: ten pounds. Her name would show as the payer.

At the reference field, she paused. Then it came to her.

Two corrupt cops. Two dead men. At least the first one certainly was; she'd investigated his murder in Birmingham.

She typed: *Say Hi to Bryn Jackson*.

She hesitated, took a breath, and then hit 'Confirm'.

CHAPTER ONE HUNDRED

"No, I don't want a lawyer," Veronica Gaines said.

"Are you sure?" DI Keyes asked.

Nina fought back the urge to kick him under the table, then gave up and did it anyway. He gave a small grunt and stared at her, but she had her eyes closed already. He'd get the message.

Veronica Gaines had been given plenty of opportunities to get herself a lawyer. And Nina was tired. She just wanted it over with.

"Yes." Veronica's response brought Nina immense relief. "So, I suppose you want me to tell you everything, yes?"

"Yes," Nina replied, delivering another kick at Aaron to discourage him from saying anything else.

"They were having an affair," Veronica said.

"Who were?" Aaron asked. Nina let that one slide. The details had to be there, on tape, out loud, even if everyone knew them.

"Erica and Simon. I think half the caravan park knew

about it, but Archie, her husband, he was as stupid as he was horrible."

"How was he horrible, precisely?" Aaron asked.

"I just didn't like him." Veronica shifted in her seat. "He had a way with him. Odd. Shifty. I didn't trust him."

Nina frowned. Coming from an actual murderer who'd just attacked a police officer and left her to be crushed to death, that was saying something.

"Was he violent towards Erica, as far as you knew?"

"Oh, no. It wasn't like that. He was just, well. He was shifty. And a bit boring."

As motives for murder went, this one lacked a certain something.

"Go on," Nina said.

"Well, he was always away. Travelling, you know? For work. But one night, he came home unexpectedly. Oh, there was the most awful row."

"You could hear it from your park home?" Nina asked.

There was quite a distance between the two locations. If Veronica had heard it, most of the other residents would have heard it, too.

"Oh, no. No, I... I happened to be passing."

"That's quite the coincidence," Aaron observed.

Veronica shrugged. "I suppose the truth is that I'd been out for a little walk and I'd seen what I thought was Archie's car heading back in. I walked over to Erica's to make sure everything was alright there. And it wasn't. He'd found out, you see. Caught them at it. Right in the act."

She sat back and smiled at them, as if that explained everything that followed.

"What happened?" Nina asked.

"Well, as I say, there was an almighty row. Archie was

CHAPTER ONE HUNDRED

saying he'd given up everything for Erica and her bloody park home. I suppose that was true. He didn't really want the new one, but Erica had her heart set on it, so he just had to work a little harder for them to afford it. And he wasn't happy with Simon, either."

"I can imagine," Nina said dryly. A sharp pain shot through her shin.

So the DI was kicking her back, was he? She ran through what she'd just said, and the way she'd said it, and decided he probably had a point.

"He called Simon all sorts. The door was open, and I was standing there watching by then, so I heard it all. Saw it all, too. He said something about Simon being a 'weird little twitcher', and Simon didn't like that at all."

Nina suppressed a smile.

"He hit him."

"Simon hit Archie?" DI Keyes asked.

"Yes. Right in the face. And then Archie hit him back. And then, well, both of them went for Archie. Erica and Simon. Archie was on the ground, and Simon was punching him. Erica was hitting him with a stapler, I think. It went on for a while."

"You didn't do anything to intervene?"

Veronica looked genuinely surprised. "Heavens, no. When they'd finally finished, they looked up and noticed me. I told them, 'Don't mind me, I don't blame you.' Horrible man, Archie. I'd always thought Erica would have been better off with Simon. Made for each other, I thought. Shows what I know, doesn't it?"

"Go on," DI Keyes said.

"Well, the new place was coming along just a few days later, so I helped them hide the body while they got hold of the concrete, and then I helped them, well, I suppose you'd say I helped them dispose of him. Him, and that stapler. It was all rather good fun, really."

She was smiling at them, as if they were all part of one big shared joke. Nina wasn't feeling inclined to smile back.

"I suppose none of us ever thought anyone would dig him up again," Veronica added with a nervous laugh. "And dearie, I am sorry about what we did to you."

She made to reach across the table to take Nina's hand. Nina kept her hands where they were and shook her head slowly. Veronica pulled her arms back.

"Continue," Nina said.

"Well, it turned out they weren't made for each other after all, Simon and Erica. It must have seemed such good fun while they were having an affair, but once Archie was out of the way, it didn't work out the way they'd hoped. It was real life, suddenly, and they couldn't stand each other in real life. Between you and me, I think he prefers birds to people."

She was looking at the DI now. She'd given up on Nina. Nina could see him looking back at her, blank-faced, and felt a sudden rush of warmth for him.

No one messed with the team. No one bashed them on the head and put them in a bag. And if anyone did, DI Keyes wouldn't be sharing little jokes with them in the interview room.

"Well," continued Veronica, "they lasted about a week, and then they decided to end it, and I think they'd hardly seen each other in all that time until all this fuss with the druggies. And then, well, they were in it together, weren't they? We all were. We had to help each other out."

CHAPTER ONE HUNDRED

Nina couldn't help wondering how long it would have lasted if they'd made it to Ireland. She found herself smiling.

She didn't care. She really didn't care at all.

Nina was alive, and they were in custody.

Before she'd come down for this interview, she'd called Elena, who'd been worrying about her all night, and Skip, who'd not been worrying because he didn't know anything had happened, but was suitably concerned when she told him. Then she'd called her mother, but not said anything about caravans or bags. She'd just wanted to hear her voice.

She had family and friends who looked out for her. And she was alive.

And the three wise monkeys were going to prison.

CHAPTER ONE HUNDRED ONE

AARON RAN a hand through his hair. "It's been a day."

Tom nodded. Nina jerked suddenly in her chair, fighting off sleep.

The boss stared ahead, her brow furrowed in concentration.

"You OK, boss?" Aaron leaned forward.

"Yes." She blinked rapidly. "Sorry. I was miles away."

She hadn't been herself during the briefing. Starting sentences only to let them fade away, asking questions they'd already covered minutes before.

"We've interviewed all three of them now," Aaron continued, determined to push through. If she needed another briefing later, so be it. "They've all admitted it. No issues whatsoever."

Tom tapped his notebook. "Erica Stern's line was the best of the lot. Apparently, and I quote, she'd 'rather spend the rest of her life in prison than spend another hour with Simon Miller'."

CHAPTER ONE HUNDRED ONE

"Ouch." The boss's response showed she was at least listening.

Nina stretched in her chair. "Having spent forty-five minutes with Simon Miller, I'm almost tempted to agree. He's admitted it all, too, of course. Says he wishes he'd never met the witch. His words, not mine. Says he's spent two years avoiding people in favour of birds, and these last few days have reminded him why."

"Unfortunately for Simon Miller," Aaron said, "it's people he'll be in prison with, not birds."

Tom and Nina burst out laughing. The boss took a moment before giving a distracted nod.

Aaron frowned. There was definitely something on her mind.

CHAPTER ONE HUNDRED TWO

"So, yes, whilst we are considering manslaughter charges, the original murder remains..."

Zoe paused, frowning as she searched for the right word. "Not exactly unsolved. We know who wielded the weapon, and we know why. But there's a duress element we can't prove, and that's down to yet more problems at our end."

"But you got your three wise monkeys, yes?" Fiona asked.

"Yes."

"Which justified digging up a caravan park and managed to make DI Knight look like an idiot. That's a bonus, if ever there was one."

Zoe allowed herself a smile. They sat in the super's office at the little coffee table with its tiny matching chairs she'd just had delivered. The idea was to suggest informality, but the chairs were so small that for a woman of Zoe's height, comfort was impossible. Her knees had protested before she'd even settled.

"Yes, I suppose so," she agreed.

"And then there's Carter. That's a huge success."

CHAPTER ONE HUNDRED TWO

"We lost Kaciaryna Ilinich. And Carter didn't admit the Daria Petrescu murder, Fiona. That's unfinished business."

"Kaciaryna Ilinich isn't your problem, and with luck she'll be some other force's problem entirely. Hopefully some other country's. And as far as Daria Petrescu's concerned, there's a man serving life for that murder, and we know he did it. Carter's involvement was never thought to be more than peripheral, was it?"

Zoe slumped in her chair, still trying to get comfortable. "I suppose not."

"So maybe it was even more peripheral than we supposed. Either way, it's a win. You should be happy. You should be out with your team celebrating. And I can't help wondering why you've chosen instead to sit here briefing me on something that could have waited until morning, and why you look like you've got other, less pleasant things on your mind."

Bloody hell. Was it that obvious?

But that was the thing with David Randle. He got under her skin, into her mind, infecting everything he touched.

"It's nothing," Zoe said. "I just thought I should let you know where we are in person and thank you for your support."

"Thank me for my support? That sounds a bit formal, Zoe. Ah, good. Coffee."

A man had entered the room without Zoe noticing.

"This is Ellis," Fiona said. "He's my new assistant."

"Just a temp," Ellis added.

He was shorter and less pale than Luke, the man he'd replaced. More healthy-looking. Zoe nodded as he slipped back out, and took a sip from the coffee he'd prepared.

Adequate. Which put it well below Luke's coffee.

"Anyway," Fiona said. "There's news from me, too."

"There is?"

Zoe sat up. News from Fiona was always interesting. Usually gossip from the assistant chief constable's office. Something about Becca Grey, the ACC's Policy Adviser, no doubt. Luke was working there now, and the channels of communication seemed to have remained open.

"I've handed in my notice," Fiona said.

For a moment, Zoe thought she'd misheard. Then she thought she'd misunderstood. There had to be another meaning.

"I'm sorry?"

"I've told them I'm leaving, Zoe."

"I can't..."

Zoe shook her head slowly, her mouth hanging open.

"Oh, come on, Zoe. You can't seriously be surprised. After all the nonsense with the IOPC, it was always coming. I've just decided to jump before I'm pushed."

Fiona was right. The IOPC report had been damning. Inaccurate, in Zoe's view, but there wasn't much a lowly DI could do about that. It had recommended a change in leadership.

Just a matter of time, really.

"What are you going to do?" Zoe asked.

Her mind had been elsewhere. On Randle, mostly. But now it was firmly back in the room.

"I'll take some time out. I'll probably end up finding another DSup job somewhere else. Make a fresh start."

"When?"

"Not for a few months. You've got plenty of time to get used to the idea."

CHAPTER ONE HUNDRED TWO

Zoe's phone buzzed, but now wasn't the time for distraction.

"Whoever replaces you will have big shoes to fill, Fiona," she said.

Fiona laughed. "I'll take that as a compliment."

"It is a compliment," Zoe assured her.

Fiona cocked her head. "But you might not be thrilled with the other half of the news."

Zoe looked at Fiona's pained expression. *Shit*.

"It's not, is it?" she asked.

"Not what?"

"Not Kiki Carnegie. It's not her, taking over your position here?"

The pained expression deepened into a scowl.

"It's not confirmed yet," Fiona said. "But it's looking likely."

That explained everything. The rumours Jake had been reluctant to expand on. And why the DCI had seemed uncharacteristically calm when she'd lost the Femi Moorhouse case to Zoe's team.

Moorhouse was a nice, juicy sea trout. But there were bigger fish to fry. Kiki Carnegie's eye had been on a shark. And it seemed she'd landed it.

Zoe chatted with Fiona for a few more minutes, but now she was desperate to leave. Desperate to shut herself away and think about it all.

Not that there was much to think about. Dorset had been an attractive proposition from the start. But the idea of working for DCI Kiki Carnegie – for *Detective Superintendent* Kiki Carnegie...

"Fuck," she muttered as she took the stairs back down to

the third floor and pulled out her phone to check the message she'd received.

It was from an unknown number, but she knew who'd sent it.

Come to the place we first met, it said.

Tonight at ten.

And four digits in place of a sign-off.

4029.

CHAPTER ONE HUNDRED THREE

AARON FLEXED HIS FINGERS, impatient. This had been going on too long.

"But you have to look at the motive," Tom said. "If you're trying to work out why something happened, that's where you start."

Nina's face twisted into a sneer. "Not if you know who the killer is."

Tom shook his head, his brow furrowed. The argument had stretched into its fifteenth minute, and Aaron had had enough.

"Why did she do it, Nina?" Tom asked.

"Well, she claims it's because—"

"Oh no. We're not having that 'she claims' nonsense. She did it because Ethan Reid forced her to do it, and she's right. And why did Reid force her to do it?"

"Because they stole his money," Nina said.

"His money and his drugs. And they used the money to buy more drugs. And they did it because they're drug addicts. And Reid's a drug dealer. Therefore, as I said all along, the crime was about drugs." Tom lifted the antimacassar from his chair. "And this, I believe, is yours."

He walked to Nina's desk and draped it over her chair with a flourish. Nina closed her eyes. For a moment, Aaron thought she'd fallen asleep – a good way to end this nonsense. Then he noticed her lips moving as she counted to ten under her breath.

"Who killed Femi?" she asked.

Tom remained silent.

"Who killed Femi?"

"Chelsea," Tom muttered.

"Exactly. His partner. His domestic partner. Which means it was a domestic killing, and I win the bet." Nina lifted the antimacassar. "And this, I believe, is yours."

She repeated Tom's actions in reverse.

"Enough," Aaron said.

Tom stood and returned the antimacassar to Nina's chair. Nina stood and returned it to Tom's.

"I said, enough!" Aaron's voice rose, but Nina and Tom were locked in a glaring contest, blind to everything but their stupid bet.

Aaron had a thought. He searched his desk drawer without success, then moved to the spare desk. Kay had left in a hurry, but she was sensible – she'd have what he needed. He found it instantly in the drawer.

Moving behind Tom's chair, where the antimacassar hung, Aaron grasped it with his left hand and lifted it.

Tom and Nina broke their staring match to look at him.

"This," Aaron said, "has gone on long enough."

He revealed the item from Kay's desk in his right hand.

"No!" Tom gasped. Nina froze in horror. But Aaron knew he was right.

CHAPTER ONE HUNDRED THREE

Starting from the bottom, he sliced through the hideous thing with the tailor's shears – ideally suited to the job, with their long blades and offset handles.

He surveyed his work – two perfect halves, the appalling bird split evenly between them.

"This is yours," he told Tom, draping one half over his chair. "And you can have this," he added, giving Nina the other half.

"Bloody hell," Tom said.

"Little extreme, Sarge," Nina said.

"I haven't been 'Sarge' for a while," Aaron replied. "And I suppose I need to start acting like that."

"What do you mean?" Tom asked.

"That printout you did. Job openings. For DI positions. Where are they?"

"You don't really have to—" Nina began.

Aaron shook his head. She was wrong now, but she'd been right before, when she'd put that list of positions on his chair.

"I do," he said. "I'm a DI now, and that means finding a proper DI job for myself."

"But maybe if you wait…" Tom's voice trailed off.

"If I wait, I'll still be 'Sarge' in twenty years, Tom. There isn't a DI role coming up here. Not any time soon, at least. It's time."

CHAPTER ONE HUNDRED FOUR

"I'd have thought you'd be happier," Carl said. The words had been bouncing around his head for an hour, and after his second beer, he couldn't contain them any longer.

"What do you mean?" Zoe turned to him with a brittle smile. She'd barely touched her stew, a dish she usually devoured regardless of her mood.

Carl stood and moved to her side. "You solved a murder no one even knew had taken place, you know what happened to the man at Grune Point, and Carter's pleading guilty to almost every charge you threw at him. To be honest, I thought we'd be out tonight, celebrating. But you seem... Well, if I had to guess, I'd say you're acting like you've seen a ghost, and you're not sure what to do about it."

Zoe let out a bitter laugh that startled him. Then she stood and wrapped her arms around him. "I suppose I have."

"You have?"

"I have seen a ghost." She licked her lips. "I think David Randle is alive."

CHAPTER ONE HUNDRED FOUR

Carl listened in stunned silence as she explained about the missing money and the finger.

They moved to the living room, settling side by side on the sofa.

"It all sounds a bit circumstantial," he said.

"I agree," Zoe replied. "It's not exactly proof. But it sounds like the sort of thing he'd do, doesn't it?"

Carl had never known Randle as well as Zoe had, but she was right. It did sound like something he'd do.

"We need to alert the authorities," he said. "Get all the agencies on it. Hunt him down."

Zoe shrugged.

"What?" he said.

"Why?" she challenged.

Carl took a moment to think. "Because he's stolen proceeds of crime that are the legitimate property of the taxpayer, and he's breached the conditions of the Protected Persons Programme."

Zoe laughed. "I think we're a bit past worrying about the conditions of the Protected Persons Programme. And if it hadn't been for Randle, we'd never have brought down Carter."

He wanted to argue, but couldn't. She was right.

"And anyway," she said, "he's probably out of reach."

"What makes you think that? Has he contacted you?"

There was a moment's hesitation before Zoe shook her head. Carl knew she was lying, but he also knew he wouldn't do anything about it.

They sat in silence, avoiding each other's gaze, before Carl spoke again. "You're going to Dorset, aren't you?"

"I don't know," she answered, though he suspected otherwise.

"I understand. And I'll miss you."

Zoe turned to him, hurt in her eyes. "You're not coming?"

"I can't. I can't leave the team. I can't leave Denise. She's still not…"

Denise wasn't better yet, despite her claims. Carl probably couldn't help her get there, but he owed it to her to try.

"I love you, Carl."

"I love you, too. But this… This is my home now. And I don't think it's yours."

That was what it came down to. Home. He'd found his. He wasn't sure Zoe had.

They held each other for a few minutes. After all the lying and evasion, these felt like their most honest moments in months.

Zoe glanced at her watch. "I need to go. There's something I have to do."

He nodded, kissed her, and watched her leave.

A few weeks ago, he might have followed her. But it was too late now. It had been fun, magical at times. But it was over. Had been for a while. They'd just taken too long to realise it. He loved her more than anyone in his life, but surprisingly, that wasn't enough.

In the kitchen, the cat mewed at the covered plates of leftover stew. Carl lifted the cover and spooned some onto a plate for her.

He was going to miss the cat. But he wasn't sure how he was going to cope without Zoe Finch.

CHAPTER ONE HUNDRED FIVE

Come to the place we first met.

The message drew Zoe back to the lighthouse on that narrow strip of land jutting into the sea near Workington Port. She'd met them there before, months ago, as darkness fell – David Randle, Olivia Bagsby, and Carl watching from his car to ensure it wasn't a trap set by Myron Carter.

But it had been a trap, in its way. David Randle had earned her trust so gradually she couldn't pinpoint when it happened. And now here she was again.

Carl was at home with his beer and a broken heart. She cared about him, but not enough to stay away.

The wind whipped around her as waves crashed in the darkness. Without moonlight, she could barely make out the angry sea, though occasional car lights or port illumination caught the black water.

She knew Randle and Olivia wouldn't be here. But there had to be something waiting for her. Those numbers had to mean something.

Fear should have stopped her, but it didn't. Something told her Randle meant her no harm.

At the lighthouse base, she started up the metal steps without calling out. Trust in Randle was foolish after everything, but still she climbed.

At the top, she turned right towards the rails overlooking Workington Port. Empty platform. She made a complete circuit. Nothing. No one.

She checked her watch: 10:01.

Taking a final look at the port lights, she turned to leave when her phone buzzed.

On the rail

Back at the rail facing the port, she shone her phone light down. There it was – a small box padlocked to the rail exactly where she'd first seen Olivia Bagsby.

4029

After one more circuit, she returned to unlock the box. Inside sat a tiny phone she knew would be untraceable.

It buzzed immediately with a video call. Zoe answered.

The screen showed what looked like an explosion at first, making her scan anxiously towards Workington. But no – it was sunshine. And sand. Then a face appeared.

"You're alive, then," she said.

"I'm sorry, Zoe," Olivia replied.

"Where are you?"

"I really am sorry. But David risked his life for me. He lost a finger saving my life."

"He lost a finger faking his own death."

"And the truth is, I love him. I'd go anywhere to be with him."

David Randle's face edged into view. "And a hundred

CHAPTER ONE HUNDRED FIVE

thousand quid in the bank and a sunny climate doesn't hurt, Zoe."

"A hundred thousand?" she said. The money taken had been a million.

He smiled. "I found a conscience, Zoe." He exchanged glances with Olivia, who smiled back at him. "Ninety per cent of the money is with the benevolent fund for bereaved widows and families of police officers. It might go some way towards correcting the damage Myron Carter did."

Zoe felt her jaw drop open. *What about the damage you did?*

"And the hundred thousand you decided to keep?" she asked.

He shrugged. "How much did it cost, keeping me in the protected persons programme for a couple of years? More than that, I imagine. I've saved the police a fortune."

She narrowed her eyes. If he got caught, there was every chance David Randle would find himself in prison this time round, not in the protection of the state.

But he had a point. That would cost much, much more.

"He's a good man," Olivia said. "He's not the man you worked with." She stroked Randle's cheek. "He's changed."

Randle looked into Olivia's eyes. "I've found what it's like to be valued."

Zoe stared at the pair of them. David Randle was alive. Hiding God knows where with the woman who should have been her star witness.

But Olivia was happy. She deserved that, at least.

Zoe just hoped it lasted.

"Don't try to find us," Olivia pleaded. "Please."

"I won't." The words came automatically, but she meant them. No more searching for either of them.

"Thank you," said Olivia.

"Take care," Randle added before the screen went dark.

For ten minutes, Zoe stood there, holding the silent phone, listening to waves crash and trying to make out distant fells in the darkness. Olivia's words echoed: *I love him. I'd go anywhere to be with him.*

Did she have that with Carl? Had she ever?

Back at ground level, she slipped the burner phone into her bag. She'd dispose of it safely rather than logging it as evidence.

She pulled out her own phone and dialled Lesley, who answered immediately.

"You OK, Zoe?"

"I'm fine."

"Only it's a little late."

She checked the time: ten-thirty. "It's not late, Lesley. You're just getting old."

Lesley laughed. "If I am, then you're not all that far behind me. Anyway, I've been trying to get hold of you for ages. How are things?"

Zoe paused. She could talk about the case – Erica Stern, Chelsea Bright, Myron Carter. She could complain about the missing Kaciaryna Ilinich. Avoid mentioning Olivia or Randle. Keep putting off what needed to be said.

Or she could...

"I've made a decision, Lesley."

Her old boss's voice brightened. "You have?"

"I have. I think it's time to put the old team back together."

"What do you mean?" Lesley asked, though surely she knew.

Zoe pulled a hand through her hair. She stared out to sea.

God, it's cold here. The wind whipped around the lighthouse and hurled her long hair into the sky.

In Dorset, there would still be sea, but it would be warmer. It *had* to be warmer.

And maybe she could make a fresh start.

Run away? Was that what she was doing? Again?

No.

"Zoe?" Lesley said. "Are you still there? All I can hear is your bloody Cumbria wind."

Zoe smiled. She'd missed her old boss.

"If you'll still have me," she said, "I'd like to come and work for you again. Join your team in Dorset."

Thank you for reading the Cumbria Crime series. We've loved writing about Zoe and Carl, but their story doesn't end here. Zoe's story continues in Dorset with the twelfth Dorset Crime book, *The Beach Hut Murders*. And Carl's story continues with *The Boatyard*, first in a brand new Whaley & Gaskill series, which features many of the characters from these books and is set around Cumbria.

Happy reading! Rachel and Joel

The Boatyard *The Beach Hut Murders*

THE CUMBRIA CRIME SERIES NOVELLAS

If you have enjoyed reading the Cumbria Crime series you might like to read the Cumbria Crime novellas. Read or listen for FREE in ebook or audio via http://rachelmclean.com/cumbria-novella or buy in paperback from book retailers.

The Castle

The Karaoke Bar

The Business

The Raid

The Liar's Inn

The House

The Pool

READ THE CUMBRIA CRIME SERIES

The Harbour

The Mine

The Cairn

The Barn

The Lake

The Wood

The Port

The Marsh

Buy from book retailers.

Also by Joel Hames, the Whaley & Gaskill series, following many of the Cumbria Crime characters after the conclusion of the Cumbria Crime books.

The Boatyard

The Viewpoint

...and more to come

Buy from book retailers.

ALSO BY RACHEL MCLEAN

The DI Zoe Finch Series – buy from book retailers.

Deadly Wishes

Deadly Choices

Deadly Desires

Deadly Terror

Deadly Reprisal

Deadly Fallout

Deadly Christmas

Deadly Origins, the FREE Zoe Finch prequel

The Dorset Crime Series – buy from book retailers.

The Corfe Castle Murders

The Clifftop Murders

The Island Murders

The Monument Murders

The Millionaire Murders

The Fossil Beach Murders

The Blue Pool Murders

The Lighthouse Murders

The Ghost Village Murders

The Poole Harbour Murders

The Chesil Beach Murders

The Beach Hut Murders

The Gold Hill Murders

...and more to come

The McBride & Tanner Series – buy from book retailers.

Blood and Money

Death and Poetry

Power and Treachery

Secrets and History

The London Cosy Mystery Series by Rachel McLean and Millie Ravensworth – buy from book retailers.

Death at Westminster

Death in the West End

Death at Tower Bridge

Death on the Thames

Death at St Paul's Cathedral

Death at Abbey Road

The Jurassic Coast Mystery Series by Rachel McLean and Millie Ravensworth – buy from book retailers.

The Swimming Club

The Empty Easel

The Shattered Bauble

The Frozen Carriage

ALSO BY JOEL HAMES

The Sam Williams Series – buy now in ebook, paperback and audiobook.

Dead North

No One Will Hear

The Cold Years

The Art of Staying Dead

Victims, a Sam Williams novella

Caged, a Sam Williams short